To whoever [...] their hands, thank you for helping me become an author like I always dreamed.

Chapter One

If I write one more word, I seriously think I am going to consider dropping out of college. Between the hard wood of the chair on my ass, making even my shoulders ache to the obnoxious clicking of the keyboard against that sorority bitch's acrylics. Aren't libraries supposed to be quiet? But no.

The oversized sweatshirt I had draped over my torso did little to make the library more tolerable. I swear the librarian thinks that I'm homeless. Every time I went in there, I always would wear my favorite black leggings paired with the gigantic grey sweatshirt with the faded red varsity lettering. It used to be his. I snuggled deeper into the fabric breathing in the scent of old detergent, imagining it still smelt like pines and the hint of smoke from his engine. The small bird nestled behind my ear twinged with the memory. I tried to swallow down the swell of sadness at the thought.

So, there I was, sitting at the chipped wood surrounded by the smell of dusty old books. I usually went to the library to get work done because there is absolutely no way that I would be able to get anything done in my dorm. It just so happens that I lived with an absolute psychopath who also happens to be my best friend, Mae. Fucking Mae. If it weren't for her, I could be typing away at this essay with a cup of tea curled in my hand and snuggled under my favorite blanket. But no, I was there in hell, trying to type about the economic climate whilst having to witness Isabella Tamlin dry hump Mick Foster in the stacks. Of course.

I rolled my eyes and jabbed away at my keyboard, trying to annoy the disgusting display of affection. Oh, great now the sorority bitch is blaring some stupid Britney spears shit. If I had to keep going to this library, I might have had to think about getting a new roommate or changing the locks on Mae. Wisps of my hair fall into my face, the rest held back in my messy bun as I shoved my glasses onto my head. I rubbed at my eyes in frustration, I genuinely didn't know how much more of this paper I could handle. Never mind the onslaught that occurred within the rows of books in front of me. I slammed my laptop shut, earning a dirty look from sorority bitch. I flashed a mocking grin as I started to shove my books into my grimy backpack.

Just as I found the tangled bundle that is my headphones to start the trek back to my dorm, in walks Maverick Fucking Foster. Not only Mick's cousin and best friend, but the campus asshole. Sporting a full sleeve of tattoos on one perfectly tanned arm, muscles rippling from what seems like every part of his body, and that annoyingly arrogant smirk he strode right over to the hump session occurring in the dust covered biographies. He simply tapped his cousins' shoulder, earning him a swift punch in the arm. Maverick simply laughed in Mick's face. Isabella seemed unfazed as she sported her own grin and waved at Maverick. I realized I might have been staring a little too long and might make him think that I actually cared about any of their lives.

I fumbled over the knots restricting my headphones until I could finally shove them into my ears. I blare classics, Jimmy Hendrix being my vibe of the day, and check the time. *Shit.* I only had an hour before my shift. Stupid economics made me waste my whole afternoon. I practically sped to my dorm to find Mae passed out in a tangle of blankets. *Typical.* I threw on a fresh pair of jeans with minimal rips and a plain red t-shirt. I slipped on my converse and run a brush through the tangled mess on the top of my head. Good enough. I snatched a pullover and my ear buds and I'm on my way.

The perks of living on a college campus is that all its inhabitants tend to rely on some form of caffeine, meaning a café on campus, meaning an easy job that doesn't require me to have a car. Once I decided to leave a life of Ritz behind me, that also meant leaving my family's funds. Hence my job at the campus café. I wrapped my hair back into a messy ponytail as I walked into the door out of the chill in the fall air.

A feeling of warmth wrapped over me as I took in the buzzing air of the café. Everything carried an aroma of coffee and gave an edge of comfort through the soft warm glow radiating from lamps set up all around the small space. Soft leather couches sagging with wear and booths littered the crisp hardwood floors. The space felt small, homey. It seemed to fill in a space I didn't know was empty.

I scanned the small café, my eyes gliding over the tables of chatting college students, until my eyes land on a small table nestled into the back corner. A head full of deep black curls is angled to watch the world scurrying by the windows, the curled edges barley brushed the collar of his letter man jacket. I could practically see the dark eyes, feel his rushed drunken kisses pressed against my lips. *Hey Birdie.* A quick turn of his head reveled a nose too short, too thin lips, and just like that the memories were gone. My chest felt hollowed out, my palms prickled with sweat. I stopped in my tracks, feeling as if I needed to shrink back from the world as guilt sucked any breath I had away. *Birdie?*

The shrill ring of the bell snapped me back to reality, bringing me back to the fact that I was standing in a café looking like a total psycho. I tried to shake it off, ignore the feeling of guilt clinging to my very being. I forced my feet forward till I found my way behind the counter and tied my apron with numb fingers.

"Hey Bill." Bill was a middle-aged man who had as bad as an attitude as I did. Due to the fact that he felt he could somewhat stand my attitude over the other perky little co eds, I was practically hired on the spot. The average person couldn't handle either of our tempers, but it just so happened that in this small café, our tempers were muted by each other's. I have no idea how that makes any sense, but it simply does.

"Grace." He nodded his head as he slaved away in the small back kitchen. I slung off my sweatshirt, and after shoving it under the counter, got to work. I scrubbed down the counters and bused all the tables. A chilly fall afternoon meant a busy afternoon for me. Small beads of sweat started to run down my neck as I got into the swing of my shift. I liked to work, it was a great distraction and of course I felt that it was a slap in the face to my parents as they never wanted me to even lift a finger never mind clean up the left-over filth that comes with college students and a public place. The familiar burn of running around the café courses through my legs. Sure, it's only minimum wage and barely allows me to scrape by but I make it work.

As I run around the café, it seems to only get busier. Each worn leather coach and small table is stock full. I even recognize the Platinum blonde hair of sorority bitch from the library, bringing what is undoubtedly a pumpkin spiced latte to her perfectly painted lips. I didn't even bother to suppress my eye roll. But I welcome it all, urging myself to get lost in the routine that comes with pumping out coffees and change.

***

The small bell fixed to the door seemed to ring every two seconds as college kids filtered in and out of the café. My hands were covered in a mixture of caramel and iced coffee after the last coed brat shoved her iced caramel macchiato back in face because it didn't 'taste fat free'. It took all I had not to throw it back into her face. While whipping my hands off on a nearby towel, I couldn't help but notice our two new customers, positioning themselves in the far back booth. There sat Mick from the library, his perfect Isabella perched next to him. Honestly despite my blatant annoyance over their constant PDA, I didn't mind these two that much which is saying a lot because most people I mind. I shoved a pen behind my ear and sauntered over to where they sat, pad clutched in my hand. The couple opted to occupy one side of the booth, cuddling close, Mick's arm slung around Isabella's frail shoulders.

Isabella was effortlessly pretty, her dark brown eyes resembling that of a deer. Pair that with her tanned skin and deep brown hair, the only thing adding to her perfectness was her right forearm displaying an intricate lace pattern of ink over the soft skin. Mick however towered over her, looking a lot like his cousin. Mick sported a floppy mop of dark hair shading deep blue eyes. He was on the paler side however tattoos laced the flesh of both arms, drawing the attention away from his pale tone.

"Hey, can I get you guys something?" I don't bother with that fake flashy grin but offer a small toothless smile at them.

"Hey I know you. You are in my English Lit class. Grace, right?" Isabella pointed a chipped red nail at me with a smile on her face.

"Yea, Professor Grundy." I nodded in response.

"Ugh Grundy, that man is insufferable. I think he gave me a lower grade on my thesis paper out of spite." She scrunched up her nose in distaste until she let out a small chuckle. All the while Mick stared at her with such adoration in his eyes. I couldn't help the smile that spread over my face at Isabella's complaint. She was known for challenging her professors, Grundy included. Last class she argued that Frankenstein was really the embodiment of current global discrimination. When Grundy wasn't having it, she proposed that he was part of the problem. That made me instantly like her.

"I wouldn't be surprised if he did." I chuckled. Isabella smiled a dazzling smile back. The pair looked so relaxed; Mick's arm slung around her shoulder giving her a quick squeeze while his own grin emerged.

"I'm Isabella by the way. And this is my boyfriend Mick." She inclined her head to Mick who turned his stare to me for a quick second.

"Hey Grace." He offered a warm smile that didn't lack an ounce of sincerity. He was just genuinely nice.

"Hey. Now what can I grab you guys?" I didn't mean not sound pushy or rush them, and surprisingly they didn't take it that way, not even missing a beat.

"Hmmmm. You know what Grace, I trust you. How about you surprise us. Anything you think is worth the hype." Isabella seemed genuinely excited about her request as her eyes lit up, dancing with a heavy dose of enthusiasm. Normally this would cause me to roll my eyes and almost instantaneously hate someone, but for some reason her reaction made me giggle.

"A challenge huh? I'll be right out with those." I gave a quick smirk and went behind the counter to make them their drinks. I really did like Isabella, although she was sweet you could tell that she didn't take anyone's shit, the same going for Mick.

It was hard to believe someone as levelheaded and relaxed as Mick could be related to Maverick Foster in anyway. Maverick was known for being a hot head. Anything could set him off, and no one wanted to be on the brunt end of the rage that that 6-foot-four frame of pure muscle could muster. He was a cocky bastard, brilliant in school but refused to apply himself in any way. And then there was Mick, just as large but seemed to be a big teddy bear. He was known as the opposite as his cousin, the kid was genuine, but he could handle himself when needed. However, both retained the reputation of attracting a lot of girls. Once Mick found Isabella, he lost that part of his reputation. But not Maverick. Together, the Fosters were a force to be reckoned with, and that didn't even include their pack of frat brothers that backed them.

I added a small mountain of whipped cream on each large mug and a small dusting of sugar and cinnamon. Perfect. I carried the two steaming mugs over to Mick and Isabella's booth, the smell of sweet pumpkin making my own mouth water.

"I present two pumpkin coffee cake brews with whipped cream and cinnamon sugar sprinkles." Isabella's mouth practically drooled as she wrapped her hands around the mug, humming softly to herself.

Without any hesitation Mick picked up his cup and took a big gulp. Pulling it away from his lips, his upper lip was covered in a froth of whipped cream. Isabella reached up and whipped it off with the pad of her thumb, the gesture seeming so intimate and yet so casual. I had to look away as my stomach turned leaden with yearning and guilt.

"Compliments to the barista Grace." Mick gave me a big toothy grin. I gave them both a quick nod before returning to my next table, leaving them to giggle over swaths of whipped cream.

Chapter Two

The hours of the afternoon started to drag into the night and soon I started to wrap up and close. Just as I finished sweeping, I heard the bell at the door chime behind me. Fucking great, don't these college kids know how to read by now?

"We're closed…." I start to turn around, but am stopped abruptly.

"Excuse me can we get two large cups of kiss my ass with extra whipped. Thanks doll." Mae says with a wink. I can't help but roll my eyes. Of course, she comes to pick me up at the end of my shift, most likely to try to convince me to go to yet another waste of space's party.

Her tall slender frame displays her tight black jeans and her fiery red tank top. Her black hair slicked back into a messy bun on top of her head. Her deep brown eyes are lined with her signature thick eyeliner. In strolls Jay right behind her. Where Mae is the embodiment of steel and nails, Jay resembles a lost puppy. Jay had been my best friend from home, he was a lost soul, sadness in those honey-colored eyes. His floppy blond hair was covered with a beat-up old baseball hat tonight and his jeans were frayed on the ends where they met his bright red vans. Our little group was a concoction of polar opposites and yet we all seemed to just work, fused together through an unknown commonality.

"Hey Grace. How was your shift?" Jay says through his sheepish grin. I could practically see the adoration in his eyes.

Another part of Jay is that he was hopelessly in love with me, but he refused to tell me. I was kind of glad he never did get the courage to tell me though. I loved Jay, but not in the way that he wanted me to. I couldn't lose him though. I just couldn't. He had been with me throughout high school and had even decided that we should attend the same university, but I could never give him what he wanted from me. There was also the fact that Jay was a recovering addict of all varieties. You would never notice by looking at him, but Jay off the deep end was a total disaster. I couldn't live with myself if I added to his destruction in any way. Not after I had already caused so much.

"As good as cleaning up after a bunch of assholes can be." I shrugged at them with a grin. "Hold up I'll let Bill know that my shift is up." I lifted up the divider in the baby blue counter behind me and grabbed at my hoodie.

"Hey Bill, I'm out of here. I just finished up the last sweep over everything, it's in tip top shape. See you!" I only got a nod and a grunt from Bill. Nothing out of the ordinary.

I stride back up to the front to see Mae typing away at her phone with those long black nails she insists make her look like a badass. Jay is standing by the window with his hands shoved in the pockets of his jeans. As soon as he hears me, he spins around and shoots me a small smile. I tried to ignore that look of love in his eyes.

"So, what are the plans tonight, please tell me it doesn't involve going to a party to stalk that frat boy of yours." That only earned me a dirty look from Mae.

"That's exactly what tonight entails Doll. Let's go get you looking like a decent functioning member of society before we drink ourselves silly, shall we?" She smirked with a wink as she extended her bony elbow toward me, replacing any feigned anger she just displayed.

"The last time you said that you tried to dress me like a goth pin up doll." I tried to suppress my giggle as I linked my arm with Mae's, Jay suddenly next to me. We stepped out into the night air and made the trek back to our dorm building.

Jay seemed a little off, staying quiet while he shuffled next to us, keeping his eyes downcast. I try to blot out the flash of him cradling the girl to his chest, his eyes broken.

I nudged him with my elbow. "You alright tonight Jay? You look a little shook up."

"Yea Gracie, I'm alright. Just a little tired."

"Pinky promise?" I said as I extended my pinky out to him.

"Promise Gracie." He gave me a smile that didn't meet his eyes as he gripped my pinky with his own. I bumped his shoulder and chuckled to try to lighten the mood. He just smiled back and kept shuffling along with us.

***

Once we got back into the room, while Mae played some of her favorite indie music, I quickly lined my eyes with a jet-black eyeliner and did a quick sweep of mascara over my long lashes. I let my hair fall down into long caramel waves. It wasn't too bad if I say so myself.

Once happy with my makeup and hair I dashed to my small closet. Mae was sprawled out on her bed typing away undoubtedly to her frat boy. It was till weird to think that Mae was hopelessly in love with a frat boy over some goth fuck-up but I guess she's friends with Jay and me, her relationships don't really make sense.

Meanwhile Jay is sitting up on my bed, his feet propped up on the headboard while he flips through the channels on our small tv. I pull out hanger after hanger, getting brief glances of disapproval from Mae. I finally settled on a black bustier top; the edges trimmed in lace. I signaled for Jay to cover his eyes as I slipped the top over my torso. I paired it with some of my favorite high wasted skinny jeans and my chunky black boots.

"Fuck, you look hot doll. Keep that shit up and you might just pick up a frat boy." Mae grinned at me. In no way was I picking up my own frat boy. Absolutely not. I noticed Jay's expression falling a bit at the prospect of me getting with someone else. I needed to change the subject before we lost Jay and got that mopey sap all night. Something was obviously wrong with him but when he acted like this, he could usually pick it up quick when we were out.

"Let's go drink shall we ladies?" I flashed them a wicked grin.

"Um Gracie, I'm not one of your ladies. But I sure do feel like getting hammered, so I'll let that slide." The light started to come back to Jay's eyes. Thank God. But I don't like the idea of him thinking about drinking. We all know he was joking, but something in his eyes tells me he might be serious.

"You? Getting hammered? Yea okay Jay. Last time you said that you nursed a bottle of beer all night and insisted that you were on your fifth." Mae cackled. I suppressed my own giggle as Jay displayed a look of insult. When he was younger and used to binge a lot after his mom died. He was an outcast, like me so I took him under my wing. Even though it was probably hypocritical of me to help him with his alcohol abuse, I did. He doesn't really drink at all now, and I on the other had liked to pretend that I was invincible.

"Ok Mae let's just get you to your airhead." Now it was Mae's turn to feign insult. Jay cackled at his ability to piss her off. I grabbed both of their hands and we walked up to Jay's beat-up old jeep.

Despite the wear in the leather seats that revealed a few loose springs and the rusting dusty blue paint job, this jeep was damn reliable in getting us to and from these parties. It sounded as if it could die any second and yet it was always reliable.

As per usual I hop into the front seat while Mae squeezes into the back, her blue-black hair reflecting the lights from the dashboard. The engine gutters to life, casting a thrum as if it were alive. I fidget with the dials until I have the heat blasting and the radio cranked. I have the odd habit of turning on the heat and rolling down all the windows. There is just something about it that's totally perfect. I stretch my arm out into the night air out the window as Jay peels out of his parking spot, his tires screeching in protest.

Mae almost immediately pulls her hair out of its bun, letting the long straight strands blow in the fall night air. There was a slight nip to the air that marked the end of summer, but it made the night that much better. Everything around me thrummed with excitement, a sense of expectation as if this night meant something big. And I felt high off the sensation.

Chapter Three

We all screech the words to each song that blasts over the small radio as we get closer to our destination. You can hear the party from a few blocks away, the steady pumping of the bass and the cheers of frat brothers. The usual thrill that comes with the prospects of the night settles over us.

Jay pulls up to park a block away from the house, the only spot available as cars line both sides of the street. We waltz up to the lawn to be greeted by the familiar sight of red solo cups littering the grass outside the house. It is crawling with college kids all hungry to get a drink in their hand. I kicked a few cups in my path and started twirling to the thrumming of the music. Jay grabbed my hand, spinning me around until his hands wrapped around my waist to dip me back. We both cackled as I punched him in the arm. Something about this night seemed different, as if everything was stuck in an oozing stillness. I didn't know what to expect but whatever it was I was excited to face it.

We finally made our way to the front door and were immediately greeted by the scene of smoke clouds hovering over barely dressed girls flirting with boys on the prowl. The lights were dim, making the led colors from the string lights that much brighter. We probably could get high from just standing there. I was in my element. Mae gave me a quick squeeze, she always did when she was excited about something. There was no doubt in my mind it had something to do with the guy she was constantly thinking about in that twisted little head of hers.

"I'm going to find Bo. I love you my babes. Let's live it up!" Mae seemed as if she was already drunk off of the energy alone. I couldn't help but laugh as she strutted away dancing as she went, to quickly find the tall muscular boy that is Bo.

Bo met Mae last year at a party similar to this one and was instantly in love. They were polar opposites, but they really did make for a cute couple. Bo had this floppy brown hair and rugged frat boy look to him while Mae looked like she walked out of a 90s grunge music video. His face immediately lit up when he saw her and swept her into a big bear hug. She giggled and smacked at his arms as he twirled her around in a circle. It was almost gross how into each other they were. Almost.

"That didn't last very long did it." Jay huffed. He followed his comment with a little glance at me and a blush crept up his cheeks. His eyes lingered a little too long on my lips before returning to the scuffed wood of the floors.

"I need a drink." I flashed him a quick smile before making a beeline to the kitchen. As much as I loved Jay, I had to get away from that sappy Romantic comedy stare down. It had been a long week and I really couldn't trust myself not to snap. That might make me a shitty person, but Jay is one of the few people that know the real me and I can't afford to lose him. I just hoped that he would be okay. He would without a doubt find someone to talk to in this crowd of people.

Just as I turned around to head to the kitchen looking for a drink, something solid bumped right into me spilling his cheap beer right down the front of my top as I rounded the corner. The sharp scent of yeast and stale alcohol stinging my nose.

"James you son of a bitch get in here! Where has your dumbass been!" The unmoving wall lifted his muscled arm gripping the sloshing solo cup high in the air. After he finally realized that I was standing there drenched in his drink his expression shifted to that of concern. I grit my teeth, trying not to lash out. *Calm down Grace, it's just a beer, just a beer.*

"Oh, shit I am so sorry. I totally didn't see you there. C'mere let's get you cleaned up." His tone sounded sincere and for some reason I immediately trusted him. He grabbed my hand in his, his own warm one seemed to engulf mine. His strawberry blond hair grazed the nape of his neck and curled up at the edges. Splashes of freckles covered the bridge of his nose and spread across his cheeks. The most intriguing of his features though was his nose, slightly too large for his face but held these deep pale eyes that seemed to melt my very core.

"I really am sorry. Sometimes I forget that I am a clumsy idiot the size of King Kong. I gotta admit though I didn't think I would knock into a girl as gorgeous as you. I really hope I didn't ruin whatever that is you got on." He gestured down to my top with interest, his eyes staying on my chest a little too long.

"Eyes up here buddy. And I hope your cheap beer doesn't ruin it either." I don't mean to be rude but it kind of just slips out. A blush creeps up his face as if he were a small schoolboy scolded by his mother. I can't help but let out a sigh. "Look I'm sorry I didn't mean to snap at you. It's just been a really long week. I know you didn't mean to assault my bustier with your beer. What I really need now though, is my own drink in my hand."

"Now that I can help you with." He said through his grin, any hurt immediately gone from his face. "I'm Finn by the way."

"Grace." I extend my hand which he swiftly envelops in his own and shakes once with a smile on his face.

"Hold up. Grace? Where have a heard that before?"

Oh great here it comes. The Inevitable recognition that comes when connecting me to my name. I am one of the Politician's kids, despite how hard I try to hide it. My stomach clenched with nerves, preparing for the inevitable array of questions and comments concerning my messed-up past.

"You're Gray!" Wait what? Gray? Who the fuck is Gray?

"So, yea, my name is not Gray and if you ever say it again, I might have to punch you in the face." I gave him a smirk even though I might have just meant every word.

"Yea okay Grace whatever floats your boat I guess." He flashes me a movie star grin that seems to have a tone of knowing behind it, waggling his eyebrows in a boyish gesture.

"Ok? About that drink?" I tried to change the subject, to do anything to get rid of that knowing look in his eyes. He flashed another grin and turned to the fridge in the corner. He threw a towel to me to clean myself up and began his search.

"What are we thinking, Wine? Champagne? Or a classic cheap beer?"

"Are Wine and Champagnes really options?"

"Nope." He turns around with a can of beer gripped in one hand. His own drink gripped in the other. I gratefully grab it and pop the top. I throw it back and it is gone in what feels like two gulps, the stale taste coating my tongue while the cool liquid glides down my throat.

"Holy shit Grace. That was badass. Want another?" I just nod, not even buzzed in the slightest. He passed me another and I pop the top again. This one takes three gulps.

"Damn ok. Was it really that bad of a week?" he asked, the metallic can still chilled despite its empty state resting in my hand.

"You don't even know the half of it." I gave him a look that he takes as I need another and soon, he replaced the empty in my hand with a full can. This time I decided to take it easy and sip it instead of chugging it like my last two victims.

"Anyway, I gotta go beat that shit out of the asshole over there. Take it easy over here, maybe I'll catch up to you in a bit." He claps a large hand on my shoulder and headed out of the door in front of me, stalking towards a pudgy guy leaning on the wall next to a completely uninterested girl.

That was interesting. I think to myself. As much as I hate to admit it though, Finn was pretty cute and charming, in a clumsy teenager sort of way. He couldn't be younger than 21 but he had this boyish charm about him. If I wasn't such a bitch, I might even have been able to be friends with him. But I am in fact a bitch.

I threw back my head and drank the other half of my beer, the cold liquid sloshing down my throat as I slam the can next to my other two empties. This week really did suck. Not only was my schoolwork kicking my ass, but it had also been Peter's birthday.

I absolutely adored my little brother and as much as I wanted to see him, I couldn't risk being caught by my parents and the inevitable lecture that would ensue. Never mind the fact that I had no way of getting there. I had called him, and he had assured me that it was okay, but I missed him. I needed to see him, but he was in unchartered territory. It caused a full-on grief situation of my old life. I didn't miss the stuck-up snobs that surrounded me during campaign parties or the stuffy clothes and roles. I missed my family. I know it's crazy that I complain about them, but I really do love my parents. My dad seemed to have two separate personalities, my dad and the Politician.

They were stuffy, into appearances. I could only hope that they loved me deep down. I just felt as if I was a constant disappointment to them. I had to get out, especially after what had happened. *Birdie?* I shook my head against the sudden onslaught of memories. Now instead of sitting at some preppy country club sipping champagne with rich snobs, I'm in a frat boys kitchen downing shitty alcohol by myself. Sounds about right.

I pulled out my phone and scrolled through my contacts until I found Peter's name. I clicked on it just to check in, I told myself, and make sure that he was alright. The phone only rang twice before he picked up.

"Hey you got Pete." He sounded happy, his deep voice bringing me back home for a second.

"Hey Pete, it's me. Just wanted to check in on you how's it going?"

"Grace! It's actually going really well. I'm captain of the team this year and- hey wait where are you it's really loud. Please tell me you aren't in trouble. You aren't in trouble, are you?" I let out a laugh. Even though I was the older sibling it seemed like Pete always took care of me.

"No Pete. I'm fine I promise. I'm at some stupid ass party with Jay and Mae. I might have had a few drinks. But its fine I'm ok."

"Alright as long as you are ok. Hey, look I gotta go the boys are here. I'll talk to you later ok?"

"Ok Pete be careful please."

"Always." I could picture him winking as he said the words.

I hang up and slipped my phone into my back pocket. I couldn't help but let out another sigh. I knew he was having fun; he was just having fun without me. I did it to myself, but it still stings.

That's it, there had to be something here that was stronger than beer. I pushed myself away from the counter that I had been leaning on in search of a new source of alcohol. I pulled open the fridge and rummaged through in hopes of finding anything somewhat strong. Pickles, cheese, beer. Really? That's it. I slammed the metallic door of the fridge, threading my fingers through my hair with a huff. I stomped over to the sink and opened the small cab underneath. Cleaner, a sponge. Score, a handle of vodka. That'll do just fine.

I gripped the bottle around the neck and stare down at it as I savor the feel of the smooth glass encased in my palm. As I turned around, I end up bumping into something solid. Of course, I bump into another frat boy. The slick bottle nearly crashed to the ground in the process.

"Do you guys travel in packs or something because I keep bumping..." I stop mid-sentence as I stared into those eyes. There is nothing I could use to even describe them. They are the kind of green that gets you excited for summer, its calming and pale yet still promises life. Not only that but they were piercing, as if they could see right through my façade. Framed by dark neat brows and settled above a long handsome nose. A swish of dark brown hair rested against his forehead. Those full lips, their only imperfection a small birthmark right above the left corner stuck in an expression of indifference.

Chapter Four

"Excuse me? Are you just going to stare at me all night or are we going to split that handle?" Maverick Foster gets out as one side of that perfect mouth quirk to the side, lifting his birthmark with them. His voice was deep and smooth, warming me down to my toes. I watched as his eyes took me in, seeming trapped where I stood. I gulped. *Pull yourself together Grace.*

He quizzically pulled a neat eyebrow up with a mocking grin as if he knew exactly what he was doing to me. As if he had the same effect on me that he did of the rest of the female population. That look alone snapped me back to reality, setting me on edge.

"I don't like sharing. Sorry looks like you're going to have to find your own." I shrugged, starting to walk away with the bottle in hand.

"That's the thing, that is mine, and I don't like to share either." I felt a hand encircle my wrist, immediately rooting me in place. I spun around to face him as he removed his hand with a chuckle. That cocky expression did nothing but piss me off. The hand not holding the handle pressed into a fist. Looking into those eyes I flipped the cap off and started to drink. As I lowered the bottle, I wiped the excess off my lips with a quick dart of my tongue, savoring the way he watched my mouth with a hunger that would never be satisfied. I shot him a look of smugness. Check mate.

He watched every movement, looking me over from head to toe, finally finding my eyes. He gripped the bottle around the barrel, barely grazing my hand as he lifted it to his own full lips. He took a big swig, his eyes never leaving mine. The beat from the blasting music thumped around us, and there I stood thankful for it because without it I swear he would have heard my heart pounding. He slowly dragged the bottle from his lips and thrust it back into my hands. His white t-shirt shifted with the movement, his tattoos visible through the tin fabric, at least the ones that didn't spill down his arms. A blush burned across my cheeks, making me furious with myself.

"Looks like we are learning to share though, huh?" He rested his hands against the counter I was just on, bracing his hands on either side of him so I was forced to face him. Those eyes danced at me drawing me in. "Now are you going to ask me who I am, or do you already know?"

What an ass. "I know who you are I just don't care." I shrugged.

"Is that so? Are you going to tell me who you are?"

"Nope. I assumed you already knew." I could feel the side of my lips quirk up.

"I do actually know who you are, Gray." He threw his own smile back in my face.

"Why the fuck is everyone calling me Gray tonight? Like what is that?" I scrunched my nose in disgust from the nickname.

"Aw poor, Gray. People actually know who you are poor you." He fake pouts, his eyebrows pulling in.

"You are one cocky bastard, aren't you?" I felt my eyebrows furrow involuntarily. I must have looked like such a bitch. My insult earned a deep chuckle that made my stomach flutter. *What the fuck, get control of yourself Grace he is an arrogant ass.* I placed the handle down on the counter to my right after taking another large swig. I crossed my arms over my chest now that they were empty and strode right up to him. I moved slowly, taking my time. Bracing my own hands on either side of his own as I leaned my face towards his. When my lips were so close to his I could practically feel them, I looked into those eyes to see surprise, and that trademark arrogance. The smell of smoke and mint swirled around me, radiating from him.

"You are lucky that you look the way you do. I'm pretty tempted to punch that pretty little face of yours, but I wouldn't want to ruin it." I give him a wicked smile, never breaking eye contact. He smirked, his eye lids starting to flutter shut. He wanted to kiss me, I could tell. I acted as if I was in his spell, our lips about to touch. The space between us was closing at a sluggish place, our breaths shared rasps. Then I pushed myself away from him right as my lips were about to graze his own. His eyes snapped open, shock taking over the sleepy lust that was just there. His lips stuck out in a pout till he quickly smoothed them back into a fake indifference. But those eyes were his flaw, they told me that he was pissed and shocked at being cock blocked. He was too easy.

"You thought I was going to kiss you, didn't you? If I don't even want to share a drink with you, what makes you think that I would kiss you?" I huffed and started to turn and walk away, grabbing the handle on the way out of the kitchen, smirking as I went.

"That was slick I'll give you that. I guess I'll see you around, Gray." He called.

"I doubt it." I didn't even have to turn around to know that he was watching me walk away from him. I couldn't help but smile.

I felt electric with adrenaline from the near kiss. The feeling of his hot breath tickling my skin. I wandered into the living room to find Mae and Jay. Some kind of hip hop was blasting through the speaker and it didn't take long to spot Mae through the writhing bodies on the makeshift dance floor. Her long arms were thrown around Bo's neck, reaching up to compensate for his height. Bo's large hands gripped her waist as they dipped and swayed to the ecstatic beat.

I could feel the adrenaline and all I could think about was what it would feel like for Maverick's hands to be on me like that. I rose up unto the balls of my feet and couldn't help bouncing to the music, taking two more big gulps out of the bottle in my hand, the alcohol burning my throat with a wicked delight. Everything thrummed with life, energy. I soon felt hands around my waist just not the ones I wanted. I turned to find Jay smiling, a bottle in one hand a dreamy look in his eyes. *Shit. Shit. Shit.* There goes our ride home. And more importantly he was drinking. Something must be wrong. Now he was here drunk off his ass. But I don't know if it was the alcohol or the adrenaline. But I couldn't focus.

My teeth were numb from the vodka as I took another big gulp, the familiar burn in my throat welcome. I turned back around and felt those eyes again. I looked around; Jay still latched onto my waist. And there he was, muscled arms crossed, the tattoos on full display propped against the doorway, watching me. If he wanted a show, I'd give him one. One more drink for good luck and I had basically finished a half of the handle on my own, throwing it to the ground. The lights around me blurred together as I stretched my arms over my head, moving against Jay to the music.

I gave a flirtatious smile and ground my ass into Jay. He was hesitant at first, but he eventually began to dance with me. I knew it was wrong but all I could sense were those eyes and I wanted to make him jealous. My vision blurred as all the alcohol set in. I reached back and grabbed Jay's hands dragging him out to the dance floor with me. We found our way next to Mae and Bo. I threw my own arms around Jay and began to sway my body to the thumping bass. Jay's beer was gone, where I don't know but it wasn't there anymore. He grabbed my arms, holding on and swaying along with me. I glanced back to the door jam to see Maverick still staring, this time his brows furrowed, and his mouth set in a hard line.

I swung my hips out more, knowing that he would see. Meanwhile Jay was becoming sloppier, his arms trailing all over me till they were cupped around my backside. I just kept dancing. Everything was fluid, moving in slow motion. Jay's eyes were unfocused, roving over me with a hunger I had never seen from him. A smile stretched across my face, my hair swinging in a caramel curtain with each sway of my hips. And just like that, everything came crashing down, Jay saw his window and took it, shoving his mouth onto mine. His kiss was sloppy, rushed. His lips seemed to engulf my face as his tongue tried to force its way into my mouth. The taste of stale beer coated my mouth, threatening to strangle me. I squinched my eyes shut. *What am I doing. I'm using him, I'm using my best friend to make a stranger jealous.* I braced my hands on his chest and pushed Jay back. His eyes shot open reflecting shock and hurt.

I could feel the sting of vodka and bile burning in the back of my throat. I clamped my hand over my mouth and ran, leaving a shocked Jay alone on the dance floor. I pushed through masses of people, running as fast as my boots could carry me. Beer sloshed around me and I could hear slurs being thrown at me, but I had to get out of there. I had to get out. I finally reached the door and barely made it out. I fell to my knees in the grass already covered in dew. I retched and retched, the vodka burning my throat the whole way.

I whipped my mouth with the back of my hand and sat in the grass, sucking the cool air into my lungs. What did I just do? I scoot back from where I just threw up, sitting in the wet grass. Feeling it begin to soak through the fabric of my jeans and not even caring. I started up at the sky threading my fingers in my hair. Only a few stars were visible, the lawn seemed quiet despite the fact that drunk college kids were all around slurring their words and stumbling over forgotten solo cups. I gulped in deep breathes. Flashes of Jay's sleepy grin replaced with broken cries and rain mixing with tears. Shattered glass under his knees. Broken, bleeding. I shut my eyes in an attempt to battle off the next wave of nausea.

"Honestly if you can't handle your alcohol, don't fucking drink it. You just made a fool out of yourself." A voice as hard as steel grit out from behind me. I could hear the grass rustling as Maverick came to view and crouched in front of me. He looked furious.

"I can handle my alcohol asswhipe. Get out of my face." My voice sounded like gravel. Each word scratching my already sore throat. That fierce gaze never went away as he shoved a water bottle into my hand. As much as I didn't want to accept it, I was grateful to have something to wash the taste out of my mouth.

"Don't guzzle the whole thing or you're going to throw up again." He commanded. I lowered the bottle from my lips. Tears pricked my eyes, but I would not cry in front of him. He already thought I was weak, and I would in no way encourage that.

"Yea thanks for the advice but I think I got it covered."

He just huffed a sarcastic laugh in my face. "Is that your definition of covered, practically fucking that guy, and then choking down your own vomit once he lands one on you?" Maverick was mocking me. Maverick. Mocking me. Hell no.

"Last time I checked I didn't ask for your opinion, my life is of absolutely no concern to you so do me a favor and get the fuck away from me." I spit at him. How dare he talk to me that way. He didn't even know me.

"Is everything okay here Foster?" Finn came around from behind me, concern lighting his face.

"Its fine Finn. Just a girl who doesn't know how to handle her liquor." Maverick growled out, the muscles in his jaw twitching.

Finn plopped down next to Maverick in the grass, seeming satisfied with his answer. He shot me a grin, but it quickly faded when he took me in.

"Grace? What happened to you? You look like you just saw a ghost or maybe an empty liquor cabinet?" Finn joked but his tone held concern.

"I told you Finn, she couldn't hold her liquor."

"I'm not sure that we are talking about the same girl here. I watched her pound back two beers and start on her third in under two minutes. She seems like she knows her way around."

Maverick's eyes snapped back to my face. His steely gaze tried and failed to corner me as he couldn't hide his surprise. I looked down picking at the grass in front of me. Flashes of what happened with Jay crowded my mind and my stomach flipped again. I used him. The combination of alcohol and adrenaline mixed with the reality of what I did hit me like a truck paired with a fresh wave of nausea. I must have blanched again because Maverick's hands found their way to my shoulders. Finn was instantly by my side, hand on my back.

"Grace take a deep breath alright. You look like you're going to pass out." Finn sounded more serious than I've ever heard him in the few short hours of knowing him.

"Finn do you mind going to find Mick. Bo too, I'm pretty sure she's here with his girl." Maverick's eyes never left my face as he spoke, the command laced with an edge.

"I came here with Jay too." It came out barely a whisper and a whole new wave of shame overtook me.

"Who's Jay? That boy from the dance floor? No, he can crash here tonight he's in rougher shape than you. Before I came out here, he was doing shots with Tug." Maverick sounded calm, calculating. I had no idea who Tug was, but I was worried about Jay. Despite my shame and embarrassment from what I did to him, having Maverick there made me feel slightly better. He nodded to Finn, who after a quick nod back jogged toward the house.

"I can't believe I did that." I whisper more to myself than him. "This is going to destroy him. I knew something was wrong. I should have known, gotten him away from the alcohol." My hands were shaking as I fisted them in the grass. I didn't need him to see me like this. I wanted him to see me as that confident girl from the kitchen, not this shocked mess crumpled in the grass. He would probably just throw it in my face anyway.

His hands trailed down my arms until one of his strong hands gripped mine. I realized how close he was and noted the sharp scent of his cologne, like mint along with the smell of the smoke. The other hand gripped my chin, forcing my eyes to meet his.

He spoke soft and low. "Grace it is going to be okay. I don't know what's wrong but your boyfriend in there will forgive you." His sudden change in tone startled me as I took in the feeling of his hand brushing against my chin.

"That's the problem, he's not my boyfriend." I sniffed. "but he wants to be, and I just dangled it in front of him and I'm going to snatch it away. I used him." Why was I telling him all of this? Maverick was a stranger, a stranger who caused this mess. His brow furrowed in confusion. Then I realized my mistake. I practically just admitted to Maverick that I was using Jay to get his attention. *Shit.*

Footsteps started to approach us, and his hand immediately left my chin. I was filled with relief, grateful for the intervention. Mae practically shoved him out of the way, placing both of her hands on either side of my face.

"Grace? What happened are you okay?" she sounded worried and I knew I was going to lose it as my throat suddenly constricted with the threat of tears. My face crumpled and I could feel the stare of the four boys behind her. She just wrapped her arms around me and let me soak her shoulder with my pitiful tears.

The hum of her voice vibrated against the skin of my cheek. "Boys, I need to get her home, I get Jay is staying here, his jeep is here, but we are going to need a ride."

The boy who I recognized as Mick took a step forward. "I didn't drink anything. Isabella spent the night at her dorm, and I'm supposed to go see her anyway, I'll bring you."

"I'll come too babe; I'm worried about you trying to get her there alone." I recognized his voice to be Bo. Mae shifted me from her shoulders and took in the mess in front of her. I probably looked terrible. The few tears that I let out had definitely started to dissolve my eye makeup. My mouth still tasted of vodka and my jeans were soaked with the dew from the ground. My top reeked of Fin's beer from earlier still.

She put her arms under my shoulders to support me while another set of hands held me from the back. I could tell it was Maverick as his minty scent mingled with sweat hit me full force. Once Mae was satisfied that I was sturdy, she snatched my water bottle off of the ground and left me to Maverick's grip. He threw my arm around his broad shoulders, the muscles shifting under his white t shirt. My feet felt unsteady underneath me as he half dragged me to a black car parked in front of the house. Maverick positioned me in the middle seat, sliding in next to me. Mae sat in the seat on my other side while the Bo sat alongside Mick in the front.

"Mick roll down the window back here but blast the heat so she doesn't get cold." Maverick ordered while he reached across me to buckle me in. My hands were still shaking but I bunched them into fists, placing them on my lap. Finn's face appeared in the now open window.

"Hey Grace take care alright, feel better. Don't worry about your boyfriend in there. I'll take good care of him." He gave me a sympathetic nod, making my stomach clench with guilt.

I managed to get a weak wave at Finn before Maverick growled out "He's not her boyfriend." Finn seemed unfazed by the outburst and simply held his hands, palms out in defeat, trying not to smile.

"Whatever." Maverick whispered under his breath. Satisfied that everyone was ready to go, Mick peeled away from the curb. The ride was silent except for the occasional reassurance from Mae. Only she didn't know what I did. It was possible that she would hate me. I tried to focus on the blurry lights radiating from the dashboard rather than the boy sitting next to me or the fact that I just ruined one of my only friendships. My stomach did flips, and I huffed a deep breath. I could feel his gaze on me immediately. He touched my arm in question, but I just brushed him off.

Chapter Five

We finally pulled up to the dorm parking lot directly in front of my building. The ride did nothing to calm my nerves and only heightened them. My legs felt like jelly as Maverick slid out of the seat next to me, poking his head back in to help me slide out. His hands left my skin, and I began to stumble, only for him to immediately catch me.

"Foster, I got her. Don't worry. You've got places to be." Bo said, obviously indicating something else with his words. He was recognized with a brief nod from Maverick, but his stare was stitched to me. Bo's hands replaced Maverick's as he walked over to Mick, who instantly handed over the keys.

With one more glance at me, Maverick swung himself down into the driver's seat and started it back up. I don't remember Mae getting out of the car, but she was there, her grip like iron yet still soft on my other arm that wasn't in Bo's grip. Mick walked around so he stood in front of us.

"You guys all set?" Mick stood in front of us, his hands shoved into his pockets.

"Yea we should be fine man thanks for the ride. I'll text you in the morning with an update. Keep an eye on him tonight he seems to be in a prissier mood than normal." Bo said as he inclined his head to the still idling car. Mick simply nodded his head and headed to the opposite building; hands still shoved into his pockets. Bo lifted me clean over the curb as if I weighed nothing and helped Mae get me into our dorm.

***

"Hey baby, why don't you go grab some water bottles I think we all need to sober up a little?" Mae questioned with a wink.

Bo immediately understood her ulterior motives. "Of course, babe, I'll see you in a bit." He gave her a swift kiss and closed the door behind him with a soft click.

Once the door closed, an immediate feeling of dread came over me. I could feel the tears well up before I could even react.

"Doll what happened to you tonight? I know it's not the alcohol because I've seen you drink almost an entire handle by yourself before. I've never seen this happen to you before what's up?" Mae slid onto the bed next to me her hand resting on my knee with nothing but concern on her face.

I didn't deserve her. I was obviously overreacting, but this week has just weighed down on me so much and tonight was the tipping point. I had used Jay's feelings against him, to help me get another guy. I was lone, my family probably despised me, Peter probably blames me for the added pressure from our family. My life feels like it's going to shit.

I flopped back onto my bed, covering my face with my hands before Mae could witness the full extent of my tears. Not only was I an awful person, but I inconvenienced five other people in the process. I could feel the blood rushing and burning my cheeks as the mixture of embarrassment and shame seeped into me.

"Honey, its ok. We don't have to talk about it tonight, ok. We are all just worried about you. Let's just get you to bed ok?" The bed shifted as she got up, and not soon after I could feel her tugging off my boots. "Um Doll, do you mind helping me out here." She gripped my hands, gently prying them from my face. I rolled up, already prepared to wallow in my self-pity. I tugged off my top and replaced it with an old band t shirt. After struggling with my damp skinny jeans, I finally found myself in my bed.

The exhaustion from the night started to weigh heavy on my eyelids, dragging them down.

"Everything is going to be alright Doll." Mae softly stroked my hair tucking it behind my ear before giving me a quick peck on the forehead. I barely heard when Bo came in as I found myself drifting off, weighed down by my own self-loathing.

I heard the soft murmurs coming from Bo, while Mae offered soft chuckles. I drifted off imagining that that was me and Maverick joking around, his hand still wrapped around my chin.

Chapter Six

I woke up to my head throbbing and my throat screaming at me. My mouth was so dry and even the soft sunlight coming through the swath of curtains in my dorm made my head pound. I looked over to Mae's tangle of purple sheets to find Bo's arms wrapped around her, cradling her as they both slept.

I rubbed at my face, stretching out, my stiff joints groaning. And then it all came back. Jay. Nausea lurched in my stomach. I had kissed Jay. More importantly, Jay was drinking again and was teetering on a relapse and I had no idea why. Instead, I was using him to make Maverick Foster jealous. Then remember the way Maverick held my chin, our lips a breath away from each other. *Fuck.*

I grapple for a pillow and hurl it over at Mae's bed. As it smacked her body, my efforts only granted a groan and an almost inaudible string of swears.

"Mae wake up." I croaked out. My voice sounded hoarse, almost unrecognizable. I rolled over onto my stomach to check my phone, a slight wave of nausea overtaking me with the movement. The screen lit up. 11:30 a.m. and 1 missed call from Pete. I'm going to have to call him back later. I shot Jay a quick text asking where he is and if he's ok, watching as the blue bubble teetered on the empty black screen.

I rolled back over, placing my phone back in its place don the windowsill. As I struggled to sit up my head protested, thrown into a fit of rage and thundering with the effects of last night's binge. I quickly wrapped my hair up into a messy bun on the top of my head and threw the blankets off of me. Padding over to Mae, armed with another pillow in case she turned violent from being woken up, I tapped her shoulder. More grumbles until one of her fierce dark eyes creaked open and she looked up at me. Exhaustion was clear from the deep bags cradling her eyes.

"Doll? What time is it?" she whispered as she started to shove the loose locks of her hair out of her face. Bo started to stir from his place beside her as Mae pushed her hair directly into his face. His eyes slowly opened as he began to realize where he is, wrapped in a tangle of bright purple sheets and sporting a fuzzy blanket.

"It's 11:30. Get up." I softly shook her shoulder. Every movement made my head pulse with pain.

"I'm up, I'm up." She stretched as much as Bo's arms allowed. Bo doing the same, reluctantly letting Mae go. I watch them, feeling weighed down by guilt and exhaustion.

"Hey Grace. How you feeling this morning?" Bo asks from his place next to Mae, squinting against the sun peppering them both. Mae seemed to suddenly remember the events of the previous night, snapping her attention back to me.

"Like shit. But nothing a little hangover breakfast can't solve right?" I lied. Mae could tell that I was ling through my teeth, but she dropped it, sensing I'd rather not talk about it in front of Bo.

"I'm starving, sounds good Grace. I'm assuming you girls need to get ready or some shit so wake me up before we go." Bo turned back around to fall back asleep, earning a quick pinch from Mae and a giggle.

I pad back to my own side of the room, scared to look at the carnage of last night. I cringed at my wild hair and the black makeup streaked across my face. My eyes were puffy, and bags hung out from under them. It was worse than I thought. I attempted to run a brush through my long strands and go to grab a quick shower. Mae doing the same. After we both shower and brush our teeth, I see my efforts wielded some results.

My eyes looked better and my face was clean at least. I twisted up my wet strands into a bun on the top of my head, swiping a quick coat of mascara on my lashes. I opted for comfort over fashion, throwing on a pair of leggings and a baggy hoodie. After finally pulling on a pair of Vans I realized how starving I was, no doubt from the phantom hangover that haunted me.

Mae was ready a whole ten minutes before me, whining that she was hungry while she tried to wake up a slumbering Bo. She looked beautiful in an effortless way as she let her long black hair drape around her shoulders, sporting a distressed pair of mom jeans and a tight t-shirt. Bo eventually rolled up, throwing on his t shirt from last night. After heaving a disheveled Bo out of bed, I was ravenous, my stomach hollow after ridding itself of its contents the night before. I clutched at my stomach with the memory.

"Doll I'm trying not to pressure you into talking here, but what the hell happened last night?" asked a concerned Mae, her hand tucked into Bo's as the cool air tried its best to wake us up. Bo peeked around her and looked at me, concern in his eyes. I quickly wiped my hand across my eyes and let it fall back to my side. After a long sigh and another wave of nausea I decide maybe I should just tell her. I had done a lot of things in my life that ruined me, could easily be considered worse than this. But that didn't help the nerves racking my mind.

"I did something fucking dumb last night. I was kind of buzzed and….."I looked down at my beat up shoes. I could feel Mae's stare knitted with pity. "I danced with Jay and he kissed me. It was my fault. I was leading him on and he was drinking and then it just happened. I ran away and then Mave- you guys found me." I stuttered out.

My confession was followed by some silence, I refused to look up into Mae's eyes. I couldn't bring myself to see the look of disgust that I was sure was plastered there.

"Grace, it's not your fault. Jay knows that you don't feel that way about him. He chose to kiss you knowing that information." Mae stated without an ounce of harshness in her voice, only understanding. It only made me feel worse.

"You don't get it Mae, I was dancing with him and I knew he was drunk and I didn't even care."

"Doll, it's not your fault he was drinking. It was a little fucked up for you to tease him like that but shit happens. You were probably just drunk and not thinking. Its ok."

"But it's not. I fucked everything up." My chest felt like it was caving in, the ghosts of Jay's hands gripping me, the burn of alcohol urging me to keep moving, keep going. The feel of Maverick's eyes on me intoxicating.

Bo cleared his throat then quickly added, "Grace, I know I don't know everything about this situation but shit like this happens all the time, you aren't the first for it to happen to ok?" He tried to give me a reassuring smile as Mae reached out and squeezed my hand once in reassurance. Only, I knew I didn't deserve their sympathy. This was my fault they have to see that. *Hey Birdie.* The memories of my past flood my vision and I have to do all I can not to crumple to the sidewalk.

Guilt still racked through me with each leaden step.

"Now about Jay drinking? We should figure that one out until he ends up right back where he started. I'll call him later, see if he wants to grab dinner?" Mae raised an eyebrow, looking at me for approval. I simply nodded my head.

Seeming satisfied, the rest of the walk to the café is spent chattering, mostly between Bo and Mae, about the night before and how Tug ended up in the hospital with a broken arm after he dove headfirst into a pong table. I still had no idea who Tug was, but I was too preoccupied with my own thoughts to care.

I offered a feigned laugh here and there, my mind still preoccupied with not only Jay but thoughts of Maverick. The way he cradled my chin in his hand. Those green piercing eyes watching mine as I ran my tongue over my vodka covered lips. A shiver ran down my spine. *Grace stop.* But I couldn't stop thinking about him. Yes, he was an absolute ass, but he had helped me. Something was lurking under that arrogant exterior and I wanted to know what. Then again, how could I bring myself to get close to him? If the previous night was proof of anything, it was that I had a tendency to mess things up. I pictured those eyes again only this time they were deep brown, lined with silver tears and reflecting the ravaging orange of fires.

Chapter Seven

The familiar smells of fresh pastries and burnt coffee tell me that we are finally at the café, snapping me out of my thoughts, my stomach letting out a low growl. The café is bustling as it usually is on a Saturday. My replacement for the day, Jenny, flutters around the small space, balancing stacks of cups on a tray. She offered me a quick smile and a wink before crashing the tray down on the counter.

Her platinum blond hair was stacked up into a messy knot, held back by a wide headband. I liked Jenny, she was snarky and quirky but not afraid to speak her mind. Her small frame made her look younger than her actual age of 21. It was hard to believe that she was a year older than me sometimes as I towered over her 5 feet. But what she lacked in height she made up for in wit. I gave her a quick halfhearted wave and led Mae and Bo to a booth in the back, the same one Mick and Isabella sat in the previous day. Only today it harbored ripped sugar packets and stray stirring sticks, but we didn't mind.

I plunked myself down into one side of the booth while the two-love birds took over the other side.

"Hiya Grace. Rough night?" Jenny said through her big toothy grin. I stuck my tongue out at her. "I'm assuming the usual right? For all you guys?" her dazzling eyes flicked around the table, staying a beat too long on Mae. Bo seemed to notice, stiffening a little but only earning a chuckle from Jenny.

"Something tells me Bo isn't going to like an iced caramel macchiato." I huffed a laugh. "I'll take two of my usual for me and Mae here and get Bo a big mug of our strongest brew, Black." I looked to him for confirmation and he eagerly nodded, Mae looking at him with adoration in her eyes. I had a knack for knowing coffee order from being stuck working here for the past two years.

Jenny shot me a wink, "You got it. I'll be right back. Try not to throw up on the upholstery would ya?" I shot her a glare but couldn't help the small chuckle that escaped. Jenny sauntered away, throwing a few flirtatious looks over her shoulder at the small table crowded with a bunch of rowdy freshman boys. They stared at her walking away, their mouths slack jawed as they elbowed each other trying to get a better view. Jenny was gorgeous and she knew it too. I turned my attention back to my two friends chatting to each other at the table.

"Ah shit, I forgot to text Mick. I told him I'd let him know how you were in the morning. I'll let him know where we are. I'm sure that him and Isabella worked up an appetite." Bo chuckled as Mae swatted his arm. He gave her a big toothy grin and stood up from our booth, his hand practically engulfing his phone as he raised it to his ear. He started mumbling into it, pacing away a few steps.

"Things are getting pretty serious between the two of you, huh?" Mae brought her gaze back to me with the words, her cheeks pink and a dreamy look in her eyes.

"I never even thought it was possible to love someone like that. I just can't help it. I mean look at him not only is he gorgeous, but he's sweet and caring. He really is a big teddy bear." She rested her chin in her hand and looked at me even though I had the distinct feeling that she wasn't really looking at me. She seemed lost in her own happiness, her eyes unfocused. I couldn't help but envy her a little. She did it, she found Bo. He was made for her.

Bo glimpsed back at us, a wide grin overtaking his face as he spotted Mae. My mind started to drift to Maverick. Those eyes and the way his hand had gripped my chin. His hands, rough and calloused yet gentle as they cradled me. *Stop. You can't get involved with Maverick.* I roll my eyes at myself and focus on the empty sugar packets in front of me instead. I knew what happened the last time I was with someone. My heart squeezed in my chest with the memory.

"Mick is gonna come down with Isabella." Bo says as he slides back into the booth. I barely heard though, stuck in a world of shattered glass and ear shattering screams. They seemed oblivious.

"Good. I like her." Mae winks and pecks Bo on the check. Geez did my head hurt. I brought both my hands up to my temples rubbing them to ease the ache. I quickly decided that right after our little jaunt to the café I was going to bury myself in my bed and not leave it for the rest of the day. The smell of coffee hit me like a truck as Jenny placed it in front of my nose. Rubbing my eyes one last time, I wrapped my hand around the cup, shoving a straw into the plastic cover. Jenny knew me too well. Next to it she placed a plain bagel, toasted to perfection and placed with the café's infamous strawberry cream cheese. I moaned just looking at it. I gave her as big as a grin as I could muster as my teeth sank into the delicious dough. Another moan fell from my lips despite my clouded thoughts and unmistakable guilt coiled in my stomach.

Jenny placed down the other two drinks, getting in return a huge grin from Bo and a wink from Mae. Bo was practically drooling over his mug, inhaling the scent of the fresh brew. Mae elbowed him once before taking a sip of her own drink. I gulped down a few sips of my coffee, savoring the richness of the caramel and the way the cool drink coated my dry throat. The comfort the drink brought was minuscule, but a comfort, nonetheless.

After I finished about half of my bagel, the door chimed open to reveal Mick, his long, muscled arm wrapped around Isabella's shoulders. Isabella once again looked effortless, sporting tight jeans and a t-shirt, displaying her lace like tattoo. Mick just gazed at her as if she were the only person around. Was everyone around me in love? As happy as I was for all of them, I couldn't help but feel jealous, I would never get that. I didn't deserve that. Isabella's eyes brightened up as she spotted us, pointing for Mick to see. She glided over, Mick following behind with his hand still laced in hers.

"Grace! Are you okay? Mick filled me in about last night. Let me know if I need to beat someone's ass, I won't hesitate." Isabella scrunched up her nose in anger and I couldn't help but smile. Mick pulled up a chair behind her, setting another one next to her for himself and coaxing her to sit.

"I don't doubt that you would for a second babe, but why don't you leave the ass kicking for me? If anyone even looked at you the wrong way you know I would have to do something about that." Mick placed a kiss on her forehead and plopped down next to her, learning his muscled figure into her side as he threw his arm around her.

"I'm alright. I'm not usually the type to lose it to alcohol but I guess I did last night." I shrugged not wanting my embarrassing truth to be aired out before I even finished my coffee. Isabella's eyebrow cocked up just a little, as if she knew that I was lying, but chose not to push me. Instead, she reached over and gripped my hand giving it a quick squeeze before entwining her fingers with Mick's.

"Hey Mick. I wanted to say thank you. I know that I was a mess last night. It was actually pretty embarrassing. So, um, thanks." I couldn't bring myself to meet his clear blue eyes out of shame.

"Don't sweat it Grace. If that were my girl, I would've wanted someone to help her ya know? Plus, I don't think Maverick would have let me live even if I didn't want to drive you guys so there is that." Mick said through his grin. Bo and Mae chuckling along with the other couple.

A million butterflies immediately filled my stomach at the mention of Maverick. Where was he? I swallowed down my question and gave my companions a quick grin. What did Mick mean though? Maverick wouldn't have cared what happened to me, I was some random girl who stole his alcohol and was nothing but a burden to him.

The rest of our time at the café was spent chatting and sipping on our coffees. My headache was still persistent, and I could feel my eyes growing heavier despite the caffeine. My mind was reeling with thoughts of Jay and the mystery that was Maverick.

As we were finishing up, we got interrupted by the vibrations of someone's phone. Mick gripped at both pockets till he pulled out his cell, staying in his seat with his arm slung around the back of Isabella's chair. He shot a quick glance at me, then answered. The look left me unsettled.

"Hey Maverick, What's....." immediately his brow furrowed. We could all hear the mumblings that indicated yelling on the other line. *Maverick.* I could feel my eyes grow wider and my heart pick up its pace. Mick looked sufficiently angry, enough so that Isabella placed her small hand on his large chest, looking up into his face. Across from me Bo stiffened, as if he knew exactly what was happening. Even the air around us filled with tension around us, almost tangible in the coffee scented air.

"That son of a bitch." Mick growled. "Look I'll be right there. I just gotta drop off Is. Ya, of course. Alright just hold tight I'll be right there." Mick ended the call. Looking at Isabella in a sort of confirmation. A question was in her eyes, and Mick simply nodded.

"Bo we gotta go. It's, um.." he glanced at me again, "Maverick needs us." Bo simply nodded.

"You girls going to be ok getting back to your dorm?" Bo asked Mae as he stood up from his seat, his brow furrowing.

"Of course, babe." Mae gave him a worried smile. He pecked her mouth before standing to his full towering height.

"It was nice seeing you again Grace. I'll see you later?" Isabella stood along with the guys. I gave her a quick nod and before I could even process what happened, they were all out the door. Was Maverick ok? What was going on?

"Eh, Doll? Let's go back to the dorm yea?" Mae fumbled to get a hold of my hand.

"What was that? Is Maverick ok?" I gripped the edge of the table as I spoke, surprised by my panic.

"Of course. Just something with his car or something I promise they are all ok." I could tell she was lying but I also didn't want to push her. I mean they all helped me so much already. I didn't even have the energy to argue with her. I could tell my frustration was showing as the blood rushed into my cheeks. I clenched my fists and walked out after Mae to head home. What was going on? More importantly why did Maverick have this affect over me?

Chapter Eight

We walked back to the dorm in silence, as a million questions buzzed around my mind. I was worried about the hotheaded yet oddly adorable boy from last night. My head began to pound even harder. Then there was the constant feelings of guilt racking through each step. *Birdie? Birdie!*

I barely noticed when we finally got back, and I flopped into my covers. As I played with a loose string on my comforter, I couldn't help but think about the look on Bo and Mick's faces during that call. They knew something. Their faces sported pure rage. I don't even know this boy. Why have I been nonstop thinking about him since last night? It's like I can't get his face out of my mind, like I can't stop hearing that deep voice that reminds me of honey, warming me to my core. Before I knew it, I was asleep with visions of green eyes and those hands cradling my face.

***

I don't wake up until 7 that night, getting up only for the need to satisfy my immense need for a slice of pizza. I scan the room to see Mae's covers ripped off her bed as per usual, but she is nowhere to be found. I swing my legs out of the comforting warmth that is my bed and place my bare feet on the cold tiles of the floor. Fuck its freezing. I pad over to the small whiteboard on our door to see Mae's messy writing scribbling out that she has plans for the night with Bo and not to wait up. I can't help but smile for her.

I note that I just so happen to still be in the leggings from earlier and a random hoodie. A Saturday night dining on a whole ass pizza for myself calls for sweatpants and movies. I rummage through my drawers, finally deciding on my favorite pair of worn grey sweatpants that are at least two sizes too big for me, I pull on a huge t shirt and fuzzy socks to complete the ensemble. I quickly place my order and scourge Netflix for my newest conquest.

The images from the previous night still rack through my mind, between Jay's lips crashing into mine to the full curve of Maverick's lips that I would have much rather been assaulted with. I need something to block them out. I select a gory film about vampires, minus the gushy romance of course, just as my pizza arrives. I sink deep into a pile of blankets and pillows, a glass of cheap wine in one hand, a slice of pizza in the other. And this right here is exactly why I would much rather not go to some of those dumbass parties. The smell of steam rose from the pie, coating the air in a mixture of spices. My mouth dripped with salvia at the prospect of filling my stomach.

Before I knew it, the end credits are rolling and not only is half my pizza gone, but so is half the bottle of wine I decided to indulge in. I feel a little buzzed and my mind can't help but wander back to last night. I snatch my phone off my bed to see if Jay ever got back to me.

Nothing. Nothing except the small script under my message. *Read.* I slapped my palm against my forehead and sighed, snuggling down deeper into my bed. I can't help but think I fucked up. I needed to find Jay. He is drinking again. Why is he drinking? I needed to find him. I punched in his name and decided to call him. It rings and immediately I found myself at his voicemail.

"Hey Jay, it's me. Um, I know you are probably pissed at me from last night," I cringed at the memory, "but, uh, I'm worried about you. You were drunk last night. Like really drunk. I just want to help you ok? Please call me back Jay. Bye." With a sigh I dropped the phone from my ear. I could feel tears pricking at my eyes. Great. One of my only friends was headed off the deep end and wouldn't even talk to me.

I quickly scanned through my contacts to find Pete's name. He once again answered almost instantly.

"Gracie! Its 11 on a Saturday night, what is your dumbass doing calling me?" He chuckled. I can't help it, I felt my eyes flood with tears.

"Gracie? Gracie what's wrong?" his tone immediately shifted to concern, probably listening to my soft sniffles.

"Mmhhhh. Um nothing. I…. I'm okay." My voice sounds thick and unconvincing to even me.

"Grace, c'mon what's wrong. Something must be up if you are crying, you don't really cry very often."

"Something might have happened last night at that dumbass party that I was at. And it was kinda bad." I sniffled out. "Um, Jay was drunk…"

"Oh no not again. Is he okay? Where is he? Is he relapsing?" Pete immediately tried to discern the situation.

"I honestly don't know. He won't answer me at all. That gets me to the second part of my story Pete. I was dancing with Jay, and he kinda kissed me. It was my fault though. I was dancing dancing with him, and I was buzzed and there was this guy…" everything began to spew out, but I know I can trust Pete for the truth on my actions. He would be honest and tell me how bad I messed up.

He heaved a deep sigh into the receiver, "Ok Grace calm down, calm down. Look Jay knows that you guys are just friends. And yes, you led him on which was kinda shitty to do but look it happened. It's not that big of a deal. Right now, your friend is in trouble and you got to do what you can to be there for him ok? And hate to be an overprotective little brother here, but what other guy?"

Now it's my turn to sigh. "His name is Maverick. I don't really know all that much about him but… I don't know he seems different."

"Oh, so my big sis has a crush eh?" He chuckles. My cheeks flamed up and if he were here, I would have swatted at his arm.

"No, No I absolutely do not. Now enlighten me, what are you doing at home talking to your big sister at 11 on a Saturday night."

"Well you know even the big leagues have to take a break every now and again." I couldn't help but laugh at his dumb attempt at sarcasm. "But I decided to have a nice night in. Dad is pretty stressed out. And, of course, that means mom is. They are asking about you. You haven't called in 6 months Gracie, you didn't even come home this summer, they are getting worried."

Last summer I opted out of going to the preppy little beach house in the Hamptons and instead decided to spend the summer with Jay. We rented out our own shit hole for the summer and did the stupid shit that college kids were supposed to. He was having some signs of a relapse, so we also had to keep an eye on that. It was still probably the best summer that I have ever had.

"I know Pete. I just can't. You know I can't." my voice broke slightly over the words.

"I know Gracie, I know. It just sucks. I miss you bud."

"Why don't you come visit me for the weekend in a couple of weeks? It could help get Mom and Dad off my case because I have made some contact with someone in the family." I chuckled through my tears.

"Hell yes! Wow can't wait to go to these wild college parties you love to attend. I'll text you later about what weekend works with football. I'll talk to you later Gracie."

"Bye Pete." I hang up the phone, suddenly feeling exhausted. It would be good to see Pete soon. I missed him. I rolled out of my blanket cocoon, shoving the leftover pizza into the fridge and tucking the now half empty wine bottle into my closet. After a quick stop to the bathroom, I found myself back in the comfort of my bed, once again dreaming about green eyes.

Chapter Nine

The shrill screaming of my alarm the next morning reminds me of my morning shift at the shop. I pulled my hair back into a sleek ponytail and sport dark jeans and a long sleeve cranberry shirt. After slipping on my old, barely white converse and snatching my apron, I am out the door.

The perks of having the early shift on a Sunday is no one strolls in till they inevitably crave brunch, meaning most of the morning the café is empty. I spent the morning goofing off with Jenny, chatting about the previous morning's hangover. And suddenly just with the chiming of the bell fixed to the door, our fun ends. It is still too early for the brunch rush, proved by the lone man who strolled in.

He practically glided in, as if he was the owner of the café himself. He sported a slick grey suit that looked like it walked straight out of a designer store. He exuded confidence, or is that arrogance? He swiftly unbuttoned his pretentious suit and sat himself at a small table. He crossed his legs in a polite manner and placed his thousand dollars watch studded wrist on the beat-up metal. His icy blue eyes scanned the café in distaste as his other hand smoothed down his golden hair, as if it needed to be fixed in the first place. I gave a nod to Jenny, my mood already shifting to bad as I approached the snob.

"Hi, what can I get you?" Something about this man felt off as I practically spit the words out at him. I don't know why I'm being so hostile, maybe it's because I have been in close quarters with this rich type before, but something dark was lurking behind those pale blue eyes.

"Why, hello there. Yes, I would very much like dark roast americano please. Black." Even his voice sounded pretentious. He twitched his wrist, urging me to comment on the watch that rested there. As he does so I noticed his knuckles are split, as if he just got into a fight.

That is unusual for his type, they usually have other people do their dirty work. He seemed relaxed yet formal. I rolled my eyes without another word, choosing to ignore the busted knuckles, and walk away. I could practically feel his gaze on my ass. Pig. I poured out his drink into a mug and with quick strides, moved to deliver it. As I placed the steaming mug in front of him, he flashed me a too white smile.

"Thank you very much." He extended his hand out to me, again making sure his watch was on full display. "I'm Connor Steel. And you are?"

I ignored his hand, looking at it as if it repulsed me, "Grace." He lowered the ignored hand, a smile still plastered on his smug face.

"Pleased to meet you Grace. I never expected to meet someone of such great beauty to be working at a place such as, um, this." He waved his hand to indicate his disgust with his surroundings.

"Why bring yourself to dine at a such a lowly café Mr. Steel?" I smiled a fake smile as I offered the insult.

He didn't even miss a beat, offering me a smile to combat my sarcasm. "Despite your perception of me, Grace, I do enjoy a quality cup of coffee. Plus being bewitched by your beauty compensates for any discomfort I might be forced to endure." I couldn't stop my eyes from rolling. "I would love to learn more about you Grace, here, please take my business card." He slid a small square of paper across the small table towards me. It seemed he only took a few sips of his coffee before he placed a crisp one-hundred-dollar bill next to the card. I am still standing there as he stood, his tall lean frame towering over me.

"Again, it was very nice to meet you Grace, I hope to meet you again." His busted knuckles worked to button back up his sports jacket. He looks me over once again with a smile and strolls out of the café. With a huff and yet another eye roll, I snatch up the tip and his dumb card and shove them into my apron. I had no idea what just happened. I also had no way to explain the gnawing of anxiety in my gut. My instincts practically screamed at me to stay away from Connor Steele. Something about him was dangerous.

***

The rest of my shift flew by, allowing me to leave the café in the early afternoon. I offered a quick wave to Jenny and another to Bill. I strung off my apron, tucking it under my arm and walk into the fresh fall air. The air still held a note of warmth, the summer sun clinging to any life it had left.

As I started the trek back to the dorm, I worked to fumble in my pocket for my tangled ear buds. I worked to untangle the knots that line the entirety of the wire, head down as I went. And with my blatant obliviousness, I managed to collide with a tall wall of muscle. I could immediately tell that it is him. The smell of mint and something earthy hit my nose, informing me of who it is before I even had the chance to look up. I lost interest in my headphones, gripping them in one hand. I moved my gaze to meet his own. I'm immediately sucked into his stare. Those green eyes that look as if they can see straight through me, those long lashes framing them perfectly. I almost don't notice the bruises peppering his jaw and the split lip.

"Maverick? What the fuck happened to you?" I reached a hand up to trace the bruises. My fingertips grazed the battered skin, lingering maybe a little too long. Maverick seemed to be transfixed by my touch, almost as much as I was. I stared into his deep gaze as little bolts of electricity seemed to erupt from my fingertips, tracing the sharp curve of his jaw. My hand moved, brushing against his warm skin, till I reach the cut on his lip. I lightly trace the gash with my thumb. His lips are soft, just as I had imagined, and all I could think was of my own crashing against his. And suddenly reality snaps into his eyes and he pulls away.

"What the fuck happened to you? I mean you looked like hell last time I saw you." His harsh words are what bring me back to reality. My stomach sinks and I can feel my own stare turn to steel as I work to tuck my hand neatly in my pocket, hyper aware of the fact that I was just rejected.

"Excuse me? I looked like hell? Look at you. Your face is totally busted." I snarled at him. I crossed my arms and tried to forget the feeling of his skin against my fingertips.

"Pfft. Yea ok, sounds about right coming from the girl who can't handle her liquor but tries to act big about it huh?" His tone is full of condescending mocking. Rage flared up in the pit of my stomach.

"Fuck you. I wish I could meet whoever did that to your face so that I could thank them." I grit as I shoved past him to leave. But, before I can a feel a grip on my arm.

"Look, shit, I'm sorry. Are you okay?" he awkwardly folded his arms across his chest, making the tattooed muscles bulge. I can't help but sigh.

"I'm sorry about that. I didn't mean to ruin your perfect little night by being a burden to you and your friends. I just overestimated myself, I guess." I run my free hand through my hair desperate to tame the awkwardness around us.

"Grace, you didn't ruin anything. I'm obviously going to help you if you need me." The words send a rush down my spine and a warm feeling curls into my stomach. Why is he suddenly acting like he cares about me?

"Well thanks. But really I'm fine it was an accident we can just forget it even happened." I turn once again to walk away and distance myself from him. This time he doesn't try to follow.

I walk back to my dorm as fast as I can rushing towards a place where I can be alone and separate from my want to turn back and kiss Maverick.

Chapter Ten

The week goes by slowly. And my mind plagued by thoughts of Maverick and Jay. Jay still hadn't answered me. He saw Mae a few times, but he refused to even look in my direction never mind willingly talk to me. Mae said its bad, he is relapsing, and he won't tell her why. I can only pray that my involvement didn't send him over the edge. And even with Jay avoiding me and his classes at all costs, it seems Maverick is doing the same. I in no way had some claim over him or anything but I couldn't stop myself from hoping to run into him again. But no such luck. But to the same degree no sightings of the jackass Connor Steel either. I guess the café was too far below his standards after all. Mix all this inner turmoil over what seems like an endless cycle of guys, I was also weighed down by an immensity of schoolwork. It felt like all I had time for was work and more work. Oh, and the rest of that bottle of wine.

Mae was desperate to get me to out but when I refused her, she simply said that if I didn't go out then she would stay in. I couldn't help but concede, along the grounds that Jay comes over too. I needed to see him and if this was the only way that I could, then so be it. Fuck this avoiding shit. I was never much for avoidance.

On Friday I decided to slip on a tight pair of distressed black jeans and a cropped bar shirt, cropped just enough that the black lace from my bralette peaks out the bottom. I opt for no shoes because we are just going to be hanging in the dorm anyway. And with that I swipe on some makeup, keeping it casual as I brush out my tangled caramel curls.

"Doll, I will never understand how you can just look flawless in a matter of seconds meanwhile I look like shit unless I undergo an extreme makeover." Mae rifles through all of her makeup drawers as I flopped onto my small twin sized bed. She doesn't know how gorgeous she is and that is what attracts most, and probably why we are so close.

"Shut up. I would kill to look like you." I chuckle. She bursts out laughing which I couldn't help but return. Immediately following our laughing session comes a short knock on the door and in comes Bo. Mae immediately rushes him catching him in a huge hug and planting her lips on his. He wraps his arm around her, bending down to give her better access to his mouth. It feels awkwardly intimate, so I quickly turn my attention to opening a new bottle of cheap wine. As I pour the cherry-colored liquid into a glass and turn I see that they are finally finished, to my relief. I don't so much mind being their third wheel, but I definitely do when they decide to make out in front of me.

"Hey Bo. Want anything to drink?" I give him a smile and a wink.

"Abso-fuckin-lutley." His tee looks like it's trying its best not to rip as it clings to his muscles. He saunters over to where I stand next to bottles and cans galore. His eyes rake over the various options until he settles on a can of beer, popping the top quickly before flopping himself down on Mae's bed. After shrugging on a red flannel, Mae did the same.

"I haven't seen you since the café, how you feelin' Grace?" Bo gives me a look practically dripping in sympathy and if I didn't actually stand Bo, I would have called him out on it. Instead, I decided to play it cool, shrugging.

"I've been keeping busy trying to keep myself distracted you know? Helps not to think about it." I tried to seem nonchalant, sipping the cheap alcohol in my cup.

"Trying to keep busy is an understatement, this girl works all day and most of the night too I don't understand how she keeps up." Mae says before taking a deep swig of her own beer. Bo simply looks at her and smiles. Mae looks back, giving Bo a dreamy look. Oh, great here we go again. Just before they can start kissing again, a knock sounds at the door.

"Come in!" Mae and I shout in unison. In walks Finn, followed by Isabella and Mick.

"Grace!" Isabella practically leaps into my arms, and her grip is surprisingly strong for such a thin girl. I hug her back, not really even sure what to say. Mick offers a silent nod before mouthing sorry for his girlfriend's attack. I gave him a nod and raised my cup behind Isabella's back, the wine sloshing from impact. Isabella finally released her grip, looking me over with a smile on her face.

"You look hot! Holy Hell!" She says through her pearly grin.

"Hey Mae! Bo!" She turns her attention to the two of them next hugging them both.

"Babe, I think they are good with the hugs," Mick chuckles, "You literally saw them less than a week ago. Hey guys." He gives a flash of a grin to everyone. Isabella pulls down the periwinkle cropped tee, so it hits the top of her high waisted shorts, going back to Mick's side to give him a swift nudge of her elbow. Tonight, her dark brown hair is pulled back into a messy bun, showing off tiny diamond earrings lining almost one whole ear. They reminded me of Jenny's.

Finn walked over to my bed, sitting down next to me before giving me his own version of a hug, pulling me to his side and slapping a kiss onto the top of my head. It was startling considering I just met him a week ago, but I was oddly comforted by the gesture. It was if I had known him for years rather than a week.

"Hey Grace, nice to see ya again. You look way better than the last time I saw you." He winks and offers a charming smile. A smile so charming that I can't help but smile back, despite the rack of guilt that passes through me at the mention of last week.

"Hey Finn. You don't look to bad yourself." I swat at his arm. Somehow his smile grew. I didn't think it was possible. Something flashed in his gaze, a deep blush creeping across his freckled cheeks, earning him a boyish look.

Another knock raps on the door. I instantly freeze, hoping and dreading that its Jay. The door drags open to see Maverick standing there. His green eyes are clouded with a tinge of hope and his usual sense of smugness. He glances around the room till he inevitably locks eyes with me. The smirk that was on his face not even two seconds ago disappears as he stares at me, clutched to Finn's side.

Finn instantly releases me, striding over to sit in the wooden desk chair on Mae's side of the room. The tension in the room is thick as it stays quiet for a few more seconds. Noticing the awkwardness, Mick strides over and shakes his cousin's hand. Maverick gives him a quick smile, but his eyes never leave mine. I froze, my breaths seeming shallow as I took him in.

"Geez Mav, intense much?" Isabella walks over and quickly embraces him, finally drawing his stare away from me. His face breaks into a grin, snapping me out of my haze.

"Hiya Is, you miss me?" He ruffles her already messy bun, earning a dirty look from Isabella, if it can even be called a dirty look. She looks like a toddler just denied ice cream. I can't help but let out a soft chuckle under my breath. Everyone seems to relax now that Maverick seems at ease and the chatter picks back up. Whereas Finn sits on Mae's chair, Maverick pulls my chair closer to me, plopping down so he sits nearly next to me. I stay perched on my bed, not wanting to get too close out of mistrust of myself. I was already reliving the feeling of my fingertips grazing his skin.

"Hey Grace." Maverick looks at me as if he is testing the waters between us. But I can't help but react to his voice, serotonin seems to course through me at the sound.

"Hey Maverick. Your face looks better." It does, the bruises faded to a light yellow and the cut on his lip already looks mostly healed. But even with the injuries he was gorgeous. His dark hair was mused, equally dark brows rising in relief at the easiness of my comment.

"So do you." That smirk returns. That arrogant bastard I giggle to myself. "I'm sorry about the other day Grace, I am. Let's just put it behind us?" His arms braced against the dark denim of his jeans.

"And what be friends?" I huffed out a laugh.

"Yea why not?" He looked genuinely confused by my question.

"Can you be just friends with a girl, Maverick?"

"And why is that the question that comes to mind?" Of course that is the question that comes to mind. Before Mick found Isabella, the Foster boys were known for their charm and their lady….. friends. Despite Mick's name being cleared, that doesn't mean that Maverick's was.

"Is that a joke?" I take a swig of my drink. Maverick's thick yet groomed brows furrow, hurt flashing across his face. *Shit.* I fuck everything up. I stand, leaving a brooding Maverick behind me. I grab a beer off the table and walk back towards the boy running his fingers through his messy dark hair.

"Friends. Here is a peace offering alright?" I hand him the can as he brings his gaze back to me and gives me the smallest and yet best smile I have ever received. He grips the can, his fingertips grazing my skin sending flames licking up my arms. Still holding my gaze, he pops the top and takes a deep drink. His tongue peeking out between his full lips to get the extra traces of alcohol that collected there.

A fire burns in my stomach and I can't help but watch. That is until Isabella snaps me back into reality when she grabs my arm and pulls me back onto the bed.

We all start chatting about the last week, Isabella favoring a cup of my wine with me as she debriefs me on her next tattoo. I can feel Maverick's eyes on me. He nods along to Isabella's words, but I can tell he isn't listening. His gaze is stitched to me, and I can't help the feeling that I'm getting drunk off of it.

"Do you have any tattoos Grace?" The attention seems to shift to me. Especially from the boy next to me.

"Of course. What do I not exude delinquent rebel vibes?" I toss back the rest of the wine in my cup, the cheap alcohol burning my throat a little. Isabella claps, literally claps like a little girl. I heave down off the bed, going to not only refill my drink but to control the blush burning my cheeks. "I actually have five." I say with my back to them as I pour myself another cup.

"No way." Finn laughs.

"Oh yes way. You better believe that this chick is a bad ass. Just wait till you hear about her piercings." Mae chuckles to the group as she lounges on her bed, beer in hand, whose mouths practically fall open as my back faces them. Maverick's eyes are practically burning into my back and I let a small smile out to the table of alcohol in front of me.

"OOOOO show me, show me, show me." Isabella practically squeals.

"Alright, Alright. But I can't exactly show you a few of them." I say with a wink. I tug on the sleeve of my tee, pulling it down to expose my shoulder as I turn. There sits the dainty script on the top of my back, right on my shoulder.

I also pull my ponytail to the side to reveal the small bird right behind my ear. I turn to give them a better look. A swirl of lust clouds Mavericks eyes and I can't help but lick my lips, savoring the stray drops of wine that linger there. My skin seems to buzz wherever Maverick's eyes wander as I deliver his show. The feeling of his eyes on me is addicting and I can't stop thinking of those lips tracing the skin where his eyes linger.

"Holy shit how have I never noticed that before." Finn stares with his mouth dropped open. I simply offer a smile over my shoulder. I pull my sleeve back into place, turning to lift the bottom of my cropped shirt. There it is peeking out from under the lace, another set of dainty quotes inked in black of the skin of my ribs. I get a few nods, and even a whistle from Finn. I can feel Maverick's eyes undressing me, taking in the lace of my bra. I want to feel his hands rubbing on the ink on my skin, his rough palms brushing against the lace. I must be drunk already. And right in that moment the door opens up.

Chapter Eleven

As I stand there with my shirt up, the bottom of my bra peeking out, Maverick's eyes taking me in, in walks Jay. My heart plummets. I didn't expect him to actually show up. I quickly drop the hem of my shirt and walk towards him. The room grows quiet as Jay stumbles into the room. On his face is a wide grin, as he lifts a bottle wrapped in a paper bag into the air over his head.

"Hello fuckers. How's it hanging?" Jay stumbles in and I'm immediately there. I hold one hand to his chest the other behind his back. I recoiled as I was hit with the sharp tang of hard liquor.

"Jay? What are you doing, how much did you drink?" All memories from the previous week disappear as my only objective becomes to make sure that Jay is safe.

He holds up his thumb and forefinger, holding them close together to indicate a small amount, squinting at them both. I shoot a look to an equally worried Mae and lead him over to my bed, placing him so he won't fall. My hands shook, flexing into fists as I tried to dispel the fear and adrenaline.

"Finn will you grab me a water bottle from the fridge?" I grab each side of Jay's face looking into his honey eyes, glazed over and red from not only alcohol. *Shit.* Finn is soon by my side, only it's not Finn its Maverick, handing me a bottle of water. I rip the brown bag from his hands and replace it with the water. I twist off the cap and urge Jay to take a sip.

"What the fuck is this?" Jay slurs, holding up the water.

"It's just some water, it'll make you feel better." I keep my hand on his arm, trying to bring the bottle to his lips. But before I can he rips it away.

"I don't want this shit." He hurls the open water across the room, spraying me in the process. "I want to dance. Remember how we danced Gracie. With your ass grinding against my dick. You liked that didn't you Gracie. You can say you didn't, but you know what they say, drunk actions are sober thoughts." His words hit their place, digging deep into my heart.

Before I could even respond Jay reaches around me and grabs my backside. He pulls me towards him, the smell of alcohol burning on his breath. "You like that baby?" I can feel everyone tense around me and I can barely even register what is happening. Did my Jay just say those words to me? No, it had to be the alcohol and drugs in his system. It had to be.

It all happened so fast, one-minute Jay was gripping my ass, my hands on his chest trying but failing to push him back, the next Maverick is holding Jay up by his collar with a murderous look in his eyes. Jay touched me. He grabbed at my ass. He's never done that before; I've never seen this side of him before and it makes me that much more concerned. But I need to save him, not just from the alcohol but now from Maverick.

"What the fuck is your problem?" Jay slurs into Maverick's face. Maverick doesn't even respond; he simply glares at him from beneath his furrowed brow. I find myself bracing my hand on Maverick's muscled arm, to do what, I have no idea. I just feel as though in order to diffuse the situation I need to be near Maverick. My hand seems small as it tries to get a hold on his massive bicep, covered in ink. His arm was hard under my hand, radiating an intense heat that seemed to sear me through to my sock covered feet.

"Maverick, I'm fine. He's drunk and he's my friend. He doesn't know what he's doing." I sound a lot calmer than I feel. My nerves rack my body, and I can't help the pit that's growing in my stomach or the small nagging in the back of my mind that reminds me that this is my fault. Maverick doesn't even look at me as he starts to lower Jay back to the ground, still keeping his strong grip on the collar of Jays wrinkled shirt. Jay slaps at Mavericks arm weakly, his face contorted in what looks like disgust.

"Maverick." My hand still on his bicep, I whisper so almost I can barely hear. "Please."

Everyone around me is wide eyed in shock, and I can practically feel the shock of it all in the air of the small dorm. I can't even focus on the embarrassment coursing through me at the idea that all my friends just went from having a fun night to me ruining it once again. Tonight, was supposed to act as a sort of reconciliation for the previous party. And now we are exactly where we started. I can feel the tears prick my eyes and I try to choke them back. I can feel my hands start to tremble as I stand there, softly clutching Maverick's arm and not recognizing my best friend in his grip.

"Please." My voice cracks over the word. He gently released his grip on Jay, and soon Bo and Finn are there, dragging Jay over to the bed. Mick stands between Maverick and Jay while moving Isabella to Mae's bed, seeming worried that he will change his mind about letting Jay go. My hand still rests on his bicep, as if I can't bring myself to let go. Before I can, the rough palms of his hands brush across the top of my fingers till his own long fingers grip mine.

"Are you okay?" His eyes are full of concern as he speaks the words in a raspy whisper. I can only manage to shake my head in response. "Hey, hey, come here." He wraps his hand around my shaking form, bringing me to Finn's now empty seat, as far from Jay as I can be in the small room. His rough hands rub comfortingly down my arms as his deep eyes search my face. I look down at my ripped jeans, playing with the frayed edges lining the rips. I can't help that small tears that spill down my face as the prospects of having a fun night are destroyed. I let out a pathetic sniffle. I can't meet his gaze; I just can't bring myself to out of pure shame. His hands are still there, running up and down the gooseflesh that covers my arms. What just happened? I couldn't even begin to comprehend what just happened.

"Gray. It's not your fault." Maverick tries to whisper soothingly. *Gray.* They keep calling me Gray.

Why the fuck are they calling me Gray? I'm too choked up to ask though. I keep trying to pull myself together despite my royal fuck up. With a quick wipe of my palms on my jeans, I rise out of the chair. Maverick is still there, transferring his hold to one of my elbows as I quietly walk over to where Jay is surrounded by Mae and a few of the boys.

Jay looked so out of place. Hs golden hair looking limp and sticking out in all directions. Those usually bright eyes are dimmed by the alcohol coursing through his veins. This is bad. He has totally relapsed, and I doubt that it is just alcohol in his system. He smirks at the boys gripping his arms as if he doesn't have a care in the world. I shake off Maverick's hold and he instantly let's go, although I can still feel his eyes glued to me.

Mae looks up with wide eyes as I come closer to Jay. I give her a quick nod and she backs off a bit. The boys stay there, pinning him so Jay doesn't repeat his previous mistake. I can feel myself tremble, not even really sure what to say. My hands wring at each other as I stand there, my legs feeling weak. Why is he doing this to himself? How could Jay do this? My Jay. A flash of wet asphalt and shattered glass rams into me, forcing me to try and blink the image away.

"Jay?" I barley recognize the meek voice that comes out of my throat. I swear he didn't even recognize the fact that I was standing there till that question made its appearance. He brings his hazy gaze to my eyes, and his grin stretches out even farther. The lids of his eyes droop down, giving him a satisfied yet oddly startling look. Maverick and Mick at my back and the two boys holding on to Jay should make me feel safe, and yet it doesn't. I feel as if the ground was yanked out from under me.

"Jay, I don't know what's going on with you right now but I'm going to help you ok? I'm here to help you." I manage to muster some authority in my voice, sounding a lot more confident than I felt. My hands that once hung loosely by my sides are now gripped into fists, trying to gain control over the slight tremor that raked through my body. "Jay. Listen to me. This isn't you. This isn't you." I take another step towards him. I slowly reach my hand out till it rests on his knee. His eyes look into mine, his mouth still turned up in that sickly grin.

"Stop kidding yourself Gracie. You are no better than me. You are simply a washed up nobody trying to prove herself through becoming absolutely nothing. Just like me. Just like Harvard." Those words found their mark, cutting me deep. I didn't even think twice. I reached out and slapped him hard across his smug face. Bo and Finn gripped Jay tighter as they blinked in shock. Mae was at my side, holding my arm as my palm prickled and stung from the impact.

"Grace. Step back. Its ok but you need to take a step back." Maverick is right with Mae, trying to coax me away. I shook of their grips. I couldn't help it. My rage was blinding. I was pissed and I wanted to snap Jay back to reality. I shoved my finger in his face, brining mine within an inch of his.

"Listen to me you selfish son of a bitch, you are never going to threaten me with my past again. Get it? Next time I won't stop at slapping you. Get yourself together. Life is hard and that is not an excuse for you to fall off the deep end."

"Wow, you are daddy's little daughter Ms Edison." He smiled before spitting towards my face. I could tell before it even happened that I was going to snap, but Maverick beat me to it. I sucked in a breath between my teeth as Maverick pushed pass me and lunged for Jay. Before the other boys could stop him, Maverick gripped a fistful of Jay's shirt and swung. His fist connected with Jay's jaw, sending it snapping to the side with a spray of saliva.

"Don't you ever, ever, treat her like that again. Do you understand?" Maverick's long finger was being jabbed into Jay's face as he spat the words. Jay simply looked to his left and spit blood out onto my light grey comforter. He turned back to the immediate threat and gave him a lazy grin. Maverick raised his fist again.

"Maverick! Enough!" I screech but it was useless, Maverick's fist was making contact with Jay's face again. Blood spurted out of his nose with the impact.

"Buddy, it's not worth it, she'll never let you into her pants. She's exactly what she tries to say she isn't." Jay grinned up at Maverick, taunting him. And off goes Maverick again, giving Jay a deep gash on his eyebrow and almost definitely a broken jaw.

"What did I just fucking say? You will not speak about her like that ever again!" Maverick yells into Jay's busted face. The veins in Maverick's neck bulge with the effort of restraining himself. His forearms are tensed, accentuating every muscle lining those long arms. His normally deep and arrogant eyes are filled with pure rage as if they alone could spell destruction for his victim.

"Maverick, I said enough." My voice sounded cold. It seemed to awaken those around me and suddenly Mick was wrestling to get Maverick off Jay. Jay let out a laugh, using the back of his hand to wipe the blood off his mouth that poured out of his nose. Mae stood frozen next to Isabella, both wide eyed and blanched. My hand reached up to my face as if I don't watch it will all go away. As I drag my hand away from my eyes I'm faced with this reality once again. Finn was looking to me, the question of what he should do in his eyes. And of course, the inevitable pity mixed in. I heaved a sigh.

"Um, Finn. I hate to do this, but do you think you can help me bring Jay back to his dorm please." I look to him hoping that he will accept. I can't risk Maverick flying off the handle again.

"Absolutely fucking not. You are not bringing that piece of shit back yourself." Maverick growls.

"I won't be by myself if Finn comes." I point out, aiming my glare at him now.

"Maverick is right Grace, its ok. I can take him alone. Just try to get some sleep tonight, I'll be fine." Finn sounds so calm and reassuring about it, heaving Jay to his feet and slinging his arm around his broad shoulders. "I got this ok? No worries. I'll call you later when I drop him off." I just nod in response, too choked up with gratitude to speak. Finn wrestles Jay out the door, leaving us all in silence for a few seconds.

Chapter Twelve

"Mick you can let go, shit." Maverick twists himself out of Mick's grasp and instantly rushes to me.

"Gray, are you alright?" He lowers his face so that it is in line with my own and his eyes seem to scan my every feature in order to decipher how I'm feeling. Those long fingers cup my chin, and I can't help but notice the cocktail of blood mixing on his split knuckles. I shrug out of his hand, pushing at him. His eyes flash in confusion.

I head toward the door, craving fresh air. I hear the heavy clunk of his footsteps behind me. I finally reach the doors and push out, the fall air instantly filling my lungs and offering some clarity to my swirling thoughts. I didn't even notice the cold as rage burned up my throat. Maverick places his hand on my shoulder, softly turning me to face him, gently cradling my shoulder.

"What was that? Why did you hit him?" I ask, praying that my tears don't make an appearance. All I could see was the way that Jay's head snapped to the side. The way I looked over Maverick's shoulder to the blob of blood soaked into my comforter. "You didn't have to beat his face in. I had it under control."

"Are you kidding me right now? Did you hear what that bastard was saying about you? He spit in your fucking face for God's sake Grace." Maverick raised his voice, those veins still bulging, standing out against his tanned skin.

"Don't swear at me. And definitely don't think that you have a right to yell at me. Don't think for even a second that you do. You didn't have to hit him. I was handling it." I sounded eerily calm, a slight edge to my voice the only thing giving me away.

He answered by throwing his hands in the air. "Grace, did you hear what that prick was saying. I could have done a lot worse."

"Don't act like you even know what he was talking about. It's my fault anyway, I led him on." I can't keep the anger out of my voice as I growl in his face.

"Do. Not. Do not pin the blame on yourself, this was in no way your fault. It was that drunk son of a bitch who touched you. You didn't do shit." Something dark was stirring in those green eyes, as if he was replaying it all in his mind and was maybe about to follow Finn and Jay.

"Don't try to act so righteous, he didn't know what he was doing! He was totally wasted. My Jay would have never done that. You know nothing about him. You can't just fight my battles for me. I don't even know you!" As soon as the words leave my mouth, something snaps in him.

"Oh, so that's what I am. Just another fucking stranger huh? That's all I am. That's not what it seemed like a week ago when you practically threw yourself at me." Shame burned up my throat and I could feel my cheeks being seared with a deep blush. I clenched my fists till my nails were almost breaking the skin of my palms.

"You know what Maverick, you are just as bad as him, so don't even act like you aren't. Get the fuck out of here. I'm done with this conversation. And you." I can't help but snarl the words into the cool night air.

"Fine, consider me gone." He swung around on his heel and stalked off towards the parking lot, not even bothering to look over his shoulder as he stormed off. I threw up my hands in frustration and stalked back towards the dorm.

I barely even knew Maverick, why did he hold such power over me. He had no right to hit Jay. But he was doing it to defend me. No, no Jay was my best friend, and he needed me. I don't care how he acted, he needed me. When I get back to the dorm, I am met with Mae and Bo sitting on my bed across from Mae's bed being occupied by Isabella and Mick. Both parties were talking quietly, all sitting rigidly with anticipation. As I creaked the door open, Mae was almost instantly there. She wrapped me up into a hug, pressing me into her small frame. I sighed, nestling my chin to rest on her shoulder, wrapping my own arms around her. I didn't know what I was going to do, and it seemed as if this hug was going to keep me grounded.

"Doll? Are you ok?" Mae murmurs into my ear. I just shake my head in return. I can feel the tears start to slip. She lets me go, grasping my hand and guiding me toward my bed, the small puddle of blood already soaked through as a reminder of what just ensued. I blankly stared at it, not even registering the tears blurring the smudge.

"Mae, we are going to head out, give Grace some privacy. If you need us don't hesitate to call." Mick's deep voice fills the room, reminded that people are here watching me dissolve into a puddle of tears. I swipe at my eyes, thankful I wore waterproof mascara.

"Bye Grace, I'll see you later. Stay strong I'm always here for you." Isabella gives me a sad smile and trails out behind Mick. I give her quick nod and they were gone. Bo shifts over allowing me more room on the small bed, enough so that Mae can slide down next to me. She wraps her arm around me, giving me a gentle squeeze.

"Do you want to talk about it?" Mae whispers as she pushes stray hairs out of my face. They must have fallen from my ponytail during the fight. I still absently stared at the deep rust. So similar to those pools on the asphalt reflecting the flames. *Birdie. Help me.*

"I..I don't know." I manage to croak out. I genuinely didn't know if I could. Fresh tears spill down my face. I try to convince myself that they are for Jay and not the Boy with the dark hair and green eyes who left my life just as quick as he entered it. Or for him. His blank eyes staring at the night sky. Broken bones and crushed hope.

Chapter Thirteen

As I survey my appearance in my small mirror, I can't even bring myself to care. My eyes are puffy from spending the remainder of the previous night blubbering around like an idiot. My hair, sticking up in all directions to the point where running a brush through the long strands might make it worse. I quickly weave a messy braid, throwing it back over my shoulder as I sweep some mascara over my lashes in an attempt to look better.

I had an early morning shift at the café and was absolutely not looking forward to it. The Saturday morning Rush was going to kick my ass today. I pull on a pair of worn skinny jeans and a hoodie. It felt like fall that day, the weak sun offering little to no warmth. The brittle wind whips my braid around, causing me to pull out a beanie, making sure both my braid and headphones are secure.

"Another rough night? Should I be concerned?" Jenny huffs a laugh at herself and continues filling the sugar containers, leaning nonchalantly against the battered metal.

"You don't even know the half of it." I grumble as I open up the countertop to get behind the bar. Jenny starts to brew coffee while I clean up for opening, taking my time as the exhaustion from the previous night sets in. I can't even think about Jay or Maverick for that matter as it simply enraged or drained me. All I could do was focus on the repetitive motions that come with the morning shift.

College students pour in, all eager to rid themselves of this morning's consequences for last night's actions. As if a pump of energy can compensate for a night of bingeing and poor choices.

***

Just as my last hour in my shift arises, in strolls the infamous Connor Steel. Today he opted for perfectly fitted khaki pants paired with a white collared shirt that without a doubt costs more than the café. Despite the noise, I can hear the clacking of his dress shoes against the wood of the floors. Of course, his hair is slicked back to perfection and that gawdy watch sits perched on his wrist.

I involuntarily rolled my eyes and fumbled to grip my notepad, headed out to take his order. Upon closer inspection I can tell he just shaved, the sting of his aftershave seeming to singe my nose. The hairs on my arms instantly raise in reaction. As if my instincts were screaming at me to get away.

"Well, hello. If it isn't Grace. I was hoping to run into your beauty again." He flashes me that too white smile yet again. His voice was coated in a synthetic kindness that in reality made me feel a growing unease.

"Yea, well I do work here. What can I get you?" I don't even bother feigning interest in the pompous ass perched on his pedestal.

"I actually came to see you. I am not going to feign indifference about you Grace. I may have done some research on you proceeding our last encounter. And you can imagine my shock to find out that you are none other than Grace Edison. Senator Paul Edison's lovely daughter." That blinding smile suddenly made me dizzy. How did he find out? My stomach clenched with dread, my heart thundering in my ears. I couldn't even focus on his slick smile. Something flashed in his piercing gaze as if he could sense what the words did to me. He knew he found his mark; it was time to pounce.

"And then I began to wonder why you are here in this small town, reduced to a waitress at a shoddy little coffee shop," he continued with venom pooling off his tongue, "And you can only imagine what I found." My heart dropped. He couldn't know. No one did. Dad covered it up. He didn't know. His eyes held a sense of dark mischief to them as he looked at me from underneath perfectly groomed eyebrows. I could feel the color drain from my face. My vision blurred with panic. The screech of metal crushing, the feeling of the concrete surging up to meet me, scraping deep into my flesh. *Birdie. Help me.* The ghosts of fire and the sting of gasoline.

"I am sorry. I don't know what you think you know, but I don't take being threatened lightly. If you are not going to order, then I am going to have to ask you to leave. Right now." I don't know how I managed the words, pinched with anger yet steady, nonetheless.

"Oops sorry Ms. Edison. I believe I will have an Americano dark roast please. And hurry if you could I am meeting someone." He grinned at me again, making me cringe.

If he knew the truth, it could mean my downfall. I gripped at my notepad to lessen the severity of the shaking in my hands. *Breathe Grace.* I fumbled behind the counter, spilling Conner's coffee on myself not once but twice. After attempting to towel the spilled drink off my apron, with fumbling hands I carried his drink towards him.

He watched me as if I were his prey as I gently placed the sloshing mug down, that sick grin still etched into his face.

"Will that be all?" my voice comes out shaky and weak, and I can't help but despise myself for it.

"Yes, I believe that will be all for now Ms. Edison." Another sickening grin as he takes a deep drink of his coffee. I stumble back behind the counter. Mumbling something to Jenny about using the bathroom.

I splash cold water on my face, trying to force myself to take deep breaths. He couldn't know about it. Dad took care of it. I left. No one should know. No one should know about what I did. Flashes of fire and the smell of smoke singe my nostrils. The bite of tar on my skin as it tore it raw.

I splash more water on my face trying to fight against the sensations. I grip the cool porcelain of the sink, refusing to look into the small mirror in front of me. *I'm fine. HE doesn't know. No one Knows.* I try not to panic, pacing around the small square that was the café's bathroom, trying to calm my pounding heart. I run my hands through the top of my hair, fidgeting with the end of my braid. I look at my face in the mirror, its color drained. I give myself a steely gaze. No one is going to control me anymore. Never again. I can't let him.

I straighten out my stained apron and headed back out. I tucked the loose strand of hair that fell out of my braid behind my ear as I walk out of the small bathroom. I wipe at my eyes, refusing to even look at the slicked back blonde hair. I busy myself with my other tables, avoiding that table at all costs.

He tracks me across the room, a smirk residing on his face. The seat across from he remains empty, but he doesn't even seem to notice. I can tell he is savoring his time making me sweat. He knows that he is making me nervous and he loves the thrill of it. His gaze is pure predator. Then the inevitable happens, he runs out of coffee. I drag my feet over to where he cockily sits, not quite lounging as to not diminish his reputation. I force myself to gulp down deep breaths as I square my shoulders and walk towards him.

"Darling, do you think that you could get me a refill, it seems my companion is less than punctual." He drawls as he examines the face of his gawdy watch. I just nod, bidding my shaky knees to step toward the bar.

"Um, Grace. Are you alright you look a little off?" Jenny places a small hand on my back peering around me to look into my face. I bring myself back to my senses.

"Yea, yea. I'm, um, I'm fine. Just a long night." Between the chaos that was last night and now this I felt as if I was teetering over the edge. I didn't want this. I moved on. This wasn't supposed to be my life anymore. Drunk kids, fights, love triangles. I moved away from this shit. I ensured that it would never happen to me again, and now I'm right back where I started. I grab Connor's freshly filled cup, offering Jenny a fake yet small smile as I turned towards my customer. What I saw almost made me drop the cup.

Chapter Fourteen

There sitting across from the only one who may know the secrets from my past, is Mick. His brow furrowed and his jaw set as he angrily gazes into Connor's mocking expression. Mick's fists were clenched, braced against the table as if he were trying all he could not to reach across the table and strangle Connor.

I stopped dead in my tracks, afraid that if I showed my face, Connor would tell Mick everything that he might know. I stared from my spot behind the counter out of self-preservation. That is, I try to before Connor catches my gaze, giving me a smug smile. He beckons me forward as if he were calling a dog, waving his hand indicating for me to move to my doom.

The heat from the fresh mug seeps into my hand reminding me of its presence. Mick sees the change in Connor's focus following his gaze till it lands on me. His eyes widen a bit as he recognizes me, whipping his gaze back to Connor. I see him growl something at Connor, however I am too far away to hear it. Connor just keeps his smug gaze trailed on me. I start to move forward, planning on dropping off the mug and getting as far away as I can. Mick looks me over, concern lighting his deep blue eyes.

I place the mug down silently, refusing to meet Connor's smug face or icy stare. Mick watched my every movement, his posture rigid as if he could spring up at any moment. Meanwhile that smug bastard just sits there as I serve him, as if I was deigned to be his lowly servant. It only made my blood boil. Mick shoved him fist in front of his mouth, leaning against it. He kept watching me, as if he were trying to warn me through his gaze. I stood up my back straight as I turned on my heel to retreat back to the counter.

"Just a minute there Ms. Grace." His grasp was strong, almost to the point of pain as he gripped my wrist. "You forgot to ask my dear friend here if he needs any provisions for our meeting." He glances at Mick and that sickly feline grin grows.

"Of course, um, M…" before I can get his name out, he discreetly shakes his head his eyes growing wide, letting me know I shouldn't call him his name in front of Connor. The problem was I did not know if it was to protect me or him.

"I'll be fine thank you." Mick's voice sounded hoarse with restraint as he holds his hand up to indicate he was okay. I gave a subtle nod and the grip on my wrist loosens. He still smiled at me, revealing those too white teeth. Another flash of blinding lights and crushed metal sweeps across my vision as I turn to leave the two.

I try to busy myself for the next few minutes, keeping my eyes on my friend while he seems to confront my new enemy. Mick jabs a finger into an unfazed Connor's face. I have never seen the levelheaded Mick lose his cool before, but he looked as if the rage in his eyes could take care of the businessman in front of him. Connor simply delicately sips at his drink, his posture relaxed as if he wasn't be chewed and spit out.

This continues for a few minutes before Connor gazes at his watch studded wrist, he quickly smooths out his collared shirt and the front of his khakis. I watch him speak to Mick as he stands, Mick never losing his murderous glare, his skin turning a sickly shade of white the only thing that gave him away. Connor neatly tucks his chair underneath the table before placing a few crisp bills down on the table. He saunters out the door not looking back once.

Once I am sure that he is gone, I stride over to Mick, burying his face into his large hands in frustration. I tap the table once with a nail and he is instantly alert. Once he realizes that it is me, he relaxes a little. He looks strained, as if the meeting he just had drained him.

"Mick, what was that whole thing with Connor Steel about?" I keep my voice low in hopes that Connor doesn't reappear with the mention of his name.

"Wait, how do you know his name? Oh god Grace, please tell me you don't know him." Mick's fists clench once again and my stomach drops.

"I don't know him perse. He comes in here on occasion. He knows who I am anyway. All I know is that he is a pompous businessman who just met with you." I decide not to tell Mick about his threats.

"Look Grace, you have to stay away from him at all costs. I'm serious. He is dangerous." His blue eyes turned to steel as he stared into my own. I mustered a nod under the heat of his stare. "I mean it Grace. He is dangerous. Look I gotta go meet Isabella. Please don't tell anyone about this and remember, stay away from him." Mick swiftly stands and heads towards the exit, looking back at my stunned form once. As he walks outside the large, window paneled door I watch as He stops, colliding with another form. My heart instantly flutters, before my blood ignites.

Maverick stands in front of a flustered Mick, his expression serious. Mick throws his hands up into the air before running one hand through his tousled brown hair. Maverick nods a few times, before slapping a hand down on Mick's shoulder.

Maverick looks into Mick's face, hand still clasping Mick's shoulder. Mick's head hangs down, not meeting Maverick's own gaze. Maverick pulls his cousin into a quick hug, patting him on his back after releasing him. He starts walking to the café calling something over his shoulder to his cousin. Just as the small bell attached to the door chimes, I revert my gaze and head back behind the counter.

Too late. I can tell he already saw me as I feel his eyes dart over me. I turn around and find him perched on a stool in front of the counter, both arms crossed and resting on the counter. His beautiful dark hair wild in a perfect sort of way. The small freckle above his lip stretching with the smile he offers, but in his eyes is hesitation, as if he is testing the waters.

"Hey Gray." His voice like silk instantly warms me to my core as he uses his nickname for me, despite the fact that I was still furious with him.

"Maverick." I give him a quick response as I turn to go find something else, anything else, to focus my time on.

"Grace, please wait. I just wanted to apologize. I shouldn't have attacked Jay, but he was assaulting you. I couldn't let him get away with that. But I was rash, and I get that ok? Just please talk to me here. I don't like the way our…. Conversation ended last night." His head and shoulders fell a fraction of an inch, as he slumped picking the skin around his fingernails.

"Well maybe you should have reasoned that before you attacked my best friend." I give him a look and I can hear him suck in a breath, trying to calm himself down.

"Gray, it wasn't like that and you know it. I am sorry about the way it happened, but I am not going to apologize for defending you. He grabbed your ass and insulted you!" His voice started to boom, causing customers to glance toward the tattooed hot head.

"Would you keep it down? I'm working. Now as for last night, he didn't know what he was doing ok? He was drunk." I hissed.

"I have been drunk plenty of times and never found myself treating a woman like that. Ever. It isn't an excuse for that type of behavior. And honestly it upsets me that you can't see that." His deep voice lowers, his eyes smoldering with pent up rage and, a tint of sadness. That look triggered something in me, I reached my hand out, placing it on his muscled forearm, the ink and skin smooth under my fingertips. I grip his arm and his eyes flash with something else entirely.

"Mav, look I understand okay? It just….. I don't know." I didn't understand my sudden need to reassure him. But seeing him slumped and wounded, it pulled at me, nagging at something in my chest. "And I'm sorry too. You aren't just a stranger. I think you know that." I could feel a blush spread over my cheeks as his mouth quirked up to the side, his freckle following.

"Like hell I do. You just called me Mav." He barks out a laugh, throwing his head back. I couldn't help the giddy feeling that rose in my chest, a giggle escaping my own lips.

"Why what's wrong with Mav?" I chuckle.

"Just no one in their right mind calls me that." He chuckled.

"Well good thing I'm not in my right mind then." I give him a wide grin, his expression becoming light and amused. "Now, Mav, I have to get back to work." I reluctantly slide my hand off his arm, drawing it back towards me. But before I can withdraw completely his hand grips mine.

"When do you get off? I want to make last night up to you?" The words made something in my chest surge. This day was so draining and now this. All thoughts of Connor abandoned.

"Not today fighter boy. I have homework. And as for when I get off, can't tell ya that." I say with a wink. This time when I turn around, he releases his grip on my hand.

"In that case I'll just have to wait for you. In the meantime, can I get a black coffee?" My back facing him, I can't help but smile.

"You are insufferable." I call over my shoulder as I pour out one of our best brews into a large mug.

I turn back around placing the mug in front of him as he quirks that damn freckle up to the side again. He brings the cup to his full lips, ignoring my warnings that it was hot. He immediately pulled the mug from his face, sticking out his tongue. I huffed a laugh as I rolled my eyes, turning to get back to work.

Chapter Fifteen

Maverick stuck to his threat, staying and waiting out the remainder of my shift. He stayed perched up on the counter calling me over every so often to make a comment about the service or make a joke about another customer.

It was the best hour I have ever had at work.

Between laughs and eye rolls, Jenny kept her eye on me, offering raised brows and snide grins when she could get my attention. After the drama of last night and this morning I was ready to move past it. Connor posed a threat, but I could barely even think about it when Maverick was looking at me. Before I knew it, my shift was up. Maverick sat at the counter watching me take off my apron, his eyes lighting up with the realization that I was done for the day. The late afternoon breeze breezed through the door sending a shiver up my spine.

"The wait is over! Let's go Gray!" Maverick cheers throwing fists up into the air.

"Hold on, not so fast." I give him a quick smile. "Don't look it's a surprise." I scrunch my nose at him as he smiles and covers his eyes with his large hands. I poured out two hot chocolates into to-go cups, covering them in whipped cream with a dusting of cinnamon on top. I slipped the lids over top, waving to Jenny before placing a cup in front of Maverick.

"Ok, open them." I grin. He peeled his hands away from his eyes, looking all too eager before his gaze dropped to the cup.

"Oh, great more coffee." He sarcastically whines. I can't help the grin that spreads over my face.

"It just so happens to be my specialty, ass." I playfully punched his arm. He gave me a warm grin before opening up the counter for me, muscles shifting under his white tee. He grabbed at his cup and we headed out into the fresh fall air.

"Now where exactly are you bringing me?" I ask before taking a sip of my drink. The warm liquid sloshes into my mouth, the rich flavor adding to the absolute bliss I was feeling.

"Now that is a surprise Gray." He winks before taking a sip of his own drink. "Holy shit what is this? Its fucking amazing." I snort out a laugh at his excitement.

"Did you just snort? Oh my god you snorted! That was the cutest thing I have ever heard." He exclaims, his own deep laugh echoing around the nearly empty campus grounds.

"Don't make fun of my snort. It's better than your bark." I giggle, slapping at his muscled arm.

We both laugh all the way to the parking lot, nothing but us and our endless teasing. How could this be the Maverick I met a week ago? He was sweet and surprisingly fun.

He leads me over to his deep black pickup truck, opening the passenger door for me. The step was high off the ground, despite the fact I was considered tall it was even high for me. Maverick placed his cup down on the gravel beside him, his strong hands moving to my waist. Warmth immediately circled me, savoring every point of pressure his fingers put on my skin, the rough calluses grazing my bare back. He effortlessly lifted me into the truck, delicately placing me so I was sitting in the passenger seat, gripping my own cup. He just smiled at me, his eyes alight with an emotion I've never seen from him. After shutting my door, in a few quick strides he is at his own, hopping into the driver's seat. Those strong hands gripping the steering wheel. He cranks the radio blaring some classics as he peels out of his spot.

The heat was blasting, and all the windows are down, just how I usually keep my cars. I smile at the thought of us both engrossed in the habit. Both taking the time to perfect the art of balance. We drive in silence besides the thumping of the radio. Only it's not an awkward silence but one of content. He whips into what appears to be an old diner with a slanted faded blue roof, a neon sign flickering in the window. The practically empty lot seeming to contradict the flashing of the word 'open".

"Wait right here, I'll be right back." He smiles before jogging into the small practically dilapidated building. I look around his truck, taking in the worn seats to the small ticking of the fake swaying plant plastered to the dashboard.

The pink plastic petals are bleached with the sun, as is the smile stretched across the center. It was an odd trinket for Maverick to have, but nothing about Maverick and his tough exterior really made sense. My mind wandered, wandered back to the feeling of his fingertips trailing over my skin, the way he effortlessly lifted me into the seat. I wondered what they would feel like under different circumstances.

I shut my eyes against the thought, forcing myself to suck air into my lungs as Maverick Jogs back to the car, a large brown paper bag gripped in his hand. As soon as the door opens, I'm hit with the delicious aromas of salt and spices. I didn't realize how hungry I was. He places the sack at my feet giving me a wink. My stomach flipped.

"Ok so food acquired. Now what?" I ask, trying to divert my attention away from the rumble of my stomach. He just winked at me before he left the lot. We drove for a few more minutes, Maverick glancing over at me with a small smile a few times.

Eventually he pulled down a small dirt path, leading into the woods. My palms began to sweat a little at the prospect of Maverick driving me into the woods alone. I mean really how much did I know him. He seemed to sense my unease, flashing me what I hoped was a reassuring smile.

"Gray, I promise I'm not going to hurt you in any way. I think I proved that one last night. I'm bringing you to my place." He says smiling. His face now is adorned with a pair of sunglasses in order to block out the late afternoon sun. I feel uneasy not being able to see those eyes, but I give him a quick nod.

***

We are surrounded by woods, the path becoming less worn as we get deeper into the thick trees, the sun becoming less and less visible through the thick canopy. Until we suddenly reach a clearing. He pulls up to the middle of what seems to be a field, the sun filtering through the surrounding trees, giving the field a golden look, as if everything were suspended in a droplet of honey sticky sweet with it. The slight breeze ruffled the small wildflowers inhabiting the space, carrying the slight flowery aroma through the opened windows. He wordlessly stopped the car, pushing his sunglasses out of his face, looking to me with a sheepish looking grin that sent butterflies in my stomach.

"We made it." He called as he hopped out, his converse clad feet causing a stirring of dust. He walks over to my door opening it for me and helping me down. Those hands wrap around my waist again, this time my shirt riding up as his calloused hands graze the sensitive skin of my hips. My feet hit the plush grasses surrounded by dust. He keeps one hand splayed on my back, its warmth seeming to melt my core, as his arm reached behind me to retrieve the paper sack.

"So, this was your big plan huh?" I say as he slides his large hand from my back to engulf my hand.

"I did have an hour to plan." He huffs as I am trailed behind him, barely able to focus on his words over the thought of his hand in mine. He lead to over to the bed of the truck, plopping the food there on the worn plastic.

Both hands free now, he wordlessly slides his hand out of my own, his fingers trailing up the bare skin of my arms, causing my skin to be set ablaze wherever his fingertips skimmed. Each one gliding over the tight fabric of my t-shirt, grazing just below the tattoo inked on my ribs. A shudder runs through me at the thought of those fingertips tracing my skin, even if a scrap of fabric blocks our contact. I'm suddenly breathless, and without a doubt my face is flushed.

He stared deep into my eyes, the wide grin and bright eyes replaced with something else, a hunger. One hand finds its way to my waist, the weight of it enough to melt into. The other explores my ribs, gooseflesh sprouting with each stroke, until it finds itself mirroring the other. Both rest on my hips as I stare into those eyes. Like the field around us, the sun gives them a lingering gold sheen, alive and dancing. His mouth, slightly parted, resting perfectly just below his handsome nose. I could feel my own lips part, as if they were urging me forward, to push my own mouth against his.

My eyes began to flutter, about to close the distance between us, when suddenly I was air born, plopped down on the hard edge of the bed of his truck. His hands lingered on my hips, now skimming the tops of my thighs. I craved his touch. I didn't want this moment to end.

Maverick's mouth quirked to the side in a smile, that small freckle rising once again and a dimple appearing next to it. His brows pulled low as if he knew exactly what he was doing to me. Before I could even catch my breath, he is gone, going to the front of his truck once more.

I gasp in deep breath's trying to cool off after the encounter. I wanted nothing more than to push my mouth against his, forget about everything that has happened in the past week, never mind the last twenty-four hours. My hands grip the edge of the truck as I try to focus my thoughts on not jumping Maverick. *Relax Grace. Shit.*

Maverick strides back over, his inked arms filled with mounds of blankets and a sweatshirt on top. He heaps the pile to rest next to me before skillfully jumping up himself.

"Here, you looked a little cold, you have goosebumps." He said handing the large black sweatshirt to me, knowing fully well that those goosebumps weren't from the fall chill. I mumbled a thank you as I pulled it over my head, trying to hide my embarrassment. As soon as the fabric rested on my shoulders I was hit with a wave of his scent. Mint and whiskey mixed with a tinge of cigar smoke. I snuggled deeper into it, hoping he wouldn't notice. The scent wrapped around me like a blanket, comforting in an odd way.

I wrapped my arms around my upper body, cuddling into the black fabric that practically swallowed me whole. I caught him gazing at me, this look of adoration on his face.

"What?" I scrunch my nose up at him with a small smile.

"I'm just admiring how good you look in my sweatshirt." His voice smooth as silk, with a hint of lust wrapped around it. My heart fluttered. *Am I really swooning over some boy like a damsel in distress right now?*

"Has anyone ever told you that occasionally you can be extremely cliché." I giggle back, afraid of the tension stirring in the air from my almost kiss. He feigned offense in return.

"I'll have you know that I am no cliché. Why, what role do I fill Gray?" He smirks at me, a dare.

"The gorgeous bad boy with tattoos and a past that no one knows about." I waggle my eyebrows at him, sending him into a laughing fit. His laugh reminded me of honey just like the setting sun around us, it was deep and sweet and golden. It oozed around us and made everything that much sweeter.

"So, you think I'm gorgeous then." He said through a sly smirk, one eyebrow raised. I couldn't help but chuckle, swatting at his arm as I did so.

"Now are you going to tell me what's in that sack or just let me sit here starving?"

"Alright, pushy, aren't we? I got us some burgers and fries. I figured you weren't the type to want a salad in some wort of 'I need to impress him' kinda way." Another breathy laugh flittered out of him.

"Perfect. And you bet your ass I would never choose a salad over a burger; who do you think I am?" I mock as I grip the greasy packaging.

"Even better, it's from a run-down diner, meaning that it is going to be amazing." I say as I start to unwrap the greasy paper. He just flashes a smile. Fingering the package wrapped around his own burger.

The smell of the burger hits my nose, making me practically drool. As I bring it to my mouth, I can't help the moan that escapes from my lips. The juicy meat reminds me just how hungry I was. I demolished it, the sun setting around us as we ate.

"Geez woman take a breath." Maverick cackles. Like actually cackles. I laugh around the mound of food in my mouth as he grips the last piece of his own burger. "I can only imagine what you are going to do to the fries."

I gulp down my food. "You mean to tell me that there were fries this whole time and you didn't produce them with this burger." I thrust what's left of the burger, which isn't much, into the space between us, staring at him incredulously. He seems genuinely confused for a second. "What person in their right eats fries after the burger and not during?"

"Good thing I'm not in my right mind." He winks.

"This isn't a joking matter, what the fuck have you been doing without me all this time, I'm going to fix this as soon as possible." I feign insult which merely brings out his deep barking laugh. He reached into the bag, procuring a fry before throwing it at me. The salty rouge, hit me square in the forehead, causing me to blink in surprise.

"Oh this is war!" I reach into the bad, grabbing a handful and throw them at him. There we sat, watching the sunset, throwing fries at each other between howling laughter. I didn't know what exactly I expected Maverick Foster to be, but this definitely wasn't it.

His large arms finally wrapped around me, the victims of our fry battle laying limp in the grass below our feet. A surge of happiness bubbled out of me as he pulled me to his chest, giving me a squeeze. I pushed him back, making him land on the mountain of blankets, me resting on top of his chest.

The firm muscles were heaving from the remains of his laughter. My hair draped around us in a caramel wave, reflecting the fractures of light that remained. Our smiles faded as we stared into each other's eyes. His lips once again parted slightly, the breath breezing out of him, so close that it tickled the skin of my nose. His long dark lashes fluttered for a second as if he were trying to recover. I gulp. I can feel my core melting.

"Um, Mav." I whisper as I look down into his gorgeous face.

"Yea Gray?" He questions, his eyes holding a note of question in them.

I didn't know what I was trying to say to him. I could only focus on the feeling of his hard chest positioned directly under my own. The feeling of my hand braced on the hard muscle directly above his pounding heart. *Birdie what are you doing?* I can't do this.

I push up from his chest rolling to the side so that my back was pressed against the back of the bed. I have almost kissed Maverick twice now. I can't do this right now. So much has happened, and I just don't think that it would be right. I didn't deserve it.

I see him out of my peripheral vision push up so that he is propped up on one elbow watching me. We sat there in silence for a moment until I looked over at him. The way the setting sun hit the panes of his face made him look like a Greek statue, his face molded to perfection. I turned my body to its side, resting my head on a rolled-up blanket.

"Do you ever feel like you are a background character in someone else's story?" I stare into his deep eyes as his brows pull in, his mouth turning down ever so slightly at the corners. I could feel the frantic pull in my chest. Remembered the last time I had this conversation.

"What do you mean exactly?" His voice sounds raspy, the deep tone spoken in a whisper.

"Like everything around you is working in someone else's favor. Like everything you do is infinitely small and just add to someone else's story?" I whisper back.

"Gray, you could never be stuck in the background." He looks at me with such intensity and certainty that I feel something inside me pang with longing.

"Do you want to know something?" I ask.

"Always."

"I always thought I might just be a background character. Everything I have done seems insignificant compared to everyone else. I've never told anyone but I just kind of felt I was just there. But, I..I don't feel like that when you are near me. I know we haven't known each other for long and that it is a total cliché but I feel like you've always been here." I meekly squeak, getting the words out as quickly as I can. I felt the weight of my words sink in, the mix of emotions flash across his features.

Tentatively he reached out a hand, cupping my face. The pad of his thumb skimmed my cheek, brushing over the surface while he looked into my face. His lips sit in a straight line, but his eyes convey everything I need. His hand moved down till it softly cupped my chin. His thumb moved to brush across my lips. My eyes stay glued to his own, unable to look away from the beautiful display of emotions swirling in them. Colors of the sunlight dancing around us. If there were ever a moment where I felt all my struggles melt away and to be seen as Grace and Grace alone, it was now.

The way he looked at me, as if he was observing a painting, taking in my every detail and worshipping it all the while. It was different from how Jay looked at me. Jay looked at me as if I was his mother, mistaking it for love. But Maverick gazed at me with a sense of wonder I could never be able to begin to explain. His full lips were inches from mine, it would have been so easy to close the distance, but instead he kept tracing the planes of my face, simply breathing me in.

A small smile played on those lips. We stayed like that for a while. Laying next to each other in the silence, and gazing into each other. Neither of us wanted to move, afraid that the moment in itself would follow suit. It was like nothing I have ever experienced. I felt understood. The flashes from my encounter with Connor fading, The struggle of Jay's relapse, missing Pete. All of it just left me as I looked into that beautiful soul. We didn't need anything physical in that moment, instead we bared our souls instead of flesh.

"Gray, to me you will never be just a background character." He whispered against the silence, bringing his lips to my forehead and pressing a feather light kiss there.

My eyes fluttered close with the sensation of his lips on my skin. "You will always be mine." He murmured while his mouth was still pressed against me, almost too quiet for me to hear. His lips slowly withdrew from my skin, it was too soon, I craved the feeling of his lips on my skin immediatly. I snuggled closer to his chest not because of the chill in the air, but because I craved his touch.

"Can I ask you something now?" he said into my hair. I just nod in response, too full of bliss to even voice words. I let out a content sigh.

"What does this tattoo mean?" I felt his fingertip graze the shell of my ear till it tentatively reached the bird nestled behind. I instantly stiffened. "I just feel like you aren't the type to get a meaningless piece." It must have felt me stiffen as he removed his finger from the ink.

"You, um, you don't have to tell me, I was just wondering." He avoided looking at me in the face, suddenly finding the sunset interesting.

The question seemed to snap me out of this dream that I was living in. I instantly pulled back, squirming up till my back was pressed up against the back of the truck bed. I covered my face with my hands, letting my hair fall around my face. *Birdie help me! Hurry Go!* Fire, squealing metal. Black.

"Gray?" He was suddenly sitting next to me, placing a hand on my forearm, his grip light and questioning. I just shake my head in response, willing the tears not to flow. I rubbed at my face hard.

"Gray I'm sorry I didn't know you didn't want to talk about it. Are you okay?" I couldn't bring myself to look at him, but I could practically see the concern in those green eyes and the set of his mouth.

"Um, its nothing really. I'm sorry for being so sensitive it just means something to me that I can't tell you. Can we talk about something else please?" I sniff, slowly drawing my hands away but refusing to look up. All I could think of was green eyes replaced with deep brown, the curled edges of his hair brushing against the color of his varsity jacket. The tall muscular frame. His eyes as the light faded from them.

"Yea, yea of course. How was um work?" he seems hesitant again.

"You were there for most of it." I huff a laugh that I'm sure didn't sound convincing, especially paired with the tears sitting in my eyes.

"Yea, but not for all of it. Did anything interesting happen?" he chuckled his own fake laugh.

Not even thinking twice about Mick I blurt out my encounter with Connor. "Some rich guy comes in a lot and today was no different only this time he had a bit of an agenda. He met with Mick, he kind of grabbed my wrist. Things got really tense." I don't know if I was blurting this information out of self-preservation, or because I subconsciously had a death wish but the words fell from my lips quickly. With each word, Maverick sunk further and further away.

"He touched you?" Maverick dragged the words out, threats and rage lacing every word, rigid. I swiped at my eyes, suddenly alert.

"I mean not really he just kind of grabbed my wrist I don't really think that that constitutes…" I tried to stutter out but before I could finish Maverick's fist connected with the edge of his truck. His face was a deep red, practically glowing with his fury.

"I am going to kill that son of a bitch. He knows better than to threaten me. He's so done." Maverick yelled, only not to me, more to the surrounding area.

"Maverick," I started to reach toward him, but he immediately shrugged out of my reach.

"Grace, not right now. All I want to do is find that bastard and bash his face in. We are leaving." Before I could even get in a word he stood and jumped out of the truck, gripping the blankets in his clenched fists, letting them drag on the ground. What the fuck just happened? This is all my fault, Mick told me not to say anything.

"Grace, let's go!" He growled from the front seat. I let out a deep sigh before scrambling out of the truck, having to leap into the dirt only to trip and fall over. The black sweatshirt was streaked in dusty smudges by the time I managed to hoist myself up into the passenger seat.

"Shit Gray. What happened to you?" His brows were still furrowed and his grip on the steering wheel turning his knuckles white. I guess it was a rhetorical question as he flew through the path that we had gone down just an hour or two before. He didn't speak, all of his features rigid, his muscles taught and standing out against fabric and ink. He flew down streets, the sun finally setting and shrouding all our surroundings in a starless black.

I didn't know what to do, sitting there fidgeting with a loose strand hanging off the sweatshirt still wrapped around me. This is all my fault. I should never have brought it up. If only I hadn't acted so weird about my tattoo. It was just too much between the reminder today, the fact that Connor knows, Jay's relapse. I just wanted to scream and punch something. But no, I was sitting in this seat next to someone who was on a mission to punch somebody. He practically burned rubber as his tires screech into a parking spot outside my building. That tight grip remains on the steering wheel, his eyes focused on the windshield.

"Mav, what the fuck just happened?" I ask not wanting to send him over the edge, but my own anger seeped through anyway.

"Nothing. Just, get out of the car Gray. I have to go." Was he really deserting me? We just talked for hours, joking around, exposing ourselves and now he wants to leave because of something that didn't even concern him. Absolutely not.

"You know what? No. Fuck that Mav. I'm not moving. Not until you tell me what is going on." I cross my arms defiantly. He looked at me as if I had just grown a head, swiveling his head to stare at me.

"What? Did I just hear you correctly?" His voice was stern, and if I wasn't so pissed, I probably would have flinched.

"Yea, you heard me."

"Get. Out. I'm not messing around Grace I need to handle this." Gone was my nickname, he was scolding me like a child.

"Neither am I." I shrugged at him, dragging my own gaze to rest on the windshield. "You don't even know who did it. What are you going to do? Go around punching every guy who looks rich?" that earned me a look like could put even Mae in her place. But I wasn't having it.

"Just get out of the damn car!" he yelled, striking the wheel of the truck.

"No! Tell me what is going on!" I whip my head to face him and see the intensity of his stare burning into mine. His rage was there, swirling on the surface and yet there it was, the same adoration and care that I had just seen in the field. I couldn't help myself.

My hands reached up, grasping the edges of his face, stubble from his jaw pricked at my palms as I looked into those eyes. I pulled his face towards mine, his brow furrowed in confusion, but I moved too fast for objection. I smashed my lips against his, needing to feel them. He immediately opened for me, allowing my tongue to slip in. His own hands found their way to my hair, one snaked through the waves while the other palmed the side of my face.

Me moved in complete harmony pushing and pulling our way into each other's open mouths. My blood rushed through me, every nerve feeling as if it were sizzling with smoldering embers. Everyplace his skin touched mine ignited into all out flames. I needed more.

I moved my hands to his own hair, running my fingers through the unkempt mess that nestled itself on the top of his head. He groaned in satisfaction and that sound was the best thing I have ever heard. Pure bliss wrapped up in a single groan. We both leaned over the middle console, both wanting more but refusing to clear that boundary. We were both breathless, but we didn't care, not wanting to break our contact in anyway.

I have been kissed before, but none compared to this. The scent of mint encased in his very being, gliding over my tongue. I wanted more, needed more. Until his hands found my shoulders and he pushed me back, panting.

"No not right now, we can't do this Gray." The look he gave me was that of a wounded puppy, his gaze downcast as if he had done something wrong.

"Mav, don't end the night this way. I have never felt like that before. Don't end it. Not yet." I pleaded, not even caring if I sounded desperate. I was desperate.

"End it? Gray I would never just leave you. Never. I was going to come back I just can't do this when I am full of this kind of adrenaline. I want to kill that bastard for laying a hand on you. I don't want to take advantage of either of us here." He returns a hand to my face, his thumb making strokes down my flushed cheek. I leaned into the touch, my eyes fluttering closed with the contact. I heard him sigh.

"Gray, I need to apologize, the way I acted was no better than," he didn't even need to finish because I knew he was thinking of Jay.

"Please not now. I don't want to fight with you. Just come upstairs for a while, cool off." I whisper opening my eyes, but still leaning into his touch.

"I'm not sure that is such a good idea." His head drops to stare at the floor. His anger was still present in the set of his shoulders, the deep crease between his brows.

"Mav, I'm not going to sleep with you. I just want you to calm down before you do something rash." With that he huffs out a chuckle before silently nodding his head. Satisfied with his answer I open my door, swinging my legs around the side and preparing to jump. I stumbled to the ground but refused to fall this time. I walked over to find Maverick closing his own door. I walked over to him, even though he towered over me, I slipped my arm around his waist, as if I was going to support him. He chuckled, gripping me to him. He kept his arm around me, walking with me towards my building. All the while I was silently praying that Mae decided not to be in our room tonight.

Chapter Sixteen

No such luck. I looked in, Maverick hidden behind me as I peeked in. Collapsed on her bed were Mae and Bo, cuddled up watching a movie. I kept the door open signaling to Maverick to wait one second. I padded in.

"Doll! Where have you been all day? I thought your shift ended at 2." Mae's head popped out from behind Bo's shoulder, a smile gracing her bare face. Bo simply turned his head to the side and waved, sporting a huge smile.

"I did get out at two. I met up with a friend."

"You don't have any friends besides me and Jay." She scrunched up her face, looking at me in confusion. At the remark, Maverick chuckled behind me trying to cover it up with a cough and failing. Mae's eyes widened and I knew we were caught. I sighed, which Maverick took as his que. He poked his head out from behind the door frame, before strolling into the room, his signature smirk returning. Mae's eyes practically popped out of her head.

"Maverick! What's up man?" Bo shifted to stand, leaving a shocked Mae on her own. He glided over to where Maverick stood, giving him a quick slap on the shoulder.

"Babe you want something to drink? I got to pee. I can stop by the vending machine for you." Bo said as he strode over to the door. Mae's mouth was hanging wide open as she took in Maverick and I's disheveled appearance. "Ok then. Be right back." Bo said as he strode out of the room.

"You know what a drink sounds good. I'm going to hit that vending machine that Bo was talking about. Want anything babe?" he waggled his eyebrows at me, purposefully making Mae's mouth open wider. I picked up the nearest pillow and chucked it at his head, barely missing my target. I could hear his hearty chuckle even as he waked all the way down the hallway. Reluctantly I looked back to Mae, still in shock.

"What. The. Fuck." Mae exaggerated every word. She scrambled off her bed reaching me in seconds, scanning me from head to toe. "Did you sleep with him? You didn't, right? You never do that but looking at you I would bet you did. How did this happen? What is going on?" Her questions poured out, I wasn't even sure how she hadn't passed out from lack of breath yet. I gripped her shoulders, staring into her face. As I silently bid her to calm down, I couldn't help gushing over the events of the night myself. Today was an absolute whirlwind.

"I don't even know. He waited around at work till I got out and then we grabbed a bite," I purposely left out the field, the fight, and the make out session, "and no I did not sleep with him, so get that out of your mind." Seeming to be unsatisfied with my answers she just shook her head.

"Of course, the one night I'm actually here you bring a boy home! Oh my God, you brought a boy home. Not just any boy but Maverick Foster. Who the hell are you and what have you done to my Grace?" She feigns horror, but I can tell her shock is genuine. I simply laughed at her. But I can't help the squeeze of anxiety that comes with the realization.

"Don't worry as soon as Bo gets back, we are going straight to his place."

"No, you don't have to do that we are probably just going to watch a movie or something." I try to protest but am immediately cut off by a raise of her hand.

"Nope, not going to happen I'm out of here. Maybe if you get laid you won't be such a bitch all the time." Mae laughs as I swat at her arm, laughing along with her.

Mae scurries around the room, collecting stuff for her sleepover with Bo, eventually him and Mick saunter in together, cackling over something one of their frat brothers did last night. Bo finally finds Mae, hidden behind a pile of clothes as she shoves them into a bag, her messy bun flopping to the side of her head.

"Um, babe? Going somewhere?" He asked from his position by the door.

"Nope, WE are going somewhere. We are going to go back to your place." Mae said while still stuffing stuff into her small bag.

"What? Why? Maverick and Grace just got here. We can all hang out." Mae's head snapped up, she looked absolutely disgusted by her boyfriend's obliviousness. She cocked a dark eyebrow at him, trying to signal for him to take the hint. He simply squinted at her in return, trying to decipher the hidden communication happening between them.

Maverick walked up behind me, wrapping an arm around from my waist from behind, planting a quick kiss at the base of my neck. Goosebumps covered my flesh with the simple gesture. Bo watching, head cocked, and suddenly understood. His eye's widened as he strode over to where his girlfriend stood, wrestling with the zipper of her bag.

"Here let me get that." Bo suddenly seemed eager to leave, effortlessly zipping up the bag and moved it to his shoulder. He grabbed Mae with his other hand, dragging her out the door. He gave a quick nod and smile to us both and kicked the door shut behind him.

Maverick looked to me and we both burst out laughing. Those two were made for each other. I gripped his hand switching off the lights as I went so only the glow from the lamps were visible. I plopped down on my bed, dragging Maverick with me. He collapsed his large frame taking up any free space the small dorm bed had to offer. In the process he accidently moved the blanket I had skillfully laid down to hide Jay's blood stain. I frowned down at it.

"Hey, what's wrong?" Maverick saw I was upset, oblivious to its cause. He tried to follow my gaze until he saw the small circle of rust ingrained into the creamy grey. He grimaced, raking a hand over his face.

"Fuck, I'm sorry." He sounded wounded. I shook my head, my mind that was full of hope and excitement crashed back into the thought of Jay. I sighed, deflating, and crashing down next to Maverick. He wrapped his arm around my shoulders. I stared up at the stained tiled ceiling feeling defeated. I wondered where he was, if he realized what he had done. What he said.

"It's not your fault. Well, it was your fault you punched him," I shrugged not trying to hide the quick little smirk that appeared, "but it isn't your fault that he is relapsing." I screwed my eyes shut, even as I felt his gaze swing to my face.

"Relapse? Fuck. I destroyed that kid, and he is obviously in a bad place. I get why you were pissed now." He sighed. I opened my eyes and nodded to him silently. "Do you know why he's relapsing?" he asks, concern lacing every word.

"No. but it happened last week and that's why I was so bent up about what…. happened." I flopped back, my back resting on the hard mattress. Almost instantaneously his head hovered above my face, those eyes gazing down into my own. While one hand propped him up, the other moved to cup my face.

"Hey, hey stop blaming yourself alright. After even knowing you for a week I can tell that you care about people and I know that you must have fought from hell and back to help him. So what you danced with him? He had no right to put his hands on you or talk to you like that. Understand?" His voice held a new edge reminding me of the rage radiating off him on the way back to the dorm. I involuntarily shuddered at the thought of his fit connecting with the metal of his truck. I reached up to my face pulling his hand away so that I could examine his knuckles. He watched me carefully as I rotated his hand in front of me, inspected the jagged splits marking every knuckle.

"Why did you do this to yourself?" As I lightly trace the edge of one of the jagged marks. He hissed.

"Well, technically I didn't do it, that friend of yours face did, and the bed of my truck." He tried to dodge the question, but I wasn't having it. I just stared at him unrelenting. He heaved a deep sigh. "Sometimes I just get so mad that I'm not exactly sure what to do." He almost looked ashamed of his revelation.

"Hey, I'm not judging you or anything. Trust me, I have punched my fair share of assholes and walls. I was just curious why you felt the need to." Still examining the cuts, I could tell his gaze was trained on my own hands, looking for any marks of their own. I shake my head. "It's been a minute since I have but don't doubt for a second that my knuckles haven't looked similar." His gaze flicked back to my face as I gently laid his hand down on my chest.

Whereas before we felt desperate and wild, now brought me back to the field, me laying there, looking at him, still wrapped in his sweatshirt. He lowered himself to the mattress next to me, pulling me into him, cradling me. I turned toward him, watching him as he sighed and snuggled down into my pillows. I curled up letting the feeling of his arms around me protect me from my thoughts and that nightmares that were ensured to follow.

"I am sorry about prying about your tattoo. I didn't mean to make you upset." He barely whispered, his chest humming with the words. My heart squeezed with the thought.

"It's okay. You didn't know. It's just… I got it for a friend." My words became thick, laced with something deeper. "He passed away." His arms tightened around me.

"I am sorry Gray. Fuck, I…. I'm sorry." He pressed a kiss to the top of my head.

"It was a long time ago."

"It still must have been hard."

I thought back to what his arms felt around me, those dimples and full bottom lip stuck in a mock pout. His grin as he threw back his beer. The feeling of euphoria that came with each breathless touch and whispered word. "It was."

Silence buzzed in the air around us, settling in the small space, urging us to keep going. The only sound our mingled breaths.

"Mav," I pulled my head from his chest, looking into his soft expression. "There is a lot that you don't know about me. I am…. I am bad. I cause bad things to happen. And I don't think you need that."

He wordlessly brought a hand to my face, thumb brushing under my chin until he softly brought his lips to mine. A simple brush of him on me that held a weight, a promise. He pulled back after lingering there against me, looking into my eyes.

"Gray, you could never be bad for me. I don't care that I don't know everything. I don't need to."

I reach out a hand, laying it gently on his face, his eyes fluttering shut. Now it was my turn to trace his features. I run the pad of my finger over that small freckle above his lip, smiling as the side of his mouth quirked up. His long lashes fell, practically grazing his cheeks. I listened to his breathing, deep and unbothered, as if he were finally at peace. His steady heartbeat reverberated in the space between us, acting as a lullaby. My hand stayed tracing his skin still his breathing evened out and he fell asleep cradling me in his arms. I felt at peace, just feeling his arms wrapped around me, till I eventually drifted off into myself.

***

I slept peacefully, not waking up in the middle of the night to nightmares as I expected after Connor's threats trudged up old memories. The soft morning sunlight filtered in through the gauzy white curtains by my bed. I lay there cocooned by Maverick's strong arms; our legs tangled underneath the cool sheets.

I looked up at Maverick, his eyes closed and a small smile etched into his face. His eye lids fluttered with tiny movements, indicating that he was deep in sleep. His mouth twitched into a soft grin, lifting his birthmark to the side. I tentatively reached up one hand, using my forefinger to brush against the side of that mouth, causing his eyes to slowly open. He gave me a lazy grin, his eyes glazed over with sleep.

"What are you doing, Gray?" He whispered through his smile. He reaches out his own hand, stroking the side of my face. I scrunch my nose at him, fighting off a grin. He ran his hands over his face, "Ugh, it is probably so late I should get going."

"It's not late its only," I twist, grabbing for my phone on my floor. I flashed on the screen reading the time, "It's only 7:30." His hands immediately left his face and his eyes snapped open.

"In the morning?" His voice raised in tone as he scrambled to sit up. I rubbed at my own eyes, sitting up and mourning the loss of his grip over me.

"Yea, why?" I raised an eyebrow at him.

"Shit!" he frantically rushed from the bed, throwing the blankets, and my legs away from him. He leapt off the bed, grappling for his keys and shoes sprawled out on the floor. "Shit, shit, shit." He muttered as he tied his laces.

"Maverick, what's wrong?" I tried to reach for him, but he shrugged out of my grip. I snatched my hand back choosing to rest it on my lap rather than be rejected again as I shivered with the sudden lack of warmth.

"This was a mistake. Fuck, I shouldn't have let this happen. I have to go." I sat there stunned, not understanding what went wrong in the matter of minutes. I just sat there, blinking, not knowing what to do as he pulled the door open, looking back at me once before his gaze fell to the floor and he walked out.

What just happened? Stunned silence buzzed in my ears, my hand grazing the rumpled sheets where Maverick was just sleeping. It was still warm and now he was just gone. Had I done something? I couldn't even call him or text him, I hadn't even gotten his number.

He just slept in my bed, we kissed. And then he runs out the door scared? It's too early for regret, usually people do that to me after at least a month, never after one night. I run through the previous night in my mind, going through every moment up until his sudden departure. I pushed myself back, leaning against the wall as I sat thinking of that boy and the night we had shared, and his overwhelming absence.

Most of all I was mad at myself. I should have known better; he was Maverick Foster after all. I had not expected the goofing off, the sparks. But I had expected the charm, only I greatly underestimated its power. I am such an idiot. Did I actually believe that Maverick would want anything more than a hookup? Especially with me? And I looked so stupid, prattling on about being pointless, I opened up to him without thinking twice about it. To a guy I have known for practically a week. With a strangled growl I flop back onto my head, burying my head under the covers. He was different, the way he cradled my sleeping form, his soft snores. At least I thought he was.

Chapter Seventeen

I received nothing but radio silence for the next two weeks. After Maverick left that morning, I didn't see him again. I was left confused, feeling used and humiliated. Mae was her usual caring self, trying to ensure me I was better than "that prick". I inevitably saw Bo and even Finn, but no signs of Mick or Isabella.

It seemed as if any and all connections I had to Maverick just disappeared. I should have been furious; I should have pushed all thoughts of him out of my mind. But instead, I couldn't stop replaying the way he looked at me in that field, or his teasing remarks, or the way his lips felt moving in sync with mine.

Pair that with the fact that my relationship with Jay was still on the rocks. Mae informed me that she talked to him, and he agreed to get help. I guess he is back in a program, only one on campus so that he can keep up with his schoolwork and life.

Knowing that he was safe now helped me to avoid him at all costs. He tried to text and call, but I just couldn't bring myself to talk to him after realizing, with the help of Maverick, the seriousness of what he did that night. And of course, there was Connor. He disappeared from the café. But that did little to ease my worries. If he did know about my past, that made him a threat to me and the life I created. I could be forced back home all because of some rich prick who for some reason finds an interest in my life.

Between trying to balance all my conflicts and trying to forget about Maverick, I was once again swamped with schoolwork. I wrote essay upon essay, trying to lose myself in the words rather than my memories. I called Pete a few times, finalizing his trip for that coming weekend. I needed to see him, not only for the distraction of babysitting him as he explores college life, but also because I missed him. I eagerly awaited that Friday, waiting for the moment that Pete pulled up.

***

Friday finally came, finding me in an oversized t-shirt and shorts, my hair resting in a messy bun on the top of my head easily resembling a rat's nest. I was watching some romance movie while waiting for the call from Pete announcing his arrival.

The movie was droning on about how they were meant for each other, earning a snort from me. Yeah right. The protagonist swooned, collapsing in her lover's strong embrace, while he brought his lips to hers. I couldn't help but reaching up to my own lips, reliving the way that Maverick's lips moved against mine. The ringing of the phone pulled me out of my haze, excitement surging through me at seeing Pete's name flash across the screen. I jumped up from my spot amongst the ruffled sheets, slamming my laptop shut, snatching my phone as I looked out the window.

"Pete? Are you here?" I smiled as I noted the anticipation in my voice.

"Look outside." He laughs in that annoyingly teasing way that little brothers tend to favor.

"I am shit head; I don't see you." I roll my eyes sporting a wide grin.

"I meant outside your door."

I run to the door of my dorm, throwing it back while dropping my phone in the process. There stood Pete, clad in cuffed jeans, converse, and a faded red hoodie. A backpack slung across his broad shoulder while his honey-colored hair grazed his chin. He looked so different, but most importantly he looked, huge. I leapt into his arms, causing his backpack to slip from his shoulder and land on the tiled floor with a thump.

"I missed you too." He laughs out while he lifts me off the ground, spinning me in a circle. I swatted at his arm laughing right along with him. He placed me back down to rest on my bare feet before examining me, no doubt for sign of injury or fuck up.

"I'm fine, no gashes, stitches, or bad ink for that matter." I give a twirl, even going so far as to flash the tattoo on my ankle to him. He lets out a gasp.

"Mom and Dad are going to kill you if they find out you have ink." He squats his massive frame, squinting at the small flowers there.

"Just wait till the hear about the other four." I gave him a snide smirk which he met with his own slack jawed expression. "Now get in here ass hat and tell me everything!" I grab his large hand while his other wrestles to grab his bag. I pull him into the small dorm room, shutting the door behind me with a loud click.

It was like seeing a stranger walk in, throwing his backpack on my floor. His massive frame towered over me now his hair longer and curled around his ears. And not to mention the chords of muscles beginning to line his arm. But he had the same blue gray eyes that mirrored my own that were unmistakably my little brother's. He flopped down on my messy bed, kicking off his shoes in the process.

"What do you want to hear about first?" He sighs, folding his hands behind his head.

"Well let's start with that girlfriend that you absolutely have, so don't even try to deny it. As an older sister, I have the right to approval." I stick my nose in the air sarcastically, earning a deep laugh.

"Surprisingly enough, I just so happen to be a single pringle." He said through his wide smile.

"Well, if you use terms like 'single pringle' I can see why." I chuckled. It felt good to joke with him again, watch his smiles and pretend they were the gap-toothed giggles of the past. But now here comes the inevitable. "How are mom and dad doing?" I gulped. His expression instantly changed from carefree to weathered.

"You know the usual. Busy. Stressed. What's new right? They miss you though Gracie." He looked at me with pity that choked me up, causing me to only nod in response. We sat in silence for a few moments before he tried to break the resounding silence echoing in the dorm.

"What about you Gracie, any boys I need to speak to?" he offered a wink. My stomach dropped as images of Maverick flooded my mind.

"Absolutely none." I could feel my nails pressing into the skin of my palms, threatening to break the skin. I avoided looking into his eyes, knowing he could pick up on my emotions. I didn't want to tell him about Maverick. Refused to relieve the embarrassment.

"Yea ok." He said sarcastically, picking up on my hesitation despite my efforts.

We sat chatting for a while reminiscing about the past and Pete excitedly prattling on about his college plans for the next year. He was planning on coming to the same university as me, knowing that he would be relatively close to home but still far enough that Mom and Dad couldn't call on him constantly. I couldn't agree with his choice more. Right as he was about to bring up the question of if I had a boyfriend again, Mae thankfully busted down the door. She rushed over to a pleased Pete, enveloping him in hug. She let out a squeal of excitement as seeing him again.

"Well hello to you too Mae." He patted her on the back, laughing at her display. She finally released her grip, swatting his arm.

"I missed you, you ass. Ok, I like the new do you got going on here, rocker chic." She twirls a few of the strands on her long fingers before ruffling it like she did when we she first met him a few years ago. Then he looked like a little kid, but now that he was grown, I couldn't stop the laugh that bubbled out at small Mae ruffling the gentle giant's hair. We all began laughing, Pete hurling pillows at us both, barking out a deep laugh I had never heard before.

"Are you guys ready for tonight?" Mae questioned, twirling around with her arm high in the air.

"Mae, I told you I'm not bringing Pete to the Frat house." I cross my arms defiantly, shooting her a look. My parents were already at odds with me, I didn't need them thinking I corrupted my little brother.

"Oh, come on Grace, it'll be fun and he needs to experience the whole college experience." She held her hands in front of her as if she were praying while flashing sad eyes up at me. I glanced over her shoulder to see Pete mocking the expression, eager to experience his first college party. I huffed out a breath. I would inevitably have to go back to the house, even if Maverick was most definitely there, plus I wanted to spend time with Pete. He needed to think I was okay, that I wasn't leaden with embarrassment and threatened by my past.

"Fine, but Pete if you drink more than two beers or find any coeds so help me God." I conceded, pointing a finger towards him as if I were a scolding mother to that beast of a boy. He eagerly nodding, busting out a huge grin. Mae squealed in delight.

"Let's get ready then!" She pranced to her closet, throwing open the doors. She picked out a long sleeved yet extremely short lace top, see through to the point where her black bra was visible underneath. Her long blue-black hair cascading down her shoulders, seeming to amplify the deep maroon lipstick she wore.

I whistled low, scouring through my own closet in search of something decent to wear. I opted for a pair of distressed jeans, tight and shredded. I found a cropped maroon tee, mirroring the shade of Mae's lips that let the lace of my black bralette peek out the bottom, as well as the quote on my ribs.

We both hurtled to the bathroom to change in a blur of lipstick and heels, leaving Pete to his own vices while we brushed out our hair and changed. When we came back, we seemed to be barely recognizable. Pete stood from his perch on the edge of my bed, eager to get to the house. I couldn't help the smile that appeared over his eagerness. We piled into his car, barely stopping to notice the slight chill in the air.

"Hey where's Jay?" Pete yelled over the booming of the car radio. Mae shot a look to me, questioning. I hadn't told Pete what happened with Jay. Jay and Pete grew up around each other and they were friends. I didn't want Pete or Jay to lose that bond over a stupid drunken night. I shook my head at Mae, pleading with my eyes not to say anything.

"He has a huge project due, plus you know how he gets." Mae shouted back, plastering a fake smile on her face. If he knew it was fake, he didn't show it, just nodding in response. In a few minutes we pulled up to the house, already booming with heavy bass and covered in discarded solo cups.

Mae instantly recognized the song turning to me and shaking out her hair, fake singing to the lyrics while me and Pete burst out laughing. I could feel my chest tighten when I hopped out of the car, scanning the block for Maverick's truck but coming up short. I shook my head, turning to grab Mae and Pete's hands and leading them headfirst into the chaos that only a frat house can supply.

My shoes kicked at cans and cups with a residual tin clink while I watched Pete's face light up with the prospects of the night. We all walked in hand and hand, preparing ourselves for what was hopefully to be a good night. The door to the frat was crowded by gossiping coeds, gripping their cups with their long acrylics and fluttering their fake lashes when anything with a dick walked by. I watched as they looked at my brother with hunger in their heavy makeup lined eyes. Like predators stalking their big clumsy teen prey. Mae gave them all a wink, sarcastically giggling as she pranced by them as she gripped to Peter tighter. As soon as we were clear of their glares, she turned to me sticking out her tongue and rolling her eyes. I shook my head stifling a giggle before dragging both inside.

"Holy shit." Pete whispers under his breath as he takes in the scene in front of him. The smell of weed and various vapes cling to the air as bodies are packed together, some writhing to the music while other busy themselves finding something to make the night less in focus.

His face held a look of pure awe, especially as a pack of girls with barely any clothing pranced by, looking him up and down with a smile as they passed. Maybe this was a bad idea. In the middle of the packed room stood a rickety old table, supporting a game of pong from the sounds of the cheers and stray ping pong balls hurtling to the ground. The opponents being none other than Finn and Bo.

"C'mon Pete! I want you to meet my boyfriend, Bo. Don't be fooled, he is a big teddy bear." She grappled for his hand and dragged him toward the table, me following close behind. As I shuffled along behind them, I scanned the room around me for any sign of Maverick, but once again found nothing. I was only met with the smell of stale alcohol and the view of lights splaying through the smoke filled air.

"Grace!" Finn's eyes brightened as they caught mine. I smiled allowing for him to walk around the table and pull me into a giant hug. Something about Finn instantly brightened my mood and I found myself actually happy to see him. As I pulled away, I couldn't help remembering that Pete was there, staring slack jawed as I gripped onto Finn.

"Finn, this is my little brother, Pete. He's visiting for the weekend." I said pushing back from his tall frame.

"Nice to meet you. Should we get you a beer?" As he extended his hand to Pete, he looked to me for permission to give him one. I gave him a nod and a small smile which was immediately returned. "Alright, I'm assuming you would need about three cans yourself Grace?" he chuckled. With that he spun to the kitchen going to retrieve our beers.

"No boyfriend huh?" Pete gave me a smug look, elbowing me in my arm.

"Definitely not dating Finn, try again." I scoff elbowing him back. All the while still searching through the crowd for that swath of dark hair.

"Pete! This is Bo. Bo this is Grace's little brother, Pete." Mae gestured between the two introducing them.

"Pleased to meet you man, I've heard a lot about you from Grace." Bo said as he gripped Pete's hand.

"Right back at you. Only Mae was the one chatting my ear off." He winks at Mae and the two giants start laughing, teasing a scowling Mae.

"Beer for all!" the pong game seeming to be forgotten, Finn handed out cold cans of beer, making sure to keep his promise and hand me three with a wink. I popped the top of one, instantly draining it and handing him the empty, double fisting the remaining two.

"That's a girl!" Finn cheered me on.

"Well, I only have two hands you know." I joked back. The little exchange earned me another raised eyebrow and smirk from Pete. I just rolled my eyes before popping the top off my next beer. I didn't want a repeat of a few weeks ago, so I chose to nurse one and hand off the other unopened can to some drunk girl in search of her next drink behind me.

"Alright, so we going to play pong or what?" Bo looks to the group throwing up both hands, almost sloshing his beer on Mae in the process. "Babe let's go me and you versus Finn and Pete, Grace you ref." I hold up my can happy to be free to wander for a minute while they kept an eye on my brother. I needed to pee. With a quick gulp, I downed the rest of my can, forgetting my plan to nurse it and slammed it down on the table.

"I'll be back. Gotta pee." I gave a small smile before I turned and headed into the throngs of bodies in search of a bathroom. Everyone was writhing to the heavy hip hop pounding out of the speakers. I elbowed my way through the crowd, earning a few dirty looks in the process. The air was hot and reeked of alcohol and sweat. I shrugged down, preparing to tackle anyone in my path, when suddenly someone was gripping my wrist. Hard enough to hurt. I spun, expecting to come face to face with Maverick, only this hold was too tight, and too placid. The touch didn't send shocks through me. My eyes snapped up to meet golden ones like limpid honey that I recognized instantly. Jay.

Chapter Eighteen

His eyes were glazed over, not with alcohol but with tears. My heart pounded in my ears. His face was weighed down by a deep frown, his eyes glowing red. I immediately withdrew my hand from his grip, acting as if I was disgusted and shoving my way to the edge of the crowd.

"Grace! Grace! Please, listen to me." He called after me, following me and weaving through the crowd if not a little haphazardly. I made it outside, which was significantly less crowded, sporting small clusters of people spread out all across the trash covered lawn.

I clunked over to the nearest tree needing to plunk myself down at its base, I covered my face with my hands, trying to calm my anger and frustration at seeing Jay. Only I was immediately interrupted by the shuffling of feet in front of me.

I could tell exactly who it was just from the short gasps of air he took in. I could feel my anger rising but instead of heat, ice ran through my veins. I stood up snapping my gaze to his own. It should have struck me how awful he looked, his usually floppy blonde hair matted and seemingly unwashed. Deep bags hung under his eyes, their deep purplish hue making him look pale and not his usual golden tanned self. His eyes looked dull, their usual kindness and tamed excitement gone.

But instead, it fueled my anger. How dare he treat me the way he did and then show up here looking pathetic.

"What the fuck are you doing here?" I snapped, not breaking my gaze. My words seemed to stun him, as if I was supposed to suddenly forgive him. My guilt nagged at me, but I kept fueling my fire. I may have started this, but I was going to end it. The beer in my system thrummed, earning me an extra ounce of courage.

"I…I had to…" he stumbled over his words, shifting one foot as if he was going to take a step forward.

"Don't come any closer to me. Back off." He instantly froze, pulling his foot back from an invisible line while fidgeting with the sleeves of his hoodies. "Jay, I trusted you. I fucking trusted you. You know everything about my past. You know what I did to earn my banishment from that shit town. And worst of all I thought you trusted me. How fucking dare, you bring him up. You had no right." The words tasted sour on my tongue, each stinging worse than the last.

"Gracie, I am so sorry. I wasn't thinking. I was drunk and high out of my mind I didn't know what I was doing. I know how much you loved Harvard…." The look in his face fragmented my heart but my anger was right there, wielding the pieces back together.

"Don't. Don't say his name to me, and that's bullshit. Jay, I have seen you at your worst before. I helped you through it. You didn't even tell me you were relapsing. Yes, I get a fucked up a few weeks ago, it was a mistake ok? But that is no excuse for what you did to me. You tried to humiliate me; you grabbed my ass!" My finger prodded the air in between us, as if I could shove his apology back at him.

Before I could stop myself, I surged forward, the tears starting to blur my vision. And that's when it hit me, the smell of weed coating him. "Are you fucking high right now?" I yelled, looking at his eyes closely. Bloodshot. I watched as his throat bobbed, reaching out to grip my hand that was pointing at him. His grip was steel, threatening to crush my hand.

"Grace. I am sorry okay? Can we just move past this?" His grip was tightening, sending pain shooting through my arm.

"Jay let go. Now. You are hurting me. Jay!" His grip just tightened, my hand twisting at an odd angle. I knew what I had to do. While he was still staring at me, pleading with me for forgiveness, I lifted up my other fist drawing it back swiftly before plunging it up into his nose.

He immediately stumbled back with the impact, gripping his now bloody nose. I shook out my hand, tingling from the hit. A quick look proved my knuckles had split as I moved to cradle it with the other. I looked in front of me, expecting to see Jay surging forward, but instead I was greeted by a tall figure gripping Jay by his collar with both hands. Muscles bulging in the moonlight, his ink absorbing any stray moon beams. His green eyes wild, matching his dark tousled hair. His mouth was set in a hard line as he stared into a trembling Jay's face.

"What the fuck did you do? Did you fucking touch her?" Maverick screamed the words into Jay's wide-eyed face, blood coating the lower half, only getting a moan in response. "What did I say was going to happen to you if you hurt her again?" Jay still just stared trembling and I had to grit my teeth not to run over to them both. To do what, I have no idea. People began to stumble outside, hoping to witness a fight. Still cradling my hand, the other soaked in a mixture of blood, I stared in horror as my friends accompanied by my little brother pushed up to the front of the crowd.

"Gracie!" Pete yelled, sprinting over to where I stood on long legs. His eyes took in my hand, gently wrapping his own around it as he tried to examine my knuckles.

"Pete, I'm ok. It's fine." I tried to wave him off, but his gaze locked onto the two figures next to me. "Did he do that to you?"

"Pete, he didn't mean to. He was just trying to talk." But before I could stop him, he was barreling at them. At Maverick.

"Get off of him you piece of shit." Pete yelled, tackling Maverick down to the ground, making Jay fall limp to the ground, still clutching his nose. "You hurt my sister!" Pete raised his fist, preparing to land a punch on Maverick's face. But Maverick had other plans, effortlessly flipping Pete over as if he weighed nothing so he landed on his back in the dry grass of the lawn. Bo and Finn rushed forward, gripping Maverick before he could hit my little brother. I stood rooted to my spot, only able to watch. Jeers and cheers rang out around us courtesy of our drunk fans, all eager for blood shed. I had enough. I marched forward, prepared to stop all of this.

"Enough!" I screamed at the figures, writhing to all gain a superior position over the others. Maverick's gaze snapped to mine, assessing and wounded. Bo and Finn took that as their chance, pulling him back while Pete scrambled to his feet, wiping at a small trickle of blood running down his chin. He jogged over to a crumbled Jay, trying to assess the damage I had caused.

"Jay, get out of here. You caused enough tonight." I ordered. Pete looked up at me with confusion splayed all over his face. The roaring of the crowd died down at the lack of violence and started to trickle back in the house, except for a few groups eager to witness an aftershock. "Pete, Jay hurt me, not Maverick. And I was the one that punched him." I closed my eyes firmly stating the words for everyone to here. Pete immediately released his grip on Jay backing away from him. Jay looked up again, all pride left. He stumbled to his feet, limping away, not even looking back.

"Gracie, what do you mean Jay hurt you?" Pete looked cared, his eyes and hair wild from his fight with Maverick.

"A few weeks ago, he relapsed, and I didn't know. I made a mistake and led him on one night. He came back pissed at me. He grabbed me and said some pretty bad stuff Pete. Maverick," I pointed to the figure struggling against his friends, "he helped me last time. Jay came to apologize but I didn't want to hear it right now. He grabbed me and I punched him." I kept my eyes closed, afraid to meet my brother's eyes. He stayed silent, looking over at a still struggling Maverick.

"Get off me!" Maverick yelled. The veins in his neck standing out and his breathing pumping up his already large chest.

"Calm down Maverick. That's her brother that you just punched." Bo yelled right back, never sounding so angry. At that Maverick's eyes grew wide. He looked to me then at Pete, his face falling. He stopped fighting, his heavy pants the only movement.

"Pete we should get her home." Mae is suddenly at my other side, throwing an arm around my shoulder protectively. He remained silent nodding in agreement. I threw a look at the three boys in front of me. Maverick had been released; his hand fisted in the grass while his head looked down. The tears streamed down my face at the realization that my drama had ruined yet another night.

I mouthed sorry at my friends who were standing rigid, ready to pounce on Maverick at any moment. They gave me looks of pity as if they felt bad for me and that just cut into me deeper. I hung my head as Mae yelled for Bo to call her later and ushered me to the car, Pete at my other side. Mae gets into the driver side, saying she only had a sip of her beer while Pete helped me into the back.

"Gracie, let me see that hand." Pete gently took my hand with the split knuckles. He turned it a few times, asking me if I could make a fist and extend my fingers. Satisfied that I hadn't broken anything, we spent the rest of the rise back in silence.

As we pulled in the parking lot in front of my building, I couldn't hold back my tears anymore.

"Mae, I am so sorry. I never meant to for this to happen. I just… I…" I let out sobbing. Mae turned around in her seat, her face pulled in concern.

"Doll, this wasn't your fault, in fact none of this is ok? You didn't do any of this." Mae said in soothing tones, reaching her hand back and gripping my uninjured one. I sniffled while the tears streamed down my face.

"And Pete, I should have told you. Mom and Dad are going to kill you if you show up with a busted lip." I cry harder at the expense of my brother. He pulled me to his side, pressing a kiss to the top of my hair.

"Gracie, I just want you to be safe. Don't worry about anything else ok? This wasn't your fault and if I ever see that son of a bitch Jay sniffing around you again, I'll make sure he understands that too." His arm grew rigid and he gripped me harder, squeezing me into him as if he was trying to protect me. I nod, tears dripping down my face. I must have looked pathetic. Utterly pathetic.

Pete and Mae ushered me upstairs, cleaning out the fresh wounds on my hand and bandaging it before placing me into bed. Pete set up a pallet on the floor, while Mae curled up beside me, hugging me as we all drifted off to sleep, hoping to forget about this night all together.

Chapter Nineteen

All three of us woke up in the early afternoon, choosing to sleep in rather than face the reality of last night. After consistently apologizing to Mae all afternoon, she finally reassured me it was fine before going to see Bo. Pete had to leave that night, so I brought him out to a late lunch, working to explain the night before as best as I could for him.

His light brows furrowed at the mention of Jay and Maverick, neither of them earning an ounce of his approval. After the heart to heart with Pete, I was forced to say goodbye to him once again. He wrapped me up into a giant hug. It took all I had not to cry onto his shoulder. I watched as his car soundlessly pulled out of the lot, and like that it was back to reality.

I slunk back to my dorm, feeling drained having not had a chance to process anything that happened. I glanced down at my bandaged fist, seeing a few blood spots that had seeped through. I clutched it to my chest, climbing the stairs to get back to my dorm.

As soon as I do, I realized that I was alone. Pete having left and Mae with Bo, I was utterly alone. I shut the door behind me, leaning my back against it and shutting my eyes. I slid down to the cool tiles of the floor, crumpling with emotion and loss. I felt alone. I lost Jay, not only to substances but I lost the old Jay to the new one. He hurt me, tried to corner me. And he knew about what happened, had been there that night so long ago in an attempt to comfort me, two broken kids trying to shield each other from reality. The tears spilt down my face, running freely as I mourned my friend.

And then there was Maverick. He had showed up to protect me. After not seeing him for a few weeks I thought I was free of him, but the minute I saw him it was like an old wound opened back up. The way he looked at me, rage and passion, until the utter defeat of his actions took over. In the bed of his truck, whispering sweet nothings against my hair, he had told me that he would never leave me, but he did exactly that as soon as I felt I had exposed myself to him. And now I was sitting here like an idiot, pinning over what could have been and craving his touch.

I don't know how long I sat there, but the soft light of twilight faded to the stark grey of early night. I heaved myself up to my feet, slipping off my jeans and flannel for a large t shirt, twisting my already messy hair up into a bun, I wandered over to my bed, collapsing amongst the tangled sheets that screamed insomnia.

I lay on my side, fingering the cool cotton next to me, imagining doing the same thing to the stubble on Maverick's defined jaw. I heaved a sigh and closed my eyes, wrenching my touch away. I don't remember falling asleep that night or sleeping well through the next morning, or when Mae strolled in and plopped down on the bed next to me. She shook my shoulder, trying to get me to life.

"Doll? You look like hell. C'mon wake up its already noon." Her voice although teasing held a note of concern. I moaned at her shaking my shoulder, grumbling and trying to shove my head under my pillow, but to no avail. Mae snatched it away before I could bury underneath it, cackling all the while.

"Not so fast, Doll. C'mon we got to get you out of this depressing ass dorm. I have a plan." I could already tell she was grinning. I sigh at the thought of one of Mae's plans, not knowing if I could handle another night of chaos. Face first on my bed, I grumbled, indicating my displeasure at the idea of leaving the shelter my bed had to offer. That only earned me a swift punch in the arm.

"Gracccccceeeee," she dragged out my name in a whiny tone, "the boys want to see you! They are worried about you." She grips my arm, shaking it again. I huff, turning myself over to face her.

"Shit, I'm up." I squint against the harsh light pouring into the room. She clapped her black tipped hands, giddy already. "Now concerning your plans for the night...." I prepared myself to let her down, not feeling up to hashing out all the details once again from the other night, living through it was enough.

"Don't you dare say no. You are coming. Suck it up. Bo and Finn are coming with us and we are going, drumroll please, bowling!" She squealed. I immediately scrunched my nose up in disgust.

"Bowling?" I flopped back down on the bed, feigning sleep.

"Grace, nooooo. It'll be fun. No drama, just us! Plus, we don't have classes tomorrow so we can hang out all night if we really want."

"Since when do you care about having class?" I snort into my blankets. She grips one of my pillows, pulling it out from underneath my head, whacking me with it. We both giggle.

"Alright, alright, bowling it is." I hold up my hands in defeat against her pillow assault. "Can we eat something first, I'm starving."

***

We order food in, meanwhile Mae debriefs me on the events of the night, bowling and drinks with the boys, no parties, no drama guaranteed. I looked at her questioningly to which she instantly responded that we would not see Maverick in the slightest, not even Mick or Isabella. I felt guilty as relief washed over me, I missed Mick and Isabella, I just didn't know if I could face them.

By the time it was time to go, I found myself showered and looking presentable, applying a quick sweep of Mascara over my lashes. My long hair spilled around my shoulders, the ripped denim of my jeans allowing for peeks of my skin to shine through. With that I wore a red tee, only slightly cropped. I slipped on a pair of white sneakers and was satisfied enough with how I looked.

Seeing the guys made me forget about everything for a little while, allowing me too to loosen up. We drank stupid fruity drinks and laughed hysterically at Bo trying and failing to get a strike. It was nice to not have to look over my shoulder for the next incoming threat to the night. No one mentioned the drama from the party, the only mention of it was when I apologized profusely for what happened. But similar to Mae and Pete, I was waved off, getting a hug in return from both boys. It somewhat lifted my spirits that I didn't totally ruin any friendships I had acquired people I actually liked.

At the end of the night, we all piled back into Bo's car, deciding that we weren't going to end the night there. Mae had the brilliant idea of bar hopping, earning an eye roll and a giggle from me. On the way to our first bar though, we were cut short.

Bo's phone starting chirping, alerting the car of an incoming call. I was in the back seat singing along with the steady flow of music with Mae, not noticing anything until Finn turned down the dial for the volume, leaving only Bo's words.

"Hey man, what's up?" Bo's deep voice tired but failed to sound casual, holding a concerned edge. I watched as his eyes flipped up to his rearview mirror, meeting my own. The look only lasted a second before snapping his attention back to the road in front of him. His brow furrowed, Finn watching Bo with a serious expression.

"Man, I'm not sure if we can right now.. He did what? Shit. Ok, ok. Alright we'll be there in a few. Just hold tight." Bo threw his phone down at Finn's feet, running a hand through his short hair.

"Babe? What's wrong?" Mae wrapped her arms around Bo from her place in the seat behind him. He shot another glance at me from the mirror.

"Guys, I am afraid we aren't going to make it to the bar." Bo said gruffly before making a quick right. He looked to Finn, brows furrowed and giving him a nod.

"Fuck." Finn whispered under his breath as he brought a hand to his forehead and leaned back as if his suspicions were confirmed. I played with the fraying edges of the seat, not understanding at all what was happening.

"Do we have time to drop them off?" Finn looked back to Bo, who simply shook his head at his friend, his mouth set in a hard line. Finn sucked in a deep breath through his nose.

"Guys? What's going on?" I asked, peering up at them from my place in the backseat. They both looked to each other weighing their options.

"Maverick ran into some trouble. And we are going to help him." Finn sighed, closing his eyes in the process.

Chapter Twenty

My heart plummeted, dropping to the floor. My eyes went wide as I slumped back into my seat, not sure what to do or think. Maverick was in trouble. What kind of trouble? I worried for him, hating myself for it. He was an ass and yet I still cared for him.

"What?" Mae asked with her voice low as if she already knew the answer. Bo's silence seemed to be answer enough to her. She slumped back down next to me.

"Are you going to be okay?" Mae peered into my face; pity obvious. It's not like I really had an option, so I just gave her a nod. We rode in silence for the next few minutes until we pulled up to a small little house, nestled between two almost identical in wear and size. The paint peeled off the sides while the top gutter hung down threatening to fall at any moment. I gulped. A sparse stretch of grass laid out in front of the small home; cage linked fence encasing the spotty lawn. Bo threw open his door, followed by Finn. Before Finn left, he peeked his head back in the car offering a grim smile.

"We should be back soon please stay in the car okay. We'll be back soon." He quietly shut the door, striding to keep up with Bo. Before they can make it to the rickety screen door, Maverick busts out. He sees his friends and walks over to them with Mick close on his tail. Maverick yells kicking at anything in sight, running his hands through his dark hair making it stick up.

Even from a distance I can see his eyes glazed over in a mixture of tears and rage. Seeing him like this pangs at my heart, urging me to go to him. Finn is there instantly, clapping a hand down on Maverick's shoulder and forcing him to meet his gaze. From our position, we can't hear a word only the muffled volume of their voices. Maverick shakes off Finn's hand with a murderous look in his eyes. I press up against the glass of the window and leaning my weight on the door of the car. My hand grips the handle of the door for support, the cool metal almost begging me to go out there. With a deep breath, I ignored Mae's protests and followed through on instinct, opening the door.

I barely made a sound and yet I knew he saw me. Maverick's sharp green eyes snapped to mine, his face filling with confusion and rage. His gaze seared into mine. He turned his attention back to his friends.

"What is she doing here? Did you bring her here?" Maverick's voice is hoarse as he jabs his finger at Bo and yells. Bo's brow dipped, giving his face a hard edge that looked like it didn't belong there. As he was about to open his mouth, I decided to intervene.

"Don't you dare yell at him or talk about me like I'm not standing right here." I growl at him; his attention turns to me once again as I become the new target for his rage.

"Get in the car, Grace. All of you, leave." His tone held ice while his eyes simmered like embers. Now that I was up close, I could see the crumpled fabric of his shirt, his jeans just as wrinkled hanging low on his hips. He looked rabid, ready to attack his prey.

"No. I don't know why we are here, but we are. And we are here for you so stop throwing a tantrum and thinking that you can order me away." I prowled right up to him, spitting my venomous words on the way.

"Leave. I'm not going to ask you again." His voice, absolutely guttural, making anyone with less of a temper shrink away, but not me.

"C'mon Maverick. She's just trying to help." Finn tries to reason on my behalf, but it only earns him a quick glare.

"If you don't turn around right now, I will throw you over my shoulder and walk you to that car myself." His hands fisted at his sides and his features ensured me that he was telling the truth.

"I'd like to see you try." I dug my heels into the bare dirt that made up the front yard, crossing my arms firmly over my chest, making sue the bandaged hand was tucked under my arm and hidden. Mick walked up behind his cousin, placing a hand on his tensed shoulder.

"Don't Mick." He didn't even turn around to threaten his cousin, he just stared at me with that stony gaze. Mick withdrew his hand but only to walk out between the two of us.

"Maverick, calm down. You know we aren't going to let you hurt her." Mick's voice was calm, but his warning was conveyed.

"I would never hurt her. Never." Maverick whirled around to lay his eyes on Mick, while I couldn't help that snort that escaped me, bringing his attention right back to me.

"Is something funny about that Grace?" His look was predatorial. Pinning me in place.

"You have a funny way of showing that. 'you won't hurt me'. Bullshit." I cackle a laugh dripped in venom. Something resembling shame flashed across his face. I could visibly see his throat bob as he gulped.

His hand flashed across the distance standing between us, grasping my wrist. My mind reeled back to Jay, the way he crushed my wrist in his grasp and the feeling of my knuckles connecting with his nose. My ravaged knuckles clenched at the memory. Only Maverick's hold was firm yet still gentle. It was as if he was cradling my hand rather than trapping me. My arm tingling with the feeling of his skin on mine, making me forget my rage. I felt rather than saw the boys around us all stiffen, ready to jump Maverick but instead Maverick only nodded his head, slipping his grip from my wrist to my hand. He sighed through his nose as he dragged my hand down, my body instantly relaxing with his touch. He wordlessly brought me towards his house, and I followed. I had no idea what to expect as I shuffled my feet following him like a lost puppy. I could hear Mick telling the boys behind us it would be okay and that they should probably head out, but I didn't stay long enough to hear their response.

The groan of the rusted hinges connected to screen welcomed me as Maverick opened the door, still grasping my hand and tugging me in behind him. I was hit with the smell of must mixed with the strong tang of some sort of lemon cleaner burning my nose. The living room in front of me featured thread bare furniture, a faded denim colored couch with its sagging cushions pushed up against the far wood paneled wall. Next to that was a worn rust colored chair, the back fabric ripped and fraying, the color muted with age. The kitchen stood directly to my left, featuring a counter, a sink and a fridge. Plastic dishes sat neatly in the corner next to a simple cup holding fake silver utensils. The shag carpet sunk beneath my feet.

Maverick's gaze was downturned, as if he were ashamed of me seeing where he lived. Finding his hand still in mine I gave a reassuring squeeze. He looked to me, seeming distraught and deflated rather than the anger that was boiling in there minutes ago.

He led me to a small staircase connected to the kitchen adorning the same blue shag carpeting from the living area. He took two at a time bringing me to a small hallway with three battered doors. He looked back to me once before taking a deep breath and leading me to the one on the end.

I entered into a small room, its light grey walls washed in light from a modest lamp in the corner. A small bed sat in the middle of the room outfitted in a quilt and a small stuffed rabbit. The room was bare, making the small heap of blond hair and shuddering shoulders in the corner obvious.

I looked to Maverick in question before letting his hand go and stepping towards the small girl. Her platinum hair cascaded around her shoulders while her face remained cradled in her hands. Small sputtering sobs racked out of her small body as she sat curled up in a ball in the corner. I kneeled down in front of her, gently wrapping my hands around her wrists.

She startled as if she just realized my presence, she dropped her wrists, looking up into my face. Bright blue eyes lined by smudged mascara looked back at me. Her petite nose a deep shade of red and full lips trembled. She was no older than seventeen but looked like a small child, helpless and alone. She looked like a doll, her perfect porcelain skin catching the light from the lamp, adding to her innocence and giving her a luminescent glow. Maverick walked to stand next to my kneeling figure. I watched as she glanced to him, then quickly back to me. Questions swirled in her deep blue eyes.

"Delilah, the is Grace. She's here to help you." Maverick's deep voice murmured in a soothing tone, stooping to crouch next to me. Delilah kept staring at me despite the tears overflowing from her large eyes. I gripped her cold hands giving them a quick squeeze. I didn't know this small girl, I didn't know her relation to Maverick, but I couldn't help the feeling that I needed to protect her.

"Hey Delilah. I don't know what's going on right now, but I am going to try as best as I can to help okay?" I coated my words with understanding, trying to calm her sobs that racked her thin shoulders. She nodded, making more tears stream down her perfect face. Her small sniffles and whimpers caused Maverick to flinch.

"Alright, let's start here by getting you off the floor okay? We can get you to bed and maybe if you are feeling up for it, we can talk." My tone holds question, trying to coax her to trust me. Another silent nod. "Okay Maverick and I are going to help you. Ready?" Maverick understands without any explanation, wrapping his arm protectively around her small frame while I do the same to her waist.

Her legs tremble, threatening to give out as we lift her to them. In a few short steps, I back off allowing Maverick to carefully rest her down on the plush quilt. He perches himself on the edge of the bed, smoothing her hair away from her face as her eyes squinch shut against fresh tears. Watching the moment feels too intimate. Who was this girl? And who was she to Maverick? I moved to kneel next to the bed, reminding Maverick of my presence. He reluctantly moved his hand from the girl's hair and moved down to allow me to sit up by her head. I silently obeyed him, taking the place where he just was. The mattress was hard and cold underneath me as I gazed down at the girl.

"Delilah? You are shaking, here cover up." I softly commanded, lifting the light quilt and wrapping it around her frail frame. She snuggled into it, creating a perfect little ball of sputtering sobs. I moved my hand to rest on her shoulder and find her to still be quivering.

"Delilah, for me to help I need to know what's going on. Can you please tell me just so I can better help you?" Another nod. She scooted herself over to the edge of the mattress as if she barley had the energy, allowing me to sit next to her. Maverick seeing what the girl did, moved himself to sit in the far corner, seating himself in a small wooden chair, the wood groaning with the sudden weight.

He sat there, arms braced on his knees as he watched us intently, a look of worry and a controlled nervousness resting on his face. It felt as if the very air was buzzing with tension. I felt as if Maverick would snap any second, only adding to my anxiety.

I shifted, propping myself to sit up next to her tiny figure. She wrestled with herself to sit up until she was cradling her knees to her chest once again but facing me. I reached out grabbing her hand in an attempt to comfort her. She let out a small shuddering sigh, the sound hollow, barely a breath.

"I don't want to leave, I don't want to leave here. But he is going to make me." Her words resembled a squeak of a wounded animal. Her voice sounded as if her throat had been scraped raw, the exertion from speaking almost too much for her to handle. I glanced at Maverick, who looked as if someone had simultaneously punched him in the gut and dared him to a fight. This time I couldn't help the small shudder that passed through me.

"Who is making you? Maverick?" I had to ask, had to know if the boy from the field, the boy who fought for me, the boy who left me was responsible for this poor girl's suffering. She shook her head, more tears streaming down, some catching on her full trembling bottom lip.

"Connor." She whimpered. And just like that my blood turned to ice. The smash of metal and the heat of the flames encases me, drawing me away from the scene in front of me and teleporting me back to my past. The hand that isn't in hers I fist in the stained old sheets till my knuckles turn white. *Connor Steel?*

Chapter Twenty-One

"Connor? Connor Steel?" I managed to gasp out. Another nod. I tried to snap my attention back to the girl, away from carnage and wreckage. The name curls around my mind, reminding me of his power over me. What he could do to me with a few simple calls. My heart pounds in my chest furiously, pounding with anxiety and rage.

"What does Connor want?" I grit out, trying my best and most likely failing to not sound threatening. The small girl'se pulse quivedr against the porcelain skin of her neck as she tried to stifle another sob.

"Me. He wants to take me away from Mav. I don't want to leave. I don't want to go." She whines, the sound shattering my heart. I swing my gaze to look at Maverick, now hugging his arms to his chest and warring with himself whether to stay here or go find Connor. I gulp, closing my eyes for faint seconds as I try to calm myself and my confusion. I was missing something, but I just wasn't sure what yet.

"Delilah, what do you mean he wants you?" I can only hope that my hushed tones come off as comforting this time. I wasn't sure I was too good at comforting others. A few more sniffles echoed around the bare room.

"He thinks Mav can't take care of me. He thinks Nancy and Jim would be more 'beneficiary to my upbringing'. But he can't. I won't let him take me." I blinked a few times, trying to let the information settle in my mind. This was the clearest that she had been with me so far and yet it was the most confused that I had been. *Maverick takes care of her? What does that even mean? And who are Nancy and Jim?* I wasn't sure what to even say. There were too many threads, none of them connecting.

"Jim and Nancy are our grandparents. But we don't really consider them to be since they haven't done a damn thing since our Dad died." Maverick's rich voice quavered from the corner, stopping my thoughts in their tracks. My heart stopped in my chest. *Our Dad? Our grandparents?* I take in the girl in front of me in a new light. Noting the way her dark brows had the slightest line between them, the obvious indent of the same dimples, the full lips.

Holy shit.

Everything began to click into place. The small girl in front of me, she was his little sister. I didn't know how I didn't see it before. She even slightly resembled Mick, the same blue orbs for eyes that Mick had, and that Connor had.

"Connor is your cousin." I whisper to no one in particular. Another nod from the girl in front of me.

"I can't leave. I won't leave." Delilah repeated, slightly rocking with the words. I didn't think twice, reaching out and pulling her to my chest. I could feel rather than see Maverick's shock radiating through the room as I wrapped my arms around her protectively, nestling her into my side. She went rigid at first, eventually easing into my grip, even going to far as to cling to the front of my shirt, already becoming soaked through with her tears.

"Delilah, I promise you, we will figure this out. I am not going to let him take you." I look down at her platinum hair, my arms giving her a small squeeze. I sat there on the precipice of my edge of the bed, holding her sobbing figure until they become less powerful and frequent, all the while holding Maverick's gaze. I could see the thanks in his eyes and that same adoring stare from our night in the field. I stare right back, not willing to break the spell for anything. Knowing the helping them both would be my demise.

***

I don't know how long we went on like that until we all slipped into sleep. I woke up to stray moon beams tickling the plain curtains, everything coated in a dark stillness, quickly scanning my surroundings and instantly relaxing when I saw Maverick asleep propped up in the chair across the room.

Delilah lightly stirred before burrowing down deeper into her blankets and letting out a soft snore. She looked so innocent and pure I couldn't even imagine the possibility of her being related to the bastard that is Connor. Then there was the whole idea of Maverick and Delilah here on their own. They must be if their grandparents were trying to gain custody. I looked back to his sleeping form in the corner. His long lashes fluttered, the lamp's glow making him look younger than he was.

He took care of his sister. He raised her. And he tried to keep her out of his partying and school. I stared in shock at this new look into the life of Maverick. I had no idea and I had freaked out about him not talking to me for a week. He was just scared, scared of jeopardizing his sister. I sighed, the noise barely audible, but causing Maverick's eyes to slowly open. He startled, swiftly examining every detail in the room till he landed on me, sprawled across his sister's bed, and cradling her slumbering form. He relaxed, his lids drooping to cover half his eyes. He offered me a sheepish half smile.

"Hey Gray." He whispered, shattering the purgatorial silence clinging to the room.

"Hey Mav." I returned his smile.

"I'm sorry Gray. For everything. I should've just told you but instead I freaked out." Keeping his voice low, looking to his sister to find her lips in a pout, her brow furrowed in sleep. He smiled lovingly at her before looking back to me. "That night, or rather that morning, I freaked out. I didn't mean to spend the night because of Delilah. I don't like to ever leave her home alone for a whole night. Especially now that Connor is stalking us." He raked a hand through his hair, slumping so his elbows could rest on his knees.

"Mav, never apologize for taking care of her. Not to me, Ever. Understand? If I had known I wouldn't have thought twice. I missed you though. I wish you didn't fall off the face of the earth." I whispered back into the room, gaining courage as I cradled the slumbering form tucked into my side. A small smile stretched across his mouth. "Why are you smiling at me?" I whisper through my own smile.

"Because you are just. You are different. Most girls would have reacted so different to this. You didn't even know who Delilah was or what she was to me and you just took care of her like she was you best friend." He murmured in wonder. I felt my cheeks singe with heat and focused my gaze on the quilt that covered my lap. "Not to mention the fact that you don't put up with my shit." He huffed a breathy chuckle.

"Anyone would have done the same." As I was still refusing to look at him.

"I didn't. When I met you brother, I was punching him." His tone sounded ashamed at recalling the memory. The image of Pete and Maverick rolling through the dirt and grass flashed through my mind causing me to shudder.

"Look, I am not going to forgive you for fighting my brother, but I understand why you did what you did that night and honestly I'm thankful you stepped in when you did. How did you even know?" I sheepishly look up to him in question.

"I didn't. I wasn't even going to go to that party, I had a lot going on," He glanced at a slumbering Delilah, "But she insisted I get out for a night. So, I headed out just to get one drink and head back here. When I parked, I saw him talking to you, then he grabbed you and I didn't even think twice. Before I could even get there though, you had broken his nose." He chuckled at the last part. "I am sorry about your brother though. I didn't know who he was, I wasn't focusing on anything besides that bastard's hand wrapped around you. I know it's not an excuse, but I wish everything had happened differently." Neither of us looked away this time, holding each other's gaze. I could swear that he could hear my heart pounding in my chest as his gaze set every inch of my skin blazing.

The spell was broken by a sudden grumble from Delilah. Still sound asleep she turned, detaching herself from her hold on me. We both held our breath, praying not to wake her up. Once I was sure she wouldn't wake up, I silently slung my feet off the edge of the bed, bringing my sock clad feet to rest on the stained carpet.

Maverick watched me wordlessly, staying in his place in the corner of the dimly lit room. I padded over to him, my breath catching in my chest as I rooted myself in front of him, reaching down to grip his calloused hand in my own. My heart thundered in my chest, my body responding to his touch. I stood in front of him, one of his hands clasped in my own. I held my breath waiting. Waiting for what, I didn't know.

After he didn't pull his hand away from mine, I lifted my other hand up to rest on the side of his chiseled face, stubble tickling my palm. His eyes widened slightly before fluttering closed and leaning into the touch. He sighed, the warm air unfurling from his nose tingling the sensitive skin on my wrist. He raised himself to his full height, standing in front of me as the rickety wood of the chair groaned in protest.

He moved his hand to my waist as I peered up into his stare. I could feel my heart flutter as he leaned his broad brow down to rest on my own. His breath tickled my mouth, reminding me of how close he was until he withdrew slowly as if it physically hurt him to part his touch from mine, only to lead me through the room. His steps where silent as he switched off the small lamp, leaving the room with nothing but the faint glow coming from the bare window. After looking at his sister one last time, he led me out of the room.

He led me to the door to the right of his sister's, the hinges whining as the door moved for us. This room was just as bare, the only decoration a single frame sitting on a chipped wooden table that acted as a nightstand. The muted red comforter was perfectly spread over the bed, located right across from a large window. Sitting in a small stack resting under the window were books, all their spines worn from multiple reads. The scent of mint and that undertone of smoke furled around my nose, immediately putting me at ease.

Maverick sucked in a breath, as if he was baring his soul for me to judge. I released my grip on him, walking over to the small frame. He made no move to follow as I gently lifted the picture. A small picture smudged with age rested within the chipped glass. In it I recognized a younger version of him, a backwards red baseball cap doing little to hide the mess of hair. His grin showed off his deep dimple, that freckle on his lip turned upward. His eyes, usually holding some kind of anger were clear, happy even. His arm was strewn around a small girl sporting platinum pig tails, her crooked smile and squinted eyes adding to her look of youth. And on the other side of Delilah was a man I didn't recognize. His hair resembled Maverick's, slightly wild and had once been the same deep rich brown, now peered with streaks of grey. His dark brows were aloft, matching his wide grin. His nose was slightly big for his face but handsome none the less. And those eyes. Like blue pools, lucid and inviting. The kindness that radiated from his face was undeniable.

"Is this your dad?" I ask, clutching the picture and turning around. His hands were shoved in the pockets of his jeans, his shoulders high as he kicked at the carpet.

"Yea, that's him. He passed away a few years ago." He said sheepishly.

"I am so sorry." I whispered, my heart breaking for the two people who lived here on their own.

"He was a great man. He tried his best you know? After mom left, he was pretty devastated, but he still tried to be there for us. He died in a motorcycle accident. He was drinking and thought he was fine, he jumped on his bike and didn't come home." He kept his voice low, as if the words physically pained him to speak. I placed the picture back in silence, the cheap plastic of the frame barely making a sound as I placed it back to its spot. Maverick's eyes stayed glued to the carpet, shame radiating off of him.

I couldn't take my eyes off of him. All shadow and dappled golden light, steel and plush grass. He was so much, everything. And he didn't even realize how strong he was. I padded over to him, hooking a finger under his handsome chin. I lifted his face, looking up into it. I stayed silent as a single tear slipped down his face, carving its path down the tanned skin.

Without a second thought, I brought my lips to his, the barest brush sending small sparks down my body. His wide mouth parted for me, the kiss soft and inviting, not the same rushed passion from our first kiss. His hands found my waist, there light weight perched on my hips, almost hesitant.

I cupped his face, dragging his lips with mine. It was sweet, reminding me of the innocence that Maverick tried so hard to hide. I wrapped my fingers in the longer stands of hair, cascading down from the top of his head. He groaned at the contact, and just like that all control was gone.

I pressed against him, my mouth suddenly becoming more persistent. I needed more of him. I hadn't even realized how much I craved his touch during his absence. One of his hands moved to brace on the small of my back, I sighed into his open mouth as the hem of my shirt began to lift. I pulled him closer to me, the feeling of his muscled arms around me making me feel safe and out of harm's way.

He was so strong. He single handedly held his family together despite the outside threats. He hid his whole life from those who could jeopardize it. This was not the hot head that I had grown to know throw gossip and inopportune sightings. He moaned my name as my hips crashed into his, wanting no space between us. I broke away for a second, leaving us both panting. Those gorgeous eyes looked tired but at the same time alert and aware of every movement I made. He flashed me a wide grin, his chest heaving as he tried to suck air back into his lungs. I smiled right back, bringing one of my hands away from his hair to stroke his face.

"What are you thinking Gray?" His voice sounded husky, not lustful but rather, loving. I shook my head, biting my lips as they curled up into a shy smile. My eyes closed as every nerve in body tingled with the aftershock of our exchange. When I opened them again, he was still staring, that smile still there only now his gaze was fixed on my teeth worrying my bottom lip.

I stepped back, dropping my hand from his face to his hands, walking backward as to never break eye contact. I kept walking till the backs of my thighs hit the bed in the middle of the room. Wordlessly, I lowered myself onto the plush comforter, scooting back to indicate him to follow. Hie eyes held question, one eyebrow crooked. I nodded, pulling is hands to get him to the bed. I shifted over, allowing him to sit next to me. He was hesitant, crawling onto the worn mattress with a groan of old springs. He scooted close to me, turning to face me. Our lips were inches away, ready to meet again.

"Gray? I just wanted to say thank you. Not just for tonight but for not giving up on me." He whispered into the little space between us. The smell of mint unfurled around us as I scooted closer, leaning towards him. In answer I pulled his face to mine, brushing a kiss across his lips.

"I would never give up on you." I whispered onto his lips. We melted together, our lips drifting over each other, tasting each other and forgetting about all of our problems. I lowered my hands, tugging and working to lift the end of his shirt. My hands roved over the warm skin. Maverick pushed back for a second, looking at me.

"Gray, are you sure you want to do this?" He looked to me, no judgement at all only question. I wanted all of him and I couldn't deny it anymore. I nodded, taking my already swollen lip between my teeth already ready to taste him again. He shook his head in response. "Not good enough. I need to hear you say it

Gray, do you want this?" He whispered, his voice still husky and with the aftermath of our activity. Eyes leaden with yearning and hope. My heart cracked.

"I've never wanted anything more." I meant every word.

"That was the most cliché thing that has every come out of your mouth." He chuckles before crashing his mouth back into mine.

Chapter Twenty- Two

When I woke up in the morning I stretched languidly, enjoying the dead weight of Maverick's bare arm stretched across my chest and the cool sheets whispering across my naked body. Maverick groaned with the slight shift, cuddling closer. His dark hair tickled my nose, making me scrunch it up. I wrapped a finger around the strands, twirling the silky locks around my fingers. Soft light filtered through the window, Soft grey clouds promised rain, perfect for cuddling in this bed with Maverick.

"Morning." Mav mumbled onto my bare shoulder. The stubble that coated his chin brushed against me, causing goosebumps to stand up on my skin.

"Morning." I nestled deeper into him, pressing my cheek against his hair. He mumbled something, his deep voice vibrating against my skin. I hummed, reliving last night.

"What time is it babe?" His voice was laden with sleep.

I scrunch up my nose with glee. "Babe?"

"What do you want me to call you, babe?" He could feel rather than see him smiling as he dragged the last out word out dramatically.

I swatted at his arm. "It's early. I think."

"Mmmhmm. I better go check on Delilah."

"Probably." As I said the words, I placed a trail of kisses over his head, tracing down his face, his jaw. A moan the only response.

"I'm glad you are here Gray. I am just so fucking happy." He stared into my eyes before placing a rough kiss on my lips, it was intoxicating.

"Mav can I ask you something?" His attention lingered on my eyes as he gave me a nod. "Why do you call me Gray?" the question made me oddly shy, making me duck my head as to shade my eyes, almost scared of the answer.

His cheeks burned with a light red and a nervous chuckle bubbled out of his throat. "Eh, well. It's kind of a long story."

"Try me."

"Ok well um, I have kind of maybe had a crush on you? For like a long time." The words sent tendrils of excitement through me, especially at the idea of Maverick having a crush.

"A crush?" I waggled my eyebrows at him, causing him to flop face first in a pile of pillows next to me.

"I saw you in one of my classes okay. I remember thinking how you seemed like a bitch," I huffed a laugh at that, "but then you spit off this crazy analysis of the book we were reading and your eyes, it was like you dared the professor to contradict you. Like you would bite his head off if he tried. I was in awe." He peeked over at me with a shy grin.

"I just knew you were the one for me. The guys have been giving me shit for the past year about it."

"The past year?" I couldn't even attempt to hide the shock in my voice.

"Yea."

I reached over, stroking the planes of his face until I softly brushed a kiss across his lips. The thought of him being so vulnerable and shy was highly ironic but oddly comforting.

"But erm, I overheard you talking to your friend there one time," at that my heart dropped, "you were talking about a guy, I think you were anyway. And you said how you were 'his and his alone' so I took that as a sign to back off." He peeked at me from under his brows as I felt every part of my body turn to ice.

My mind reeled. Bronze eyes examining me, smoke pouring from his lips as he chuckled at me. His large hands stroking my bare skin. That curly hair a constant mess piled on his head, a deep chestnut brown, warm like his eyes. *I love you Birdie. Forever.*

I felt the tears pricking at my eyes, hyper aware of Maverick's gaze as he watched me struggle, stroking his broad hand over the bare skin of my stomach. Trying to comfort me. Only I didn't deserve to be comforted.

"Yea, um." I took in a shuddering breath, my voice thick with tears.

"Hey hey, Gray you don't have to tell me." His voice was soft, as if it could caress away my pain.

"His name was Harvard." The words felt forced, burning their way up my throat. Maverick stilled; his fingers frozen on their spot on my stomach. "He…he died."

"Is that the friend that…." His large thumb brushed the bird at my ear. I could only nod as the tears slipped down my cheeks. He sucked in a breath.

"Fuck I am sorry Gray. So so sorry." He brushed kisses all along my face, fingertips skimming my skin. I melted into his touch, savoring any ounce of comfort he offered even though every touch acted as a burn reminding me, I didn't deserve this.

"I loved him." He stilled, bringing his eyes up to my face even though all I could do was look at the white chipped paint on the ceiling. "I loved him so much. I thought…."

"Shhhhh. It's okay Gray. I got you." He whispered the words, pulling me against his bare chest. I burrowed deeper into his embrace, as if it alone could protect me from the onslaught on memories.

We lay there, embraced while he pressed soft kisses against my hair, whispering sweet nothings in an attempt to soothe my broken form. Stroked the skin of my arms till they stopped shaking with sobs, till my tears dried against his skin in salty patches.

Once I was calmed, I forced myself to meet those green eyes. "Thank you."

"You don't have to thank me. If anything, I should be thanking you."

I placed a soft kiss to his mouth, savoring the way they curled into a smile with the contact.

"I should go check on Delilah be back in a flash." He gave me another quick peck before rolling off the bed.

He shifted his weight off of me, the cool air hitting me and making me miss Maverick's warmth. I pulled the sheets up to my chin, breathing in the minty scent that can only be described as Maverick.

I watched his naked form walk to his small closet, grappling to find a pair of dark sweatpants and pulling them on so they rested low on his hips. He shot me a grin over his shoulder, aware of my gaze. He sauntered out, closing the door behind him. I sighed, rolling to my side.

And yet I couldn't ignore the pit furled in my stomach. Harvard. I couldn't, wouldn't let the same fate destroy Maverick. The touches, soft kisses like ash choking me, coating my tongue.

"Shit!" I could hear Maverick yell from the other room followed with a loud bang, making me sit up with alert, forgetting my train of thought. Maverick stormed back into the room, throwing back the door. He ripped back the door to his closet.

"Mav? What's wrong?" He punched at the wall, leaving a small dent. I got up quickly, throwing on my clothes as quick as I could, watching as Maverick pulled on a tight fitted hoodie and grappled for the keys of his truck.

"She's gone." He heaved the words in angry gasps and it was then I noticed the small piece of crumpled paper clutched in his fist.

"What do you mean she's gone?" I struggled to get the words out as I work up my jeans. He ran the hand not gripping the note through his tousled hair. Wordlessly he shoved the paper toward me, the small paper crinkled from the strong grasp of his fist. I worked to smooth the deep creases encasing the smudges of ink. I squinted at the smudged script, so small it was hard to read.

Mav. I'm going to fix this. I love you. -Delilah

My heart dropped. The paper fluttered from my grasp, cascading till it nestled softly on the shag carpet. What did she mean she was going to fix it? Before I could even think, Maverick grabbed my hand tugging me out the door, not even bothering to lock it before practically running us towards the chipped black paint of his truck. He ripped open the door with such force it quivered.

He effortlessly picked me up, setting me in the high passenger seating and slamming the door in what seemed like one motion. Before I could even register the cool morning air or the fact that I had no idea where we were going, Maverick was whipping out of the small patch of dirt he used as a driveway.

We hurtled down the street, taking each corner on two wheels. Maverick's hands gripped the steering wheel so hard his knuckles turned white; his arms riddled with veins from the tension in him.

"Maverick, slow down. Where are we going?" I didn't dare touch him, but I said the words with force trying to snap him out of his rage and worry. I got nothing in response, just more silence. He didn't slow down at all, the blurs of trees and golden leaves streaking by the spotty windows of the truck. I slid against the seat, digging my nails into the worn leather for even an ounce of stability. My teeth grinded together, trying to think of a way to calm Maverick down.

He suddenly slammed down on the brakes, the tires squealing in protest. I whipped my head to the side, after regaining my posture from being lurched forward with the impact. We stopped in front of an expensive looking house, its massive double doors standing ominously against a perfectly manicured lawn. The grass was so green it looked unnatural. The massive house featured giant windows, all expertly shadowed as to not see inside.

The pale blue paint had not a single chip, the shutters painted an elegant red to correspond with the landscaping. I turned to ask Maverick where we were, but instead I saw an empty seat and the door slamming shut. I grappled with my seatbelt, cursing it as I finally wretched it free. I jumped to the cement of the road, the bare soles of my shoes thudding with the impact.

Even the cement was even and perfect. My legs buckled at the slight impact, but I quickly regained my footing and ran after Maverick. His broad shoulders were tense, his long legs moving in quick strides as they carried him to the door. He looked ready for battle, the tension in his body clearly ready to spring.

He reached the massive doors, me trailing and struggling to catch up with him. His fist rose, banging on the door, making the whole thing shudder. I thought the door was going to cave in.

"Open the damn door now. I know you are in there Connor!" Maverick's deep voice tore across the silence of the morning. He pounded again. This time the doors swung inward, and Maverick instantly reacted, wrapping his hand around the pressed collar of Connor's pale grey shirt. Connor didn't seem fazed, offering a half-lidded gaze paired with a lazy grin. The sight of him made me blanch suddenly, my brain screaming at me to get away from the threat Connor posed. Maverick dragged Connor from the door, throwing him down into the grass. He loomed over his cousin, his tall frame casting a shadow over the crumpled businessman. Connor simply let out a breathy laugh.

"Where is she? Huh? What did you do?" Maverick's face turned a deep shade of red, spit flying with the force of his words. Connor moved his hands, dusting the grass stains on his palms on the dark wash of his expensive jeans.

"Cousin, nice to see you as well."

"Don't. Where is she?" Maverick snarled back. I stood wide eyed, thankful that Connor hadn't noticed me yet. I gripped the fabric of my sleeves to prevent digging my nails into my palms.

"What do you mean?" genuine confusion spread over Connor's face until something clicked. He rose to his full height, towering over me but still significantly smaller than his cousin. "She ran away from you, didn't she? She saw how unfit you were to be her guardian." He chuckled out a dark and bitter chuckle. Maverick's jaw feathered; his fists clenched.

"Just tell me where she is." Maverick's voice came out low, threatening.

"How should I know? You are the little bitch's legal guardian after all." And just like that Maverick snapped. His fist struck Connor across his jaw, knocking his head to the side. Connor met the blow with another bitter laugh, spitting blood onto the unnaturally green lawn. I couldn't help but think of Jay.

"Don't you ever call her that again or so help me.." Before Maverick could land another punch, Mick shoved past me coming from what seemed like thin air. He ran to his cousin, jumping in front of Connor.

"Maverick, don't. Don't let him have power over you. You got to get out of here. Now." Mick, gripped Maverick's shoulders trying to get him to focus. "Maverick, look at Grace, she's worried and you need to find Delilah." Maverick looked back at me, that wild look still ragging in his eyes. Just like that though, Mick made the situation worse. As my name slipped out of Mick's mouth, Connor followed Maverick's gaze, sliding his own icy stare right to me. A wicked smile spread across his lips.

"Well, what a surprise. Grace. Lovely Grace." Connor drawled, his voice sending chills down my spine. I knew it was coming he was going to expose me. "Does my cousin know your secret? Does he know who you really are? What you did? I bet he doesn't considering he can still stand to be near you."

Connor's words made Maverick's gaze snap back to the disheveled man. "But then again disasters attract disasters." With that he was knocked to the ground with a quick jab from Maverick. Mick had been distracted watching me with confusion and what seemed like a tinge of recognition. Maverick's outburst saved me, Mick returning his focus to his quarreling family as he shoved at Maverick, forcing him back from his target.

"Now Maverick go. Before he calls the cops or finds her first." At that, I snapped out of my own stupor, walking over to him and placing a shoulder on his heaving shoulder.

"Mick is right. We have to go." I practically whispered the words, only receiving a slight nod. I pulled at his hand, dragging him with me. We quickly strode to his car, trying to distance ourselves from the threat that Connor posed. I could feel the tense air surrounding Maverick but all I could do was suck down breaths, trying to calm my hammering heart.

I had thought that Maverick was finally mine, I belonged to him just as much as he belonged to me especially after last night. And now I was at risk of losing him right when I had found him. I forced Maverick into the driver's seat, not trusting myself behind the wheel right now. My hands were quivering as flashbacks bombarded my vision, each breath coming out shakier than the last.

"Fuck!" Maverick's sudden outburst snapped me back to the present, his large fist connecting with the already banged up wheel. He opened both hands, slamming both palms against the top of the wheel, face scrunched into a sneer of frustration.

Without another word he grappled for the clutch and threw it into drive, racing down the street. I fumbled for words but came up short. What could I have possibly have said? If this was Pete missing, I would be reacting the exact same way. All I could think about was blinding lights, crushed metal, and the small girl curled up in the corner of her room weeping.

Maverick, eyes never leaving the road, gripped his phone, punching in a few numbers before bringing it up to his ear.

Almost instantly he got an answer, "Bo, It's me. It's Delilah... Yea. You didn't hear from her did you?.... Shit. Look just keep an eye out and if she contacts you let me know." He slammed his finger on the screen ending the call.

His full lips were set in a straight line, his dark strands of hair flopping into his face. He looked as if he had been carved from steel, all hard edges and sharp lines. Even the air around him felt cold, metallic and energized.

I fisted my hands in my lap, not sure what to do and if I was supposed to comfort him. I was absolute shit when it came to this, it was a miracle that I was able to connect with Delilah like I did in the first place. My hands twitched, my fingers aching to reach out to him, to touch him, to do anything that could offer him even an ounce of comfort. Just as I was about to reach over though, his phone began to buzz.

His eyes immediately filled with hope, they made him look almost like a child, ready to receive a gift or a sweet. He glanced at the screen his eyes closing for the briefest of seconds with a sigh of relief before answering.

Chapter Twenty- Three

"Delilah? Are you okay? Where are you?"
Despite the edge to his voice, he tried to maintain a
sense of urgency while also trying to calm the possible
flight risk that was currently Delilah. 'I'm on my way.
Do not move understand? I'm coming." He threw his
phone back into the cup holder, bringing a hand up to
rub at his forehead.

"Was that her?" My own voice came out as a
squeak, making me flinch. It was obviously her, but I
was at a loss for words. He sighed through his nose as if
he suddenly remembered that I was there.

"Yea, that was her. She's in the center of town."
He didn't even look at me, his eyes glued to the road. It
was my turn to heave a sigh now. I slumped back in the
worn leather of the passenger seat, relieved that he found
Delilah, she seemed so small, so frail as if a breath of
wind could have carried her away, and I was worried for
her. I hadn't even realized how tense I had been till my
legs and shoulders ached with its release.

We drove through winding back roads in
silence, making it there within minutes as Maverick held
true to his promise. The cool air seemed to seep into the
car, sending an involuntary chill down my spine as

Maverick whipped into a space directly in front of the small building that acted as town hall.

Sitting on a small metal bench in front of it sat a small girl. Her platinum hair wrapping around her small body donning a giant grey hoodie and leggings. Her big eyes were red, her freckled cheeks tear stained, and her nose and cheeks tinged with an unnatural red. And clutched in her small pale hand was a stack of crisp papers. Everything about her screamed defeat. My hands twinged with the ache to hurt whoever did this to her.

Maverick barely put the car in park before he rushed Delilah, dropping to his knee in front of her shaking form. It seemed to intimate, I shouldn't be there, but I swung myself down from the truck, staying put on the edge of the curb. Maverick peered into the girl's face, wrapping his big hands around her to cup her head in his hands.

I could only watch him scanning her, making sure there were no injuries or signs of any type of distress. More tears spilled out of her now closed eyes. I could hear his slight murmurings, Delilah's only response slight nods. I forced myself to step forward, rounding up so I was on Delilah's side. I perched down next to her, the metal from the bench biting into my jeans.

I scooted closer; Maverick's eyes still locked onto her face as Iwrapped my arm around the girl's shoulder hugging her to my side. I could feel how cold she was as I started to rub my hand on her arm, tiny tendrils of cold seeping into my fingertips with the contact. I was only there to comfort, I didn't have a part in this and that was fine, but I wanted to be there for the both of them. Maverick looked to me, a fleeting glance but the flash of a smile that he gave me was enough to warm me to my core. To signal he was back in his right mind.

"I am just happy that you are ok. Never do that again, understand? I don't know what I would ever do if something happened to you." Maverick continued his soothing words towards his sister, still cupping her head in his grip. More silent tears spilled down her cheeks.

"Mav, I need to tell you something." Delilah's voice came out hoarse and small, her grip on the papers in her lap tightening. The movement drew his attention to them as well. "I had to leave this morning because I had to do something. I knew that if I told you, that you wouldn't let me do it. But I had to. It was the only way." Her small voice cracked over the last word.

"Delilah, what is it? You can tell me." His words were soft, tender, questioning. I squeezed her to my side, trying to offer my reassurance, despite my own grim expectations.

"Um, in order for me to, to avoid any ties to Connor or their side of the family, I had to, um, I had to…." She stumbled over the words; her gaze downcast at the papers buckling under her grip. "I had to get emancipated."

The words struck Maverick like a blow, his confusion lighting his features. "You, you what?"

She sniffled in response, trying to muster courage, "Mav, there was no other choice, they weren't going to stop. You know that. I have a little under a year left before I am eighteen, but until that we were both at risk. This was the only option." She was trying to convince herself with the words, growing paler by the second, each word a sentencing for the siblings.

"I...I don't understand." I could see the hurt in Maverick's face before I could hear it in his voice. Those eyes were now robbed off all signs of earlier hope and relief. The only emotions in them now were defeat and hurt. I sat there frozen. Unsure what to do, this small girl who meant so much to me for some reason, and the man that I loved crumpling before me.

"I am my own guardian now. They can't take me."

"I know how emancipation works Delilah," Maverick's tone slipped, making him snap, "I just don't understand why. Was I not good enough? I am so sorry Delilah I am so sorry about everything." Any rage that had just bee there was gone, leeched out to him in a huff of defeat. His broad shoulders slumped, making him look smaller than before, too weighed down.

"Mav, I love you. You were the best guardian I could have asked for. But it was unfair for you. It was my turn to protect you." Silent tears slipped down her round cheeks with the words, tugging at my heart.

Maverick dropped his gaze, not able to meet her eyes and just nodded, not able to believe the words. My heart broke for him, for his sister who was now legally alone in this world.

"It's ok, It's ok. We don't even have to acknowledge it; you will still live with me. We will still be together. Only this piece of paper will say any different." Maverick said more to reassure himself then his sister. While Maverick still stared at the concrete, Delilah looked to me. Her full lips pressed together to suppress a sob. Her big blue eyes told me all I needed to know. She just shook her head. I felt my own tear escape and slide down my face.

"Maverick, I can't stay here." Delilah's words penetrated this barrier of silence none of us knew was there. I watched as a tear quivered and hung to her long dark lashes. With the revelation, Maverick's gaze snapped to his sister. "You know as well as I do that they won't stop. They can hire the best lawyers, try to refute the emancipation. I have to leave. I have to find a place of my own. I won't let them take us both down."

This girl clutched to my side was so strong and she didn't even know it. So much like her brother. She stuck her chin out despite her quivering bottom lip. She was willing to sacrifice everything to save her brother without a second thought. Maverick's hands dropped, his head falling down as he slumped to sit on the pavement. His silent tears stained the worn fabric of his sweatpants, some slapping onto the concrete. I knew this was breaking them both and all I could do was watch. Watch as they both crumpled in a mess of steel and loss.

I turned to face Delilah, throwing both arms around the brave girl and holding her close to me. I could feel her silent sobs rack her body, she had to have been out of tears, but she collapsed herself into my arms. I hugged her tighter, resting my head on her platinum hair as if I could protect her from the next challenges she would have to face.

In that moment I decided I would help in any way I could, even if that meant unburying my past. If she was brave enough to sacrifice herself, so could I.

Chapter Twenty- Four

I don't know how long we sat there, all with our cheeks stained with tears and the cold working its way into us. Eventually I shifted to find Maverick unmoving in his defeated state. I unfolded my arms from around Delilah, chucking her chin with as much of a smile as I could muster.

I looked up to find the truck still idling, a steady stream of smoke billowing into the winter air. Maverick had left the keys in the ignition. I helped Delilah to her feet, guiding her to the car and setting her on the bench seat nestled between Maverick's and my seats. I gave her a small smile which she tried to return but failed. After making sure she was ok, I cautiously approached Maverick, sitting next to him and angling my body to face his own.

I hesitantly reached out a hand, placing it on his large shoulder. He had stopped crying, but I could tell he was still devastated as he refused to look to me.

"Maverick, it's cold out here. Let's get you back to the house ok?" He responded with a nod and nothing more. "Ok, I'll drive ok? It'll be ok." He dragged his eyes up to mine and the wounds reflected in them broke my heart even further.

His dark lashes were matted with tears, his tanned skin featuring blotches and slightly blanched. I reached my hand up, tracing the path of a stray tear. He nuzzled into my hand, accepting any sense of comfort he could get. This was destroying him. For a brief instant those green eyes were replaced with deep brown ones, lifelessly gazing at me. They pleaded with me, but I was helpless. Just as I am now.

"I just wish I was enough." He whispered, the words so silken and fragile, it was if they weren't even said to begin with.

"Maverick, you listen to me, you never say that again. You are so much more than enough. You did everything you could. Everything. Don't doubt that for a second." My voice came out all fire, passion igniting every word. His eyes found mine, His lips slightly parted and I did the only logical thing I could think of. I brought his lips to mine. Not rushed or clashing but soft, delicate, a promise of his worth.

I tasted the salt of his tears streaked over the soft skin of his full lips. I brought both hands to cup his face, delicately framing his strong features. It also held the promise of goodbye, when he inevitably discovered who I was, what I did and what I was going to do. My fingers intwined in his hair, the silken strands shifting through my fingers. I worked my lips, wanting to memorize each curve, each movement. I finally pulled away, looking deep into those green fields of longing and defeat, mixed with the slightest tinge of adoration and desire. He looked so vulnerable so exposed, and I only knew how threatened he actually was.

***

I drove the three of us back to their house, none of us able to talk even if we had known what to say. I tried to think, to formulate a plan. I knew I had to reach out to them. I didn't know if they would hear me out, I had put them through hell after all. But they were my parents.

I reached the small gravel parking space that acted as a driveway in front of the Foster's small home. With a glance next to me, I saw that Delilah was fresh out of tears, her eyes wide in her blanched face. Her hair fell around her frame in delicate cascades so blond they could have been white. She just stared at her hands, gripped together in her lap. Next to her sat an equally disheveled Maverick. His dark lashes stood out, tear stained, framing his pale green eyes. Deep bags hung from his eyes, making him look weathered. He leaned against the window, both hands gripped into loose fists, as if something had just slipped out of his grasp.

I wordlessly killed the engine, waiting for a recognition or movement, but they both just stayed silent. I reached tentatively to Delilah, placing my hand on her thin shoulder. She startled, looking up quickly and relaxing once she saw she was home. I gave her a grim nod, pushing open the door and sliding to the ground. She hopped out; arms wrapped around herself. I walked over to Maverick's door, giving a small knock on the window in an attempt to break him out of his stupor. Even behind the dusty glass of his truck with stained cheeks, he was beautiful.

He looked to me and I could only give him a grim smile. The sky above me had turned cloudy, the air holding an electrical and muggy charge promising a storm. He met my eyes and simply nodded, pushing himself up as if it pained him to do so. The door swung outward, Maverick effortlessly leaping to the crushed gravel beneath him. I needed to touch him and comfort him, but my arms hung at my sides, their weight seeming awkward as he gave me a nod and walked to catch up with his sister's form that was shuffling to the door. I knew I only felt this way for what I was about to do, but it didn't hurt any less. With a brief sigh. I turned on my heels and helped them into the house.

I threw the keys to the truck on the small, chipped counter, dingy with age yet clean nonetheless. Both brother and sister stood in the center of the dim living room not able to meet each other's gaze and fidgeting with their clothes.

"Delilah? Why don't you go and get some rest? Maverick, you should do the same. I'll walk Delilah up and I'll meet you in your room in a minute." They both look exhausted, which only aided in what I was about to do. I strode over to Maverick, quickly planting a kiss on his cheek and pushing at his chest to herd him towards the stairs. He turned, about to leave but stopped dead in his tracks. It was as if he had stopped mid step before he quickly turned back and crashed into his sister.

His arms effortlessly wrapped around her, seeming to swallow her. He buried his head in the crook of her neck. He clung to her, as if she was his only tie to the world. At first, Delilah was startled, her hands pinned at her sides until she gripped him back, just as fiercely. Two statues carved from the same stone.

"We'll get through this; we'll find a way." He whispered into her neck, sending my stomach to my feet as it weighed with guilt. Delilah was too choked up for words, only managing a nod against her brother's massive shoulder. As he pulled back, he tucked a strand of her hair behind her ears and headed back up the stairs.

He took the stairs slowly, not turning once as he found the hall. Delilah just stood rooted to her place, watching him disappear around the corner. I felt so attached to them both, even though I had only known them for such a short period of time. All I wanted was for them both to be okay. And I would make sure that that would happen.

Maverick couldn't let her go, he would never be able to let her do what needed to be done, both me and Delilah knew that. I was their only hope. I walked up to her; she was practically my height, but she seemed so much smaller. I pulled her to my side, knowing what I had to do next. I urged her forward, bringing her up to the same small room I had held her in last night. I left her side for a few seconds, only to pull back the small quilt for her. She slid in, snuggling in as I gently pulled the cover over her. I placed my hand on her hair, the silky strands grazing my fingertips as I looked into those deep gentle eyes, she was so vulnerable, so young and yet she was so strong, capable. I smiled a closed lip smile in an attempt to ease her and turned to leave, before I could get the chance, I felt a grip on my wrist. I turned back, seeing Delilah's small yet surprisingly strong grip on my arm.

"Thank you, Grace." She whispered, loosening her grip and cuddling back into her blankets. I felt tears prick at my eyes, my throat suddenly tight as I choked back tears. I just nodded to her, turning to shut the door behind me.

I stayed there for a second, hovering outside her door, my hands gripped in fists, my back pressed against the aged wood. I had done a lot wrong in my life, I had done wrong by my family and by Pete, by Jay and even Mae. But I would not do wrong by Delilah, or Maverick. I was not a good person, in fact I was the opposite, but I could do this for them. I had to do this for them. All I could see was Maverick's crumpled form on the sidewalk, flashing next to images of oil-stained concrete and that lifeless form splayed in a similar manner.

Before Maverick could hear me or realize I was no longer in with his sister, I padded down the stairs, my sneakers sinking into the shag carpet with each step. I pushed the door open as slow as I could, willing the rusted hinges not to squeal and reveal me.

I stepped out, the cool air moist with the promise of rain. The smell of the damp air did little to calm my nerves as I gripped my phone and pulled it from my back pocket. I could do this. It wasn't for me, it was for Delilah, for Maverick. He would hate me for this, but it had to be done. I scanned through my contacts till I found his name, my shaking finger hesitating over the dial button. For them I would do this. I slammed my finger down. Small rain drops plastered their way to my skin.

Each ring felt like my damnation, urging me to end the call while I had the chance.

"Hello, you've got Senator Paul Edison." Even hearing his voice sent me into a panic, maybe I couldn't do this. His voice wasn't unkind, warm actually, the perfect embodiment of what a politician could be. I stayed silent trying to will my lips to move. He beat me to it his words coming out a breathy gasp, "Grace?"

"Um, yea. Yea, it's me." My voice sounded shaky unsure, bringing me right back to stuffy dresses and a perfect plastered smile. It made my stomach roll with panic.

"Where have you been? Your mother and I have been worried sick. You know how much stress we are under." Just like that his voice was all hard edges and demanding.

I forced myself to swallow the harsh words that were ready to bubble out of me, "I'm fine. I know and I'm sorry."

"And let's not forget the fact that we let your brother go to see you and he comes back with a busted lip. Is that the type of company you keep now Grace?" His tone was full of disdain, disgrace. How ironic that their beloved Grace had ended up to be the biggest disgrace they had ever encountered.

"I'm sorry. I am. But I need your help." The words tasted bitter, as if I was begging for him to smile down on me with his politician kindness.

"Grace, what is it? Are you in trouble again? Please tell me you are okay?" I knew exactly what he was thinking because I was recalling that same night.

"I promise I am not in trouble and I am doing well. But one of my….. friends. They need help." I was just met with a sigh; I couldn't tell if it was of relief or disgust.

"It's bad. There is this girl, she's a year younger than Pete. D.." I stopped myself, "it's pretty bad. She had to get emancipated because her grandparents and snobby ass uncle are trying to get custody over her. She needs a place she can go, a place where she can be safe." I finished, my eyes squinched up with the inevitable rejection.

Another sigh. "I'll see what I can legally do. As for a place to stay," he paused, it seemed infinite, this pregnant silence that could damn these people I loved or be their salvation. "Our house in Maine is available. She can stay there until everything is figured out." I blew out a breath I hadn't been aware that I had been holding.

"Thank you, Thank you so much. You have no idea what this means.." before I could finish though I was interrupted.

"I have a condition Grace. I want you to come home." And there it was. Of course, he couldn't just do something out of the goodness of his heart, he had to make some kind of profit. He had to benefit in some way.

My eyes grew instantly wide, dread surging through my veins at the prospect of returning to my past.

"Not permanently of course, as you are still attending school. Just for a few weekends and events and such. Look, Grace it has been a long time since the- the accident," I gulped at the images that flooded back, "you need to come back. For our sakes."

I stayed silent. It was fair. A fair sacrifice for those I loved. But it was so hard. I was faced with returning to my past. But I had to in order to save them.

"Ok. I'll do it." The words felt like my condemnation.

"I'll get the Maine house in order, I'll send Pete to get her. He'll be there by tonight. I'll see you soon Grace." Without another word I slammed down on the end call button. A few hours. I had a few hours to say goodbye to the boy upstairs, sick with dread over losing his sister. He would hate me for my part in this, and worst of all he would find out about me. I couldn't stop the tears that glided down my cheeks. I swiped a hand at them, jamming my phone back into my pocket and turning back towards the house. I was covered in a fine mist from the outside, but I was numb to it, taking the stairs two at a time. I carefully turned the knob to Maverick's door.

Chapter Twenty-Five

The soft gray light filtered into the room, the broken spines of the classic books by the window seemed to mock me, proudly displaying Maverick's love for them, a love I would be stripped of, left bare and alone. He was sprawled out on his bed, his eyes closed. His hand twitched slightly, indicating he was deep in sleep.

That perfect full mouth was in a tight line. Everything about him screamed power, ferocity and yet as he slept, he resembled a boy, a shattered boy who had been forced to grow up, forced to carry burdens no one should have to face. I padded over to him, refusing to wake him up. I had too much to do and he couldn't bear witness to any of it. I brushed the pad of my thumb over his broad cheek, those long lashes curling and brushing against the same plane of his face. I pressed my lips to his temple, lingering there before breaking away and forcing myself back to Delilah's room.

I slunk through the dark room to kneel down by her side.

"Delilah, wake up. We have to talk."

Delilah's eyes fluttered for a second before snapping wide open, instantly alert.

"What is it? Is Maverick… What time…." I could practically see all the questions clouding her mind, as I reached out gripping her hand.

"Shhh, no no everything is fine. It has only been about ten minutes, but I have to talk to you about something."

"Grace? What is it?" Her paranoia was still clear in her juvenile voice. It still shocked me to think that she was seventeen, that she was only seventeen after the decisions she had to make.

"There is something about me that Maverick doesn't know. Nobody does. But I am going to tell you because it allows me to help you ok? But we have to keep quiet because Maverick can't know, not yet." I kept my voice to a whisper trying to coax the sleep out of her while making her alert all the while. Her brows furrowed but she nodded. The gesture was so Maverick that I had to suck in a quick breath.

"My full name is Grace Edison, my father is Senator Paul Edison." He owl like eyes widened, which I didn't even think was possible. "I told him about what happened, and he agreed to help. We are going to let you stay in our Maine house till everything is figured out. My brother is going to be here in a few hours to pick you up and bring you there."

"Don't tell Maverick. He won't let me go." Delilah's voice suddenly held an edge, she was commanding me, demanding my secrecy. Little did she know that she already had it.

"Of course." As soon as she was satisfied with my response, she pulled me into a bone crushing hug. Her arms were thrown around my neck, holding me close. Hesitantly I wrapped my own arms around her, squeezing her back.

"Thank you, Grace. For everything." She whispered into my ear; sincerity evident in every word.

"Of course, Delilah." I whispered back in the darkness.

* * *

Within the next hour, I texted Pete to find out he could be there within two hours, enough time for Delilah to pack and comprise a note saying goodbye to her brother. We both worked quickly and quietly, stuffing stacks of clothes into an old dusty suitcase that hadn't been used in years. I watched as she tucked the same picture displayed on Maverick's nightstand into a copy of a book before shoving it in an old backpack.

Just as Pete was about to show up, Delilah extended a small envelop to me, her loopy handwriting spelling out Maverick's name on the front. "You need to give this to him. Tell him I love him. That I'll see him soon."

The words were so sure, yet her eyes spilled over with tears. I reached out, gripping the small envelope and pushing it into my pocket with a silent nod. We stood looking at each other for a second, considering the aftermath of what was about to happen. Just then my phone vibrated, alerting me that Pete was there.

Delilah let out a deep sigh but never looked away from my gaze, no more tears. All iron and courage that looked so much like her brother. She gripped my hand as we walked out into the lawn. Pete's jet-black expensive car looked out of place on the small block and I could hear Delilah suck in a breath. Pete was there, a grim smile etched onto his face, his floppy hair covered by a red baseball cap. He was instantly in front of us, crushing me into a hug.

"I know how hard that was for you. They must mean a lot to you." He whispered into my ear, his form crushing me against him. He stepped back, releasing me and seeming to just then realize why he was there.

"Delilah, this is my brother Pete. Pete, Delilah." I gestured between the two, feeling rushed and praying that Maverick would not wake up. Pete's eyes widened, his mouth going a little slack jawed as he took in the beauty that was Delilah. I smiled a little at his reaction despite my panic.

"You are going to catch flies with your mouth open like that." Delilah let out a tired giggle, coaxing Pete back to reality. He snapped his mouth shut and I couldn't help the chuckle that escaped at Delilah's comment. He extended his hand, still quiet with wonder.

"This is going to be a long ride if you don't talk to me." Delilah giggled again, she sounded tired, but the undertone of quiet excitement was undeniable.

"Uh.. Uh yea, here let me grab those." Pete leaned over, grabbing Delilah's small bags containing her whole life besides Maverick. I gestured for her to follow us as I followed my not so little brother to the popped trunk.

Delilah stopped by the passenger door, staring at her childhood home, absorbing every detail, every chip in the paint, every piece of rubble torn up from the small gravel driveway, the sloping gutters. Her life before she was pried away from it. I wanted to give her privacy as I moved with Pete to the trunk, pretending to help him. After a few minutes I walked back over to her, Pete close behind.

"Welp I guess this is it." Delilah sighed out, a single tear escaping before she could quickly wipe it away. I crushed her into a hug.

"No, it isn't. We are going to fix this." I said to her, hoping to lift her spirits.

"We should get going. We have a decent drive ahead of us." Pete's deep voice sounded sympathetic, soft. I pulled back from my embrace with Delilah, chucking her chin before Pete opened the door for her. She wordlessly slid in, ripping her gaze away from her house.

"Take care of her. I mean it." I said to Pete as I pulled him into a hug.

"I will. I heard about the condition. I'll help anyway I can. Dad set up the house with maids and everything, even called the local high school for her. She'll be fine." Pete's words vibrated his chest, buzzing against my cheek.

"I'll see you soon." I pulled away looking at Delilah crumpled in the front seat one more time.

"I'm counting on it." He shouted over his shoulder as he got back into his car. I watched for a few moments as he adjusted the heat settings for Delilah, making sure she was comfortable before setting off.

Rain started to pelt the cracked asphalt of the road, but I was too stunned to move. Delilah might have left but my job was not over yet. I had to still face Maverick. Tell him everything, about me and his sister.

***

The rain clung to my skin, as if it were trying to act as armor for my impending battle. I walked up the stairs, turning the corner to find Maverick exactly as I had left him, sprawled across his faded bedding. He looked so peaceful, unaffected by the pain that was about to ensue.

I slipped off my sneakers, padding in sock clad feet to his bed. I pulled the small envelope from his sister out of my pocket and propped it against the picture of the three smiling faces that resided on the table next to his bed. The image made me feel sick with the loss that this family was forced to face. The small mattress groaned as I sunk my weight down to sit on the edge of it. With the movement Maverick's eyes fluttered, his arms twitching with alertness as he began to pull out of his sleep. His head lifted off his pillow, his eyes heavy.

"Gray?" He flopped back down, seeing that it was me, wrapping his arm around my waist in the process. Its weight was a comfort I didn't deserve.

"It's just me." My voice sounded too thick, too hoarse from holding back tears.

"Is everything okay? I mean I know it's not but are you okay?" despite everything that had happened to him, he was still worried about my wellbeing. I nodded; afraid I wouldn't be able to control my tears if I spoke.

"Gray, thank you for everything you did today. I just can't imagine my life without her. She's what's left of my family, my dad you know? And it drives me nuts that I can't be what she needs." His voice was heavy with sleep, but his despair was evident in every word. I gulped down my guilt, preparing myself for the inevitable. "I should go check on her." Maverick started to shift, sitting up to reveal the rumpled clothes he threw on that morning. I pushed my hand to his chest, my eyes downcast.

"Gray? What is it? Is she okay?" Maverick's words were serious, to anyone else they might have thought them to be calm, calculated but I knew them for the panicked question behind them.

"I have to tell you something. I need you to listen to me." I whispered into the room, unable to accept that I had created my own downfall. His brows instantly furrowed, his arm moving from my waist to prop himself on the bed. The touch had seemed so normal, so easy, and yet he hadn't noticed the weight of what it was, the last time he would touch me like that. Lovingly. "I'm not who you think I am. My full name is Grace Edison." I peeked up at him, the confusion evident on his face.

He tried to throw a grin at me, trying to pry any positive reaction from me. "Is that supposed to mean something to me Gray? To me you are just Gray. I don't care what you full name means; I just care about you."

"No, listen to me. My father is Senator Paul Edison." With that his mouth formed a small *oh* but his brow was still furrowed in confusion. "I belong to a wealthy political family. I had to come here to, to get out of something. There was an, an accident. It was my fault. But I had to leave." I couldn't bring myself to tell him the details right now and further taint my image to him. He grew rigid, tense and still wildly confused. I sighed. "I haven't been back since then. But when I heard about what Delilah did, I knew I had to help. So, I called in a favor." I was trying to stall, to delay the inevitable.

"Grace, what did you do?" His voice was stern, all sense of comfort vanished.

"I promised my dad that I would go home. In return for legal help. And a place for Delilah to stay." I swallowed as the last few words came out as a squeak. At that moment his eyes filled with rage as silence overtook the room. The only sound was the pounding of rain on the roof. "She left, she's on her way now. She will be safe. She had to go." The words were just tumbling from my lips as Maverick just stared at me with that rage filled stare lighting those green eyes storming with an emotion I couldn't pin point.

"She's. She's gone." It wasn't a question, more of himself trying to convince himself. I nodded as tears spilt down my face.

"Mav, she had to. She'll be safe. In the meantime, we can figure out what to do." I tried to reach for his hand, but he pulled it away before I could reach it. "Please Mav."

"Get out." He growled out. Shock filled me, I wasn't even sure that I had heard him correctly.

"Mav…."

"Get. Out." He wasn't even looking at me, as if my presence alone was enough to disgust him.

"Maverick, please." I was begging and I hated myself for it, but I would gladly beg if I could convince him.

"I said get the fuck out!" Maverick exploded in fury, hurtling his pillow so it hit the wall with a thump. I recoiled as he leapt to his feet, threading his fingers behind his head.

"Please." I sounded broken.

"You had no right! You didn't fucking think! Get out. Now." He screamed as the tears fell. I didn't even recognize him. His eyes were wild, his veins prominent against his skin as he strained to contain his rage. I felt my own shame raise in my throat, the bitter taste coating my tongue.

"It was the only option. She had to go, and she knew you wouldn't let her." My voice sounded like ice. I couldn't tell if I was trying to protect myself or him from anymore hurt.

"Bullshit that was the only option. You are right I wouldn't have let her leave, because she is a kid!" He screamed as he threw his hands up in the arm in exasperation.

"Connor was going to take her." I screamed right back, not even knowing where I found the strength.

"Don't." He pinned me with a look. "Don't you dare say that name in this house. You had no right. I was such an idiot. I should have never even let you know about her. And you just went and fucked everything in less than twenty-four hours." The rain thundered against the sides of the house now, covering the window in a cascade of dirty water. I just looked at him. Not even knowing what to say or do. He turned away from me, seething before sending a fist straight through the wall of his bedroom. I jumped with the sudden violence.

"Maverick! Stop." I commanded him, mustering any strength I had into my voice.

"I told you to leave. So, leave!" He yelled as he turned. I backed up, tears blurring my vision, almost tripping over my discarded shoes. I fumbled to pick them up as he turned his back to me again. His muscles strained under the wrinkled fabric of his t-shirt; the gaping hole punched through the plaster in front of him.

There I stood in the doorway, clutching my beat-up converse to my chest, staring at the devastation that I had caused. I had to get out of here, it physically hurt me to leave him, but I had to.

"I love you." I whispered before backing out of the room. He didn't turn, his arms braced against the wall as he took in heaving breaths.

I felt numb as I stumbled out into the storm, not even bothering to put on my shoes. The wet asphalt slapped against my socks as I distanced myself as fast as I could from his house. The rain immediately soaked through my clothes, sending a deep chill straight to my bones.

I couldn't tell where the tears and rain started or ended, which was which, as I fumbled through the curtain of water to the road. I wouldn't turn back, I couldn't. My wet feet slapping against the asphalt and the down pour were the only sounds. I don't know how long I walked, I didn't even know if I was going the right way, but eventually I stumbled up the steps to my building, exhausted and soaking wet. And more importantly alone and broken.

Chapter Twenty- Six

I didn't hear from Maverick for the next month.
I felt numb, going through the motions. I avoided
parties, desperately not wanting to run into him. I went
to work, school, and bed, feeding myself enough to
sustain me and not bothering with much else. I refused
to go hang out with the guys, despite Mae's pleas.
Everything reminded me of him, the feeling of his skin
on mine, our lips pressed together, his eyes. But he just
was gone. I know that this was my fault, I messed up
everything that I had come into contact with and it only
made sense that I would destroy the family of the boy I
loved too.

I didn't even see Mick, Isabella, or Connor for
that matter. I was stuck in a perpetual state of self-pity.
Partner that with the looming devastation that came with
inevitably having to return to my home and reopening
the wounds that came with it. I hadn't even told Mae
what had happened. I hadn't told her that seeing her and
Bo so happy made my chest tight with longing for
Maverick. I was just a shell, a shell of who I had been
and not able to fill myself back in.

I did however hear from Pete and occasionally
Delilah. It seemed that my efforts had been worth it on

Delilah's end at least. She was working on finishing her senior year, inhabiting a house that fit at least ten people by herself. She was happy. She missed Maverick of course but Pete made sure to keep her distracted. From what I heard he was up at the house almost every weekend, taking her out to explore her new town or to help her fix some part of the house. I guess he was able to talk to her now.

Hearing from them was the only good thing it seemed, knowing that I had at least helped her in the process of destroying her brother.

As I hurried in for my morning shift, I managed to throw my hair in a messy bun, stray strands tickling my cheeks as I burst into the small café. It was finally cold weather, meaning that the heat was blasting, a welcome feeling as I rubbed at my arms to ward off the cold.

"Hiya." Jenny barely looked up as she threw me the greeting, knowing that I probably wouldn't respond anyway. I grunted back at her as I took my place behind the chipped counter, the smell of stale coffee wrapping its way around me.

The soft glow from the various lamps around the room reflected across the rain plastered windows. It looked cozy, comforting even in the small café, the leather couches draped in rich fabric blankets that signified colder weather.

A few stragglers hung around the few wooden tables in the corner chatting softly enough that the heater's mind-numbing drone drowned out their voices. Lounged out on one of the dark leather chairs, sagging with wear were a couple, draped over each other as they munched on a shared pastry.

I watched as the guy reached out the pad of his thumb to wipe away a spot of powdered sugar off the girl's lip. She giggled in response, planting her lips on his own before plopping a small dusting of powdered sugar on the boy's nose. They both giggled, snuggling into each other as if there were no one else in the room. Something sharp stabbed at my heart, remembering the time Maverick cuddled up to me like that in the back of his truck, french fries scattered on the ground in front of the bed. The small chime of the bell affixed to the door brought my attention back to the present, snapping me out of the memory. But as my eyes went up, my heart dropped.

There, rain dripping off his windbreaker, was Jay. His wet sandy hair stuck up in all directions looking windblown and disheveled. His eyes flicked around the room, scanning the area as if he was searching for something. His bright eyes were cradled by purplish bags, but his eyes looked clear and alert, he wasn't drunk or high. I let out a breath I hadn't realized I had been holding as his eyes snap to mine, his face falling a little as he recognized me. His brow furrowed in a grimace as he shook some of the water off his arms and started to walk over to my place behind the counter.

I didn't react at all as he gingerly sat on the stool directly in front of me, his eyes glued to my face to see if his presence gauged any reaction from me. He looked wounded, hurt and sheepish, cowering in front of me.

"Hi Gracie." His voice was hoarse, the usual rich and happy tone completely replaced by broken and cracked words. I started to back up, the small of my back hitting the counter behind me.

"Gracie, I have to talk to you. Please. I'm begging you." His eyes were pleading, his voice cracking over as the words worked to shatter what little of my heart had remained intact. I let out a deep sigh out of my nose.

"Jay, why should I?"

"You shouldn't. I was a dick. I…" He gulped, "I touched you. I grabbed you. Even if I was drunk or high, it was no excuse for what I did. I betrayed you. I used your past against you, I knew what that would do to you, but I didn't care." The words lingered in the coffee scented air, every one wrapping around me and threatening to choke me.

"You touched me Jay, you hurt me. Yes, I know I messed up by dancing with you," I flashed back to what Maverick had told me, "but it is not my fault that you did what you did." The words felt strange coming from my mouth. It felt wrong to say, to blame Jay. But I know that I was not to blame for his behavior. "You relapsed and you didn't even tell me. I still don't know why." Customers started to flow in, occupying the couches set up by the windows, cackling over something that was probably unimportant.

"I know. I am sorry. I just felt hopeless you know? I just, I don't know I don't have an excuse to give you besides I screwed up." His eyes were downcast as he said the words into the counter.

"I...I can't. I can't do this right now. I have to work." I scooted back against the counter as tears started to blur my vision. "Jenny will get your order. I just can't." He just nodded into the table and gestured to Jenny to collect his order for me. I felt raw, as if I had been shredded to ribbons. I felt destroyed and every moment that I had spent thinking about Maverick worked to amplify the pain. And now Jay, trying to apologize, apologize and I couldn't even look at him without wanting to cry, or scream, or punch something.

I moved to the opposite counter, trying to make myself busy. The bell at the door just kept chiming in a steady rhythm, reminding me that I needed to pull myself together, I had a job to do. I swiped my hands under my eyes, trying to wipe away any stray tears. As I straightened my apron and turned, I was greeted with the café bustling with activity and at the center stood a lone man, disheveled hair not bothered to be slicked back. His collared shirt was rolled to expose his bare forearms, not as wide as Maverick or Mick's but muscular non the less. And those piercing blue eyes were trained on me.

Connor Steele marched over to me, his brow furrowed and his face practically glowing with rage. I felt too small, too trapped behind the counter. I could feel Jay watching me, watching as Connor came up to me.

"You little bitch." Connor growled out as he slammed his hands down on the counter. Customers snapped their heads to find where the noise had come from, watching Connor's heaving shoulders.

"Where is she? Huh? What did you do?" His voice was like venom. I just stared wide eyed, only making him angrier. He slammed his hands down on the counter again.

"I don't know what you are talking about." I managed to squeak.

"Bullshit! You are going to tell me what you did right now and then you are going to tell me exactly where she is. Understand? Your family might be powerful but so am I." The words dripped with demand and threats and all I could do was stare.

"Hey man, back up." I hadn't even realized that Jay had come over, towering over Connor. Jay might have been all legs, but he was strong none the less, he could be intimidating.

Connor's eyes snapped between Jay's hard expression and me, a venomous smile stretching tight over his pale skin, "Oh I get it, screwing him, too are we? I should have figured..." but before he could finish Jay was shoving him.

"That's enough. You aren't going to talk to her like that." Jay roared, customer's whipping their heads to watch the two men. I was rooted in place, too shocked to move. I had never seen Jay like this, so ready for blood. Apparently I really didn't know my best friend at all.

"If you knew what was good for you, you would keep your distance from that little slut!" Conor sneered as he pointed to me. I felt my cheeks seer as everyone turned their attention to me now rather than the fight. Jay took a menacing step forward, an obvious threat for Connor to keep talking. The damn bell at the door went off again.

Mick was there, taking a handful of Connor's shirt in his hands before he could get to Jay. Connor struggled against his younger brother. How did Mick get here? Everyone was staring at the commotion, even Jenny pressed herself against my side to let me know she was there to protect me. I had never felt so humiliated.

"Enough!" Mick screamed at his brother, still struggling to get out of his brother's grip. Mick worked to wrestle him out of the door, half dragging a flopping Connor to the sidewalk outside.

The café was absolutely silent, save for Jay's heaving breaths echoing against the dingy paint of the walls. Everyone was contesting with themselves on where they should direct their attention, the two men outside words flying and fingers jabbing at each other, the tall, frazzled boy with his eyes pinned to the man he had just threatened, or the small girl cowering behind the counter. This was hell.

I pushed past Jenny and the prying eyes, rushing to the back before my tears could become the next spectacle. I reached the small brick wall at the back of the café, crates and trash cans lined across it. The small nook was used for storage the smell of must and mold unfurling around me. I slid to the floor drawing my knees up to my chest, wrapped in a ball of self-pity. Wet hot tears burned my eyes as I pressed my back into the bite of the cold brick. My life was beyond screwed up. It was as if I was living in a twisted teen soap opera, everything I did ending in my misery. I let out a strangled sob, the sound ripping up my throat before I could stop it.

I picked up the nearest object I could find, I half crumbling piece of brick and hurled it at the opposing wall, screaming with the anguish of the last month, the last few years. All my misery propelling the brick forward till it smashed into the wall with a loud thud. Tears flowed down my face in a never-ending stream. Footsteps sounded in the doorway. I swiped at my eyes, shame burning my cheeks. I looked away at the concrete floor.

"Gracie?" Jay's voice was soft, questioning.

"I'm fine." I bit out. He moved forward.

"Gracie, I know you aren't. Look you don't have to tell me what that was about I just needed to check on you." He slid down next to me, close enough to comfort me yet still far enough not to make me angry. I missed Jay. I hated to admit it, but I felt so alone without him, without anyone, without Maverick.

"He knows." I sniffed. I could feel Jay stiffen with instant understanding.

"He knows?" Jay asked, still refusing to touch me. I turned my tear-stained face to look at him. A clouded look overtook is eyes, till he quickly blinked them back.

"He threatened to expose me. I wasn't sure why until, until. Um, until I found out he was related to Maverick." Jays eyes widened at my words, trying to process the information quickly.

"But why would he threaten you? I don't understand."

I heaved a breath, "Look, you can't tell anyone. Maverick has a sister that he has… had…. Custody over. She had to leave so that prick you just met couldn't get to her."

"So where is Maverick now?" my silence was answer enough. Jay tentatively reached out a hand, lightly placing it on my shoulder. The small gesture destroyed any resolve I had left. I turned, throwing my arms around his shoulders, and hugging him close.

"I can't forgive what you did to me Jay, I can't. But maybe with time? I miss you." I murmured into his shoulder, having courage now that I wasn't faced with that broken look in his eyes.

"I know Gracie, I missed you too. And I will do everything to prove I am better." Jay pulled me into a deeper hug, protecting me from my own misery for a few seconds.

"A-hem." We both turned to see Mick, bouncing between both feet and hands shoved into his pockets. He looked uncomfortable at seeing me.

"Mick." I pushed Jay away for a minute, looking to him and giving him a nod to tell him I would be okay. Jay nodded back, shifting to stand, eyeing Mick as he walked out.

"Grace, I wanted to say sorry for my brother out there." Mick looked grim, serious.

"It's okay." I couldn't help but compare him to Maverick. The similar set of their shoulders, or the similar swirls of ink spilling down their muscled arms.

"No, no its not. I also wanted to say thank you. I heard what you did for Maverick and Delilah. You risked a lot, even if Maverick can't see it yet." The mention of Maverick's name made my stomach clench.

"Well, thanks. But I'm not exactly sure how gallant my actions can be considered."

"Grace, what you did saved them. Maverick is going to take some time to understand that, but Delilah and I are both grateful." His voice was deep, reminding me of Maverick. I just nodded.

"He'll come around Grace he will."

I didn't have a response, even if I did my words would have been strangled by my tears anyway. Another nod. He just nodded back, before backing out and leaving me alone again.

Chapter Twenty-Seven

It was nice to have Jay back, despite our tenuous relationship. It was still a little awkward with everything that happened within the last few months, but we worked past it. Mae was more skeptical than I was, giving Jay the cold shoulder until I explained what he had done for me. I still felt a little numb, but having Jay back helped slightly.

A few more weeks went by, filled with more school, more work, more rekindling my friendship with Jay. But it all came to a standstill when he called me. I was lounging on my bed, feet propped up on my headboard, with my head on Jay's lap watching a movie. My phone let out a shrill vibration, tangled in the blanket wrapped around myself. I fumbled for it, looking for the small phone, preoccupied with the romantic comedy flashing on the computer screen. I didn't even look at the caller id before putting it up to my ear, eyes still glued to the screen, as the protagonist gallantly saved his girl.

"Hello?"

"Grace." My father's gruff voice sounded on the other line. I immediately shot up, knocking the computer over in the process.

"Um, hi." I murmured while Jay looked at me questionably, I just mouthed to him, 'my dad'. He looked just as shocked as I felt.

"It is time that you held up your end of our bargain. There is an event this weekend. It's in Massachusetts, it's the Gala. I will have Pete pick you up tomorrow to spend the weekend." My stomach dropped. Tomorrow. I would be faced with my worst memories, tomorrow.

"Grace?" My father's voice held an edge of impatience.

"Oh, um yep, I mean yes, I will go. I'll be there." I stuttered out. The exchange took seconds, seconds to destroy me once again.

"I'll see you then." And then the line buzzed as he hung up on me. The call had been brief, commanding and just like that I felt my world dissolve. I gulped. I was going home. Or what used to be my home anyway. Back to Massachusetts. I get that I wasn't far from there now, but it felt like a universe separating me from my past, that is until Connor decided to blur those lines with his threats.

"What was that about?"

"Um, I'm going home." I couldn't even fathom the words. I was going home. What did that even mean? I was being forced to attend a gala for saving my ex-boyfriend, if he could even be considered that, from legal battles and inevitable heart break? Why not with the way everything else was going.

"You, I'm sorry it sounded like you just said you were going home." Jay said in confusion.

"I did." I couldn't help the gulp that followed.

***

I threw things haphazardly into a small suitcase, opting the best clothes to hide my tattoos. I would have to wear my hair down, unless I wanted them to see the small bird resting behind my ear. My mind was buzzing. Would they disapprove of my appearance? My ears were studded with several earrings and rings, my nails were short and jagged from working and my habit of gnawing at them. I was a different person than what they remembered, and I could only hope that they realized that.

"I can't even believe this." I muttered, Jay propped up on my bed, Mae somewhere off with Bo. I scourged through my clothes to find my more conservative pieces, lots of jeans and a few baggy t shirts would be fine. Better than my cheap beer stained bustier. I scrunched my nose at the bundled fabric that still reeked of liquor. I tossed it to the back of the small closet, opting to not even give it a second glance.

"Neither can I. I mean you swore you would never go back." Jay flipped through his phone, trying to act like my sacrifice for Maverick didn't bother him.

"I had to Jay; you know that." I tried to sound nonchalant despite my panic.

"I know. Just be careful alright?"

"Always am." I said throwing a wink his way. I was trying my best to act like I wasn't panicking at the prospect of seeing my parents again. Or the idea of having to deal with their stuck-up friends at some overpriced Gala. I knew that before I left, Dad had kept what happened a secret, opting to maintain his appearance then spoil it by revealing the screw up that was his first born. At least I wouldn't be bombarded by pitiful stares and whispered comments. I shook off the thought refusing to think about that as I packed not and adding to the stress.

At least I would get a chance to catch up with Delilah. I wanted to see her, see how she was doing rather than having to fill in the lines between calls and texts. I wondered if she texted Maverick yet.

I shoved my last shirt in my bag, having to force it close to coax the zipper shut. I stood back, hands resting on my hips gulping in air, while Jay gave me an incredulous smile.

"What?" I giggled. I didn't even remember the last time I giggled.

"I believe you over packed by a long shot Gracie." He chuckled. We both laughed for a few minutes before returning to our movie, finishing the night with a quick, yet surprisingly not awkward hug, and the promise of a phone call.

***

"Call me when you get there, Doll." Mae squeezed me into a tight gripped hug. The smell of roses strangled me almost as much as her grip.

"Of course. I'll see you in a few days you know that right?" I chuckled into her glossy black hair.

"Geez babe you are crushing her! Let the girl go!" Bo cackled, his giant figure doubling over at his girlfriend's display. She shot him a look. "Bye Grace!" he got out between his deep laughs.

"C'mon Grace! We don't want to be late." Pete called from the idling car in the lot.

"Okay, I really have to go, I'll see you soon!" I released myself from Mae's grip, tugging my bag behind me, my backpack already slung on my shoulder.

"Call me!" Mae yelled as I hopped in the front seat of the car. I flashed her a grin.

"Off we go. Are you ready for this?" Pete asked with a mixture of excitement and anxiousness.

"Ready as I'll ever be." I huffed.

Chapter Twenty -Eight

I don't know how long I had been asleep, but I felt the car lurch to a stop. My eyes fluttered open to be burned by bright sunlight streaming through vibrant colored leaves. I squinted against the harsh light, trying to regain my senses and grasp an understand of where I was. We were parked in front of a massive house, all the siding a deep red wood accentuated by black trim. Long grasses waved in the slight winds smelling of fresh mountain air. The lawn was a perfect green, small orange flowers springing up along a granite path leading to a large black door. My eyes flew to Pete's. He sat in the driver's seat with a smug smile plastered on his face.

"A quick pitstop."

Before I could even open my mouth to mention this wasn't really a pit stop as we way overshot our destination, the front door flew open, and a platinum blonde blur raced towards the car.

"Grace!" Delilah retched open the door, hauling me out and into a massive hug. My mind was still foggy with sleep, trying to keep up with the shock that was the girl in my arms.

"Delilah? Oh my God! Delilah!" I crushed her back, almost barely recognizing her as a giant smile lit her face. Whereas before she looked like a sad little girl, struggling to hold up an unbearable weight, she now looked stronger, healthy, happy.

"Come on! You have to come inside you are probably starving!" She tugged at my hand, flashing a huge grin at Pete. I allowed her to tug me into the giant house. I was instantly hit with the scent of lemons, the smell oddly comforting when paired with the light cream of the walls. The giant windows lining the back wall were all thrown open, allowing the unusually warm fall air to breeze by the gauzy white curtains. Next to the couch was a small stack of books, resembling those in Maverick's room, worn and well loved. A pair of old sneakers were neatly arranged at the door. The small elements gave life to the house, making it oddly Delilah's. I couldn't help the smile that overtook my face.

"Do you like it here?" I asked, almost dumbfounded by the sight of this once cold house full of signs of life.

"Is it that obvious?" She chuckled.

"She doesn't really like the fact that she has to wait till Fridays for me to reach the books on the top shelf for her." Pete teased. Delilah scrunched her nose at him, faking anger until swatting at his arm. I was even more happy to see the relationship budding between the two. He reached for her, tickling her until she shrieked out in laughter, darting away with him hot on her heels. I flashed Pete a knowing look to which he rolled his eyes with a huge grin on his face. I followed them to the large living room, sinking into one of the plush beige couches. I watched the two as Pete threw her over his shoulder and twirled her, all the while she pounded on his back cackling.

I was so full of relief at the fact that she was here, safe and happy. Pete threw her down on the couch, flopping down next to her with a hearty laugh. She looked to him and stuck out her tongue to which he only gave a lazy grin.

"Anyways," another fake dirty look in Pete's direction, "I really wanted to thank you Grace. I love it here. I miss Mav, like a lot. But I had to go. He knows that."

I tried to control myself from asking about him, from demanding every detail, "Um, have you talked to him?" I tried to avert my gaze; my shame was probably peppered all over my face. Thankfully, Delilah understood and didn't call me out on it.

"I've called him a few times. He's taking it pretty hard you know. It's hard for him. We are all each other have, its hard being separated." Her words held a pregnant sadness to them. I watched Pete scoot over an infinitely small amount.

"I know he is."

"I'm sure you know how difficult he can be, hell you are the one dating him." I froze at that. Delilah seemed to notice my reaction and swung her gaze to Pete. He gave her a small shake of his head. Her large eyes got even wider. "Oh my, Grace, I'm so sorry. I had no idea. What did he do?"

"It's not really what he did, more of what I did. I shouldn't have gotten involved with you guys, but I had to help you, I wasn't going to let Connor take you."

"Wait, wait, wait. He left you for helping me?" Delilah screeched, making me flinch. "That son of a bitch! I am going to kill him! He finally finds the perfect girl, and he dumps her for saving his ass? What even is that?" She swivels her head in every direction, as if she was looking for her phone to call him right then.

"No, No Delilah. It's okay. I shouldn't have gotten involved, I am just happy you are safe, both of you are safe." I tried to get out the words before she could have a chance to call him. She still looked enraged and slightly skeptical.

"Well, I am still mad at him. And you did the right thing, don't doubt that for a second. He'll come around." Delilah looked at me with a twinge of sadness in her eyes.

"Enough with the depressing stuff, how's school?" I quickly changed the subject.

Delilah droned on, so much more talkative and outgoing then I had seen her. She talked of her senior year, and how she was practically the head of the school paper. She talked about putting the 'mean girls' right in their place. All the while Pete just watched her in awe. I could not have been happier for her. She was so animated, so different. She was no longer broken. Occasionally she relapsed into a moment of sadness as she remembered her old life, but she was strong, steering herself back on track.

"Alright we better get going." Pete shifted to get up as he groaned the words, reaching a hand behind me to reach for Delilah. The sun started to dip behind the snow peaked mountains outside the window, casting orange and pink hues across the spotless walls, I suddenly appreciated the color scheme that the designers had chosen.

Pete pulled her into a swift hug, planting a quick peck on her forehead. She scrunched her nose, grinning up at him. I walked over, pulling her into me and hugging her tight.

"Grace, don't give up on him." Delilah whispered so low so only I could hear.

"Never." I whispered right back, gripping her tighter.

"Come on ladies, we have a gala to get to Grace."

I nodded pulling away from Delilah and giving her a quick smile. I took one last look around the room, swathed in light from the sunset. I sighed a breath of relief. I waved and followed Pete out.

As Delilah waved to us from the door, I couldn't help but watch as a deep blush spread across Pete's cheeks.

"So, you and Delilah huh?" I asked, cocking my eyebrows at him.

"Shut up." he said through a grin.

***

We drove the last hour or so back to Massachusetts chatting about meaningless nothings in an effort to distract myself from what was to come.

I watched as grassy fields drenched in moonlight waved in the wind, watched as we veered down a familiar road. Large houses sneered at me, taunting me as I was forced to return. I felt my chest tighten, leaning against the cool glass of the window. Panic bubbled in me but all I could do was try to force it down as my past came screaming back at me.

The crunch of gravel under tires was achingly familiar as we rolled up the long path of driveway that led to a monstrous house. The soft moonlight swathed the light blue paint, amplifying its sense of entitlement and prestige. The landscaping around the house was trimmed to perfection, not a single blade of grass out of place. There parked in the massive driveway sat an expensive array of cars, the golden light from the outside light system shining on their glossy exteriors.

I sucked in a breath. The last time I had been here, I was crusted in a mixture of mud and blood, my hair dangling limply as my dad forced me into the shiny SUV parked on the edge of the drive. I had begged him to help me, the rage and disappointment like a punch in the gut. I tried to shake it off, tried to focus on the present, I was back.

I glanced into the large windows encasing the front of the house, showcasing a winding staircase and frivolous decorations that no doubt could have been just as expensive as the row of cars in front of me. And there, against the golden glow of the interior lights was the outline of two figures, gazing out expectantly, awaiting the return of their only daughter.

Pete was wordless, sensing my anxieties without having to ask. He went to get my bags as I tried to force my shaking legs to support me and carry me out of the car. The gravel crunched over my wrecked shoes, already seeming out of place against the elegant back drop in front of me. The front door swung open, revealing a grand entry way as a weighed down Pete and I strode to meet our parents.

It was late, late enough that any normal human being would have preferred a pair of sweats to the formal attire my parents showcased. I saw my father first, strongly resembling an older version of Pete. His once blond hair was now peppered with gray hues. His face was no longer smooth, sporting few wrinkles that indicated an immense amount of frowning. His eyes were the same steel gray I had remembered, making his appearance come off as severe, as if he possessed all power in the room. His muscled frame however remained young looking, his deep periwinkle dress shirt hugging his muscles with every step he took to meet us.

Standing next to him, never looking out of place, was my perfectly groomed mother. Her heels clicked against the marble tile of the foyer as she moved to greet her children, her blazer clad arms outstretched as if to receive me in a hug. She put on a dazzling too white smile, framed by her deep hazel eyes, heavily lined with cosmetics.

"Darling, My Grace, how I have missed you." My mother's voice was ever polite, echoing off the silent men as she wrapped me in a light hug that lacked any sense of warmth. I was caught off guard. I had expected two ways of this encounter, and both had involved extremes. I was not expecting the polite contact and words seeming to lack any sense of emotion. But then again what did I expect, my mother had always acted as if she were simply an accessory, not able to possess any emotion of her own, especially if it contradicted my father. I was immediately hint with the strong scent of roses that was her expensive perfume, the smell wrapping around me and only working to suffocate me more.

"Hi Mom." I gasped out. I tried to return her half-hearted hug, giving her a light squeeze. She stepped back, still clutching my arms. I watched as she took in my appearance, looking at me up and down to scrutinize over any small imperfection. She tucked the hair behind my ear, to anyone viewing the display it would seem like a gesture of affection, but I knew it for what it truly was, her checking to see the multiple piercings lining my ears. She recoiled in distaste, quickly recovering.

"What have you done to your ear? It looks like a pin cushion." She said the words with a joking tone, but I watched her tight-lipped smile twitch in anger.

"What? You don't like them?" I couldn't help but antagonize her. She huffed, stepping back to allow my dad to step forward. He looked as if he were a statue, his hands gripped behind his back.

"Grace."

"Hi." I felt uneasy under his steady stare. He didn't look me over like my mother had, he simply looked deep into my eyes. Somehow that made me more uncomfortable. I fidgeted with my hands, transfixed in place by that look alone.

"Pete, I suspect you drove carefully." Even though his deep voice was directed at Pete, he still stared at me.

"Yes sir."

"Good. I expect you are both hungry after your trip. There is food in the kitchen. Grace we will let you get settled and talk to you in the morning. Good night to the both of you." And with that he turned on his heel, sauntering to the grand staircase. My mother flashed me another fake smile before obediently following her husband. I was startled to say the least, but what did I expect really.

They both just seemed too cold, especially for supposedly worried parents who had seen their only daughter crumble before their eyes. I hadn't seen them for nearly two years, and that's the welcome I get? Figures.

"Don't worry about it. I'm starved." Pete seeming to read my thoughts effortlessly carried my bags to the bottom of the stairs before gesturing for me to follow him to the kitchen.

I hadn't been in that house for what felt like an eternity, but as soon as I stepped into the four cream walls, my senses were flooded with familiarity. I followed Pete to the marble encrusted kitchen, the smell of bleach and a hint of vanilla sucking me right back to my childhood. I watched as Pete navigated the fridge, grappling for sandwich ingredients while I sat at the breakfast bar, taking in my surroundings and the nostalgia that followed. The cold counter tops brought me back to the multiple nights I sat here, my forehead pressed against the smooth surface drunk out of my mind. My body had been numb, while the cool from the surface seemed to be the only thing that kept me grounded.

The brief interaction with my parents was lacking, I felt hollow. I hadn't known what to expect really, but it definitely wasn't what I received. My mother acted as if I was someone she needed to impress with her status, also looking down on me as I didn't fit into her cookie cutter world anymore. And of course, my father. I literally saw them both for a total of two minutes before he retreated to the sanctuary of his overpriced scotch in his luxury lined study.

There had been a time, so long ago that the memories seemed foggy, age clogged, that my parents had been considered somewhat normal, caring even. Memories of ripe apples plucked from trees, fuzzy gap-toothed giggles with pudgy fingers clasped around the red fruit. My father's deep laugh echoing around us. But now everything was obscured by pills, alcohol, wealth, and twisted metal.

"What kind you want?" Pete's voice snapped me back. In his hands was a bag of bread while assorted meats and cheeses lay haphazardly along the polished marble.

"The works." I said with a fake smile. The weight sucked away my appetite, but I didn't want to alarm my brother.

I felt empty, numb. All nostalgia replaced with white noise. I didn't belong here anymore. I knew I didn't. My ink, piercings, my tone alone made me stand out against this posh world like a sore thumb. No doubt I was the epitome of my parent's embarrassment. My skin crawled with the thought of what tomorrow would bring. I should have stayed away. I didn't belong here anymore.

Pair that with the sudden resurgence of grief I felt at losing Maverick. Seeing Delilah's gestures and expressions so like the boy who raised her physically hurt me. I could picture the quirk of his lips, that small freckle raising with the movement. His tattoos stretching across his skin as he reached for me. I craved his touch, but more importantly, I craved his presence.

With Maverick came drama, occasional bloodshed, and anger. But pair that with adoration, protection, love. Every hard ship was worth it just to see that dazzling smile that warmed me to my core. Without it, I felt lost. I tried to suppress it, the need of Maverick, this past month but I couldn't hide the deep nagging within me. I tried to pretend it wasn't there, but it was. He was a proud selfish bastard, but I belonged to him. The problem was that I was just as much of a proud selfish bastard.

He turned me away, for helping him. He fought the people I loved. He wrecked me. How could I let that stand? I didn't want to go whimper at his feet, plead for his attention like half the other girls at his beck and call. I was determined to prove I was somehow better than them, that I was above an infatuation with Maverick Foster. Little did I know it was too late for that resolve. I was already utterly in his grasp, and there was no way I would be able to escape.

Chapter Twenty-Nine

After a night spent haunted by my own insomnia over having to face the Gala and the lack of Maverick, I rolled out of bed. I dreaded going downstairs to face the day despite the nagging at the back of my mind telling me not to let them win. I would not look weak to them, I would not conform to them.

I strutted down the stairs hiding my nerves with feigned indifference. I sported wrinkled sweats and a cropped shirt with my hair haphazardly thrown into a bun on the top of my head. If I was forced to be here so be it but I would be damned if I tried to blend in, especially so early in the morning.

Whereas last night the house looked daunting, all sharp edges and cold against the dappled moonlight, it now looked somewhat inviting. The crisp scent of sweet apples floated in on sharp fall air from the open windows. Warm sunlight coaxed its way through gauzy curtains, bathing everything in a soft golden hue. I heard soft humming, no doubt from my mother, as she nursed a cup of tea.

My bare feet against the cold floor mad me wince. I padded across the foyer, waiting for my body to adjust to the cold seeping into my skin. There in the kitchen, exactly as I had predicted, was my mother, her face perfectly painted, her hair effortlessly slicked back into a sleek blonde ponytail. She gazed admiringly over one of her trashy romance novels, her tongue shooting out to graze her dark red lipstick.

"Mom?"

"Hello darling. How did you sleep?" She seemed unbothered, not even taking the time to lift her gaze from her book.

"Uh, fine. Is there any coffee?" I was irritated at the fact she thought my presence was so unimportant she couldn't look at me over those pitiful words about true love.

It looked as if she had to pry her gaze away, "There is some in the pot on the counter….." She stopped in a look of horror at my appearance. "Grace, what are you wearing?"

"Sweats?" I feigned confusion as if this totally normal occurrence for most individuals wasn't astronomical to my mother. My mother would never be caught dead in sweats, or god forbid, be seen in her pajamas.

"Grace, you need to look presentable today, no sweats." I rolled my eyes at her disgust.

"Mother, I don't know if you are aware but some of us do not wake up in a complete pant suit ensemble. Some of us are normal." I turned towards the cabinet grappling for a coffee cup. If this is a preview of the rest of my day, I would need caffeine.

The smell of the dark brew washed over me as the deep brown liquid sloshed into my mug. I couldn't help but sigh as the rich scent teased my nostrils.

"Do not use that tone when you speak to your mother. Now what do you plan on wearing tonight?" My mother's eyes dropped back to her book, losing interest in me.

"Oh, I was thinking just like this?" I hid my smile as I brought the mug to my lips.

"Very funny Grace." My dad's deep voice filled the room instantly, taking with it any comfort I had gained. My spine stiffened as he rounded the corner, working to tie a deep red tie around his neck. His dress shoes clicked against the tile as he walked over to my mother, planting a quick and cold kiss on her brow. All for appearances of course.

"Hello dear." It made me feel slightly better that she didn't favor him over her novel either as she spoke the words. He walked over to the same counter I was just digging through, selecting a metallic travel mug. He filled it to the brim, clamping a lid on the top.

"I have to get to the office; I suspect all will be well while I'm gone. Grace, be nice to your mother please."

"Wait, you are going to the office?" I sounded more hurt then I meant to.

"Yes, there are matters that need my attention. I won't be long." He fumbled with his tie as he spoke. As he finally seemed satisfied with its placement, he wrapped his large hand around the mug before striding to the large double doors that led outside. "I expect you to behave. I will see you when I get back." And just like that, I was left alone with my mother and her novel. Why was I even here?

"Nice to see you too, Dad." I mumbled into my cup.

"What was that darling?" My mother asked as if she cared.

I started to stalk out of the kitchen, mug in hand. "Nothing."

***

I spent the remainder of that morning scrutinizing my dress that I had bought, the more I looked at it, the uglier it became. I worried at my bottom lip, tugging it between my teeth. I was already under stress; I didn't need my parents ridicule over my attire. I threw on a pair of jeans, swiping some mascara over my eyes before grabbing my purse.

"Mom, I am going into town, can I borrow the car?" I called, my voice echoing in the empty house. I didn't need to look long to find her nursing the same cup of tea from hours ago, now focused on her perfectly manicured nails.

"Sure darling. Just be careful." Still, she didn't look at me. I snatched the keys off the key ring and hurried out to the luxurious sports car gleaming a deep cherry red in the fall sunshine. The engine purred, the steering wheel vibrating under my fingertips. I blinked away the panic, turning up the radio to drown it out. The engine revved again as if it was coaxing me out of the driveway. I sucked in a breath before slapping the gear shift into drive.

The street was lined with giant houses practically screaming wealth. Pedigree dogs walked on bedazzled leashes as their owners gabbed on the newest smart phones trailing after them. My grip on the steering wheel was hard, trying to quell any sense of panic present. It was a quick ride, finding me in front of a small store front with delicate dresses draped over mannequins in the window. I sighed a deep breath I hadn't realized I had been holding as I flung the car in park. I pushed my head back against the head rest forcing myself to breathe. Finally feeling recovered enough to go in, I went in to find a suitable replacement for the atrocity of a dress I had left behind.

As I pushed back the heavy window paneled doors, I was greeted by racks upon racks of flowing fabrics, all strikingly delicate and colorful against the pale white walls. I grazed my hand against a rack, admiring the feeling of fabric beneath my fingertips. My options were almost overwhelming.

I scanned the rows of clothing, seeing if anything caught my eye when I saw it. Until my attention was snagged. There on a headless mannequin sat the most gorgeous dress I had ever seen. The flowy satin shone with a pale grey, snugly hugging every curve. It was simple, sporting thin straps across a straight neckline. The back was low, small interlacing straps crisscrossing delicately to hold the smooth fabric up. The long skirt flowed out, billowing out around the floor. My heart fluttered as I took in the dress. I imagined stepping into the gala, my hair pinned back and confidence at proving my parents wrong about me. I purchased it without a second thought. The lady behind the counter gaze me a fake dazzling smile as she wrapped the silk dress in a protective bag, happy to have just made a sale of that size.

I was too thrilled with the dress to even acknowledge the preppy pack of girls whispering as they recognized me. I waltzed out of the store, happy for the first time in a long time. I had always enjoyed clothing and I couldn't help the thrill that came with the purchase I had just made.

"Grace is that you?" I froze at the sound of the voice behind me.

I felt my spine stiffen as I immediately recognized the voice. My grip on the garment bag clutched in my hands tightened. My heart began to race, my hands pricked with sweat. Flashes of sirens, a growing pool of blood, broken glass. I turned around towards the voice.

"It is you! It's been so long." She looked the exact same, her jet-black hair short and fringed to frame her face. Her nose ring reflected the sun, similar to the ones in her eyebrow and ear. Her short slender frame looked a little fuller, her hips and breasts protruding more than they had in high school. Despite the harmless look of innocence wrapped around her every feature, I couldn't help but notice the predator underneath. A wolf in sheep's clothing.

"Beck. It's been a while." My voice came out raspy, but strong none the less. Despite the anxiety squeezing my every nerve, I worked to fake indifference. If I let one second of my anxiousness shine through, she would pounce.

"Geez the last time I had seen you was, oh wow, was it really that night?" Her smile grew, her toothy grin making me more unsettled. I gulped down my fear.

"Yea, I guess it was." I pretending to pick at my nails as if they were more important than coming face to face with my nightmare. She fumbled for her jacket pocket, pulling out a packet of cigarettes. She placed one between her cherry lips, extending the pack to me. I just waved her off. She shrugged before returning the pack to her pocket and lighting the butt.

"You never really were a smoker were you. I know Harvard is…. Sorry was. Anyway, where have you been? We missed you during cleanup." Her voice reeked of fake sincerity. I tried to keep my cool mask in place, refusing to fumble in front of her. Even if that name sent a fresh stab of pain through me.

"I had to get out of here." I said, refusing to look away from her dark eyes. They just took me in as if they knew all my secrets. The screech of tires, the small red square hitting the ground, rasping breaths. Her dark orbs for eyes watching me as if she knew exactly what I was thinking.

"I had a feeling you and Daddy had a plan." She stuck out her bottom lip in a pout. I bit my tongue to keep from spitting venom.

"I guess you could say that." I opted for a cold gaze instead. That just seemed to ignite her more.

"How is your little pet there, Jay. Still a devastated alcoholic pining for your affection. Such a shame that he disappeared with you. He was a cutie." The words broke all sense of restraint I had had. A tire rolling, a scream, deathly quiet.

"You shut your fucking mouth." I spat, springing forward a step. I towered over her, looking down into her amused expression.

"Ah there she is. Thought I lost you there for a second." Another charming smile. "Especially after I didn't see you at the funeral." My eyes scrunched shut, trying to ward off the memories that flowed through my mind. The revving of engines, Beck's eyes as she dropped the flag. Jay's broken sobs as he crawled over to her small broken body. Me rolling onto concrete with a wet smack as I crawled out of the back seat.

"Fuck you." I growled. Every inch of my body yearned to strike her. To feel my fist connect with her nose with a satisfying crunch.

"Especially considering you were so close with the both of them." She knew exactly what to say to get me to crumple. I had pushed my hands through his sopping wet hair, slick with rain and the deep red of blood. Her crumpled body lay a few feet over, looking broken and small against the wet asphalt. "You blame yourself, don't you? I certainly would. I mean whose idea was it?" Her words wrapped around me.

I grimaced, clamping my teeth down to stop myself from attacking her. "What do you want Beck." It came out as more of a statement than a question.

"Oh, don't you worry, You'll see. Till then." And just like that she waltzed away.

What just happened? My past had been buried and now it was all coming back to haunt me. I stood on the sidewalk, feeling absolutely devastated at the encounter that just occurred. Any happiness I had just had was gone, replaced with despair and anxiety.

What did she mean I'll see? Nothing made sense. I forced my numb legs to carry me to my car, flopping into the seat while placing the garment bag in the seat next to me. I squeezed my eyes shut, trying to fight the images pressing in on me. I swore I could smell the deep metallic of blood mingled with gasoline and wet tar. Could feel the crunch of glass under my shoes as I was hauled back, could see the flashing blue lights of the cop cars. Before I even knew what I was doing I grappled for my phone, thumb poised over Maverick's contact.

"Damn it." I swore under my breath before throwing the phone to the floor of the car. I forced down my fear and started the engine.

I drove the familiar path there, my hands quivering against the leather of the wheel. I reached the abandoned area, old planes rusted over with years of neglect. The long path looked unoccupied, absolutely bare and void of any trauma that had occurred there. I rushed out of the car, slamming the door shut behind me. The soft fall air teased at my shirt, pulling the fabric.

Bits of dried grass peaked though the old tarmac, revealing the wear of the strip. I closed my eyes, allowing the night to replay, forcing myself to relive it.

Chapter Thirty

The deep black of the summer night coated the air around us. The echoing cicadids flitted through the air, accompanied by a symphony of the chirping of crickets. The warm air thrummed with the possibility of rain, lightening striking in the distance. We were high out of our mind, Jay and I passing the joint between our lips as we laughed at Jill and Harvard in the front seat. Jill's nose septum piercing twitched as she scrunched her nose against the sting of the vodka. Harvard chuckled that deep chuckle, his dark eyes flicking to me every so often.

I remembered our light laughter as we parked there, waiting for the others to show up. We were in for a night of cheap weed and even cheaper alcohol. It was the summer before my freshman year in college and I felt lost. I was going to be thrust out of what I knew. I was happy to get away, to leave my family behind but this was all I knew. Harvard and Jill were three years older than Jay and I, townies intent on showing us the ropes of our own future townie lives. They had the opposite upbringing of me, no one cared where they were, they had no rules. It was thrilling.

I smiled a drunk smile back at Harvard, dying for any ounce of attention he would offer me. It was fitting that his name was Harvard, he didn't attend college and took education with a grain of salt. The irony was undeniable. He was ruggedly handsome, looking as if he was meant so much more to this town but he was stuck, the embodiment of how I felt.

I loved him. Loved the thrill of his calloused hands brushing over my bare skin, of his lips pressed to mine. He was my salvation, a reminder that I was human, alive.

We joked, giggling and chuckling with the summer storm as our backdrop. Jill had passed the full bottle of sloshing alcohol to me. I still remember the deep burn of it crashing into my stomach. Just as I was about to take another deep swallow, more headlights came whipping up to the tarmac, bringing with them the jeers and yells that come with delinquent teens looking for a good time. I felt electric, like nothing could stop me. Just like the lightening flashing in the sky.

With a mischievous grin at me, Harvard hurtled out of the car just as rain began to pelt the dented metal of the roof. His cheer was followed by other's jumping out into the rain, headlights glistening through the streams. I tugged on Jay's hand; the bottle pressed to his lips. The rain cradled me, clinging to me as I basked in it. I spun, feeling the cascading drops slide down my skin. Soon Harvard's hands joined them, his fingertips gliding on my slick skin. I leaned into the touch, savoring every ounce of pressure that they had to offer. Music bumped from car stereos, vibrating my very bones. We lost all sense of abandon, dancing in the down pour, the smell of smoke clinging to the air.

I didn't want to lose my high and wanted to keep the fun going. That's when it came to me.

A race.

I remember tugging on Harvard's hand, whispering my plan to him. He smiled a mischievous grin, his black hair glued to his forehead from the rain. His eyes danced with excitement. It all happened so fast, all a blur, barely registering, people cheering at the proclamation of a race, people piling into cars, engines revving. I sat in the back of Harvard's car; Jay's eyes wide next to me with fear. He tried to question me, to protest. But I wasn't hearing it. Jill's cackle filled the car as the windows were all rolled down, saturating the smoke-filled air with the smell of exhaust fumes. My head was buzzing on my shoulders, my stomach lurching with thrills.

I watched as Beck flounced in front of the line of racers. Her small frame was supported by thick heels, her mid drift clearly exposed in her tight top. I recognized her from school, her clothes plastered to her from the rain. She gave a seductive pout, met with cheers and more purring of engines. She worked a deep red scarf free from her neck, soaked through with summer rain. She flicked the makeshift flag up, the air pregnant with expectation. Harvard tipped the bottle back, downing the cheap alcohol before passing the bottle to Jill. The flag fluttered to the ground.

We tore down the tarmac, wind and rain and lightning. Nothing could stop us we were invincible.

Too fast.

Everything was too fast. It all happened in slow motion, glass passed across my vision, fragments looked as if they were suspended in time. The car rolled, metal groaning as the car flipped. I clung to the seat; my other hand clung to Jay's. I don't remember if I put on the seatbelt, but I felt the scrap of fabric straining against gravity. I watched in horror as Jill and Harvard flung forward, the impact shattering their chance of life. The car somersaulted, leaving it like a crushed can, left on its side on the wet asphalt. I couldn't even comprehend how it happened, maybe we took a corner too fast? I didn't know. My ears rang, my nails gripped into the leather as I felt blood trickle in a steady stream from my forehead.

We were suddenly still, the smell of gasoline burning my nose. I let out a strangled sob, letting out a croak instead. I shifted, glass glittering with my movement. Jay looked to me, hanging onto consciousness. I dragged him out, both of us landing in a heap on the asphalt with an unsettling wet slap.

That's when I saw them. Crumpled a few feet from the car I recognized Jill's shaved head, red coating the ground around her. Bile burned the back of my throat. My head hummed from the impact, I was confused, so confused. I didn't remember screaming his name, didn't remember crawling to his limp form.

I gripped at him, shaking him and sobbing, praying he would wake up, give me a hazy smile. The rain pelted in a steady rhythm around me as I wailed, praying for anyone to hear me. The metallic scent of blood mixed with the sharp scent of wet asphalt. His eyes stared unblinking into the sky. Jill's crumpled body half lay in Jay's lap, him stroking her buzzed hair and murmuring soothing nothings. I screamed again, praying, praying for anyone to help me. But it was too late. They were gone.

I brought trembling stained hands to my mouth, trying to suppress my growing sobs. I couldn't register as the heat from the flames began to lick at my skin. I didn't care. *I love you Birdie.* I would never get another stolen moment with him. Never spend a night in his car listening to music or catching his mouth quirk up into a smile. He was gone. I didn't register as hands wrapped around my arms and tried to pry me away from him. I clawed at them; I couldn't leave him. I wouldn't. Jay dragged me away, me fighting him all the while.

The cries of anguish, flashing blue lights, none of it mattered. All I could see were those dark lifeless orbs once filled with so much life now empty. I was nothing. I am nothing. A killer.

Chapter Thirty-One

I snapped back to the chill of the afternoon, my fingers barely grazing the small bird tattooed behind my ear. I took in a shuddering breath, surprised to find tears running down my face.

My fault. That was my fault, everyone knew it, hell even I knew it. But I was a coward. I didn't even go to their funerals. Instead, I ran, packed Jay into a rusted old car and took off, hoping to forget the past in a haze of alcohol and drugs. Jay used it to try and turn around, taking responsibility for his indiscretions, facing them head on. Yes, Jay was messed up but at least he embraced it.

I had once told Maverick one of my biggest fears was to be stuck in the background, forced to be a detail in someone else's story, only I knew the truth. I was scared to be forced forward, to be discovered. I was scared of being in the spotlight, wholly exposed and naked for all to see and judge. As soon as my reputation was tainted with my reality, I would be tainted. Everyone would flee. Jay couldn't, he was already in too deep. Mae knew brief details, choosing to ignore them, saying that the past is the past or some bullshit. I was always secretly convinced she refused to hear the rest of the story out of fear of discovering the real me.

I imagined the blank stare of Harvard, my father's brow furrowed and tears lining the deep silver of his eyes when he found out about what happened. He didn't embrace me, he didn't cry with tears of relief, he just looked at me with those eyes holding a thousand insults. He looked at me as if I was a monster, they took me in how I expected most would have if they knew the truth.

And that is what made Connor and Beck's threats so real. I don't think I could bare if I lost everyone. I gulped down my own disgust at my selfishness. Because of me, Harvard and Jill's friends would never get to see them again. I shut my eyes against the thought of Maverick's handsome face twisted in disgust as he found out the truth. Even though he was enraged at me now, even though he could not stand to be near me now, if he only knew the truth, he would be disgusted at even the thought of me. I held out hope that he could at least remember me fondly now. The wind breezed around me, lifting the small pieces that slipped out of my bun. I would never come out of the background, because I was scared of the foreground.

***

I don't know how long I stood there, just watching the empty tarmac whisper the ghosts of the past. I only knew I was there long enough for the cool fall air to seep into my hands, burning them with an icy numbness. I was there long enough for my phone to buzz with multiple texts from my mother, asking me where I was and that I only had a mere three hours to prepare for the Gala. I huffed a sigh, scanning the area once more as if I hadn't already memorized every detail.

"I am so sorry." I whispered for no one to hear but the ghosts of the past. A tear slipped out of my eye, dripping down my chin. I slumped back in the car, hands only shaking a little as I tried to leave my past behind. Maybe losing Maverick was redemption for what I had done, a retribution of losing the life I took from others. Maybe I was meant to lose him.

Only, I didn't want to. Maverick represented the only thing I had in life that seemed worth it. I messed up the lives around me, I was a walking disaster, but so was he. I may be banished to be a minor detail, but he chose to occupy the forefront. We were a beautiful balance of mess. Maybe I was meant to find Maverick just as much as I was meant to lose him. I gripped the steering wheel in resolve. Maybe Maverick wasn't my damnation, but my salvation.

I drove home pondering the anomaly that was Maverick. I still felt heavy with guilt and panic from my encounter with Beck, but I also felt light with the determination of my decision. I glanced at the garment bag delicately draped across the red leather of the passenger seat. I felt a sad smile play at my lips.

As I walked into the front foyer, cradling my purchase, I was met with the steady hum from my mother's hair dryer as well as the soft curses of my father as he searched for his missing pocket square.

"I'm back." I said to no one as I glided up the stairs to my room.

I worked to loosely curl my long caramel waves, taming them back into a loose updo. Pinning the strands together and tucking a few stray pieces behind my ears. I skillfully brushed eyeshadow on my lids, creating a smoking storm framing my deep gray eyes. My father's eyes. I looked, put together. Like the old Grace Edison, politician's daughter. I stared at my reflection, pondering if that girl still existed. Wondering if she could be redeemed, reborn. Wondering if Maverick could accept her, imperfections and all.

"Grace! Hurry please, we have to be out the door in twenty minutes!" My mother's shrill voice called from somewhere downstairs. I stepped up and away from my haunting reflection, slipping on the dress.

I was right, it was perfect. The fabric clung to my body in the perfect places, the long skirt flowing softly to swish against the hardwood at my heeled feet. Despite its lack of glitter or detail, it still shone and was breath taking in its simple beauty. I smoothed down the silk, pleasure coursing through me at the whisper of fabric over my fingertips. With another glance at my unrecognizable reflection, I set off to join my family.

"Oh, darling." My mother rested her hands under her jewel adorned neck as her face crumpled with emotion. Her own soft blond hair was pulled back, exposing the elegant pale column of her throat where a single thumbnail sized diamond rested. Her frame was draped in a deep navy gown, all simplistic elegance, she looked beautiful. Next to her stood Pete, adorned in his own Navy suit, fiddling with a pair of silver cuff links. I couldn't help but smile at the attempt to tame his wild brown curls with some kind of gel. And then, there was my father. He looked as if he were intimidation incarnate, a deep blue suit hugging him, perfectly shaped to his form. His deep pure blue suit worked to reflect the varying grays of his eyes. The deep wrinkles of his face revealed how much the man liked to frown. But his eyes held a light when they looked at me. It was slightly unsettling.

"Grace, you look stunning." My father's words of approval should have brought with them a swell of pride, or happiness at finally earning praise. But instead, I stayed numb, offering a small polite smile as answer.

We all stood there awkwardly for a moment as if no one knew exactly what to do. All of our family was here, in one room once again and yet everything was so different.

My father cleared his throat to break the awkward silence. "We should probably get going. Shall we?" Ever formal, my father extended his elbow out to my mother, who graciously wrapped her hand around it and started to the door. I looked to Pete and rolled my eyes at the display. In return he dramatically offered his own elbow to me, mocking our parents. I barked out a laugh before taking it and following my parents to the car.

After a short ride, we found ourselves pulling into a grand horseshoe shaped driveway, the white gravel bathed in the bleeding pinks of the sunset and the beams from hanging lanterns edging the driveway.

White gauzy fabric adorned the outside of a grand white house large enough for at least five families to live in. At the front of the house, groups of people buzzed, groups of elegantly dressed older women and servers intermingling. The soft sounds of string instruments carried into the air, filtering through the golden hues of the trees. The very air smelt of champagne and elegance. Or maybe that was just my mother's own pungent perfume wafting from the seat in front of me.

At the sight of all the graceful strides and pretentious clothing, my throat tightened in panic. Flashes of Harvard's dark eyes, Jill's full pink lips, Maverick's shock of dark hair and bold green eyes. I sucked in a breath through my painted lips. I felt Pete's hand drift to my shoulder, its weight slightly reassuring as I battled with my thoughts. I fidgeted with the smooth fabric of my dress, hoping that I would have the ability to do this.

My father pulled the car up to the front entrance, opening the door and helping my mother to her feet. Pete did the same to me in his overly mocking fashion. My father handed the keys to the nearest valet and led us into the party in front of us. A king headed to battle.

I felt rather than saw the looks thrown my way followed by awed whispers. Old ladies gawked at my dress, searching for any aspect of my appearance to tear apart. I held my chin high as I hid behind a forced smile. Men nodded towards my father with respect in their eyes, their wives practically swooning with lust in their own gazes. My mother either didn't notice or refused to acknowledge the latter.

All those expressions changed as they took me in, piercings lining my ears, the small, tattooed bird the only one of my tattoos visible. I heard the small intakes of breath. I felt the looks of the same men who just held the highest respect for my father look me over with hunger like wolves ready to sink their teeth into my flesh. I let out a small shudder.

I would not show weakness though. This dress would act as my armor, my smile my weapon. I walked side by side with Pete, clutching the solid arm he outstretched to me. I focused my thoughts on Maverick. How he would have laughed at the whispers pertaining to him, how he would have glared right back at these clucking hens. I rolled my shoulders back as I imagined Maverick would. Maverick wouldn't have even tried to seem confident; he just was.

As we entered the large dining area, I felt myself gasp. Long tables lined with varieties of delicate cakes with pastel frostings, and small sandwiches featuring savory meats, lines of bubbling champagne. I took in the sight hungrily. The only thing that I missed from these events was the food. I licked my lips. But before I could reach the table we were swarmed.

"Oh, senator Edison, how lovely for you to come!"

"Is that who I think it is? Gracie?"

"Oh, Pete you look so dashing."

"So Grace, I'm assuming you are in college?"

"You are stunning, you must have to fight off the boys!"

"That dress is certainly interesting."

It seemed everywhere I would look was another painted face, a shrill voice behind it. I tried to answer, but before I could another question was thrown my way. The rest of my family had no trouble keeping up with the question overload. My heart raced as I stumbled over my words.

"Yes its me."

"Yes I do attend a university, it's a bit of a ways away."

A chuckle.

A smile.

I tried to keep up but it seemed as if I was just being flooded with more people, more questions, more compliments. I shut my eyes once again, picturing Maverick holding my hand, by my side as I fought off the crowd. This was dangerous territory I was encroaching on, relying on the idea of someone who most definitely hated me. But I couldn't help but recall how his calloused skin felt brushing against me. I opened my eyes, scanning all these faces. All these faces who did not care about me in the slightest, just the gossip that would follow. I watched my parents offer handshakes and fake flashes of smiles.

I did not belong here. If my encounter with Beck earlier showed me anything, it was that I could not take anything for granted. Why was I here? The endless drone of preppy jargon and the ever-present buzz of judgement meant nothing to me. And yet he did. He meant everything.

I shoved through the crowd with appalled gasps and startled comments.

"Grace? Where are you going?" My father's attention was momentarily diverted as I raced out of the crowd and back to the grand entrance I had just walked through. People jumped out of my path with appalled gasps, but I couldn't help but smile. This wasn't me; Maverick knew the real me. I wasn't just a background detail to him. Even if he hated me, I needed to tell him, needed to show him that he was a piece of me.

I ran through the glistening twilight, slipping off my heels as I went.

"Grace!" My father's voice called again. But I didn't stop. I just kept moving. I ran, my dress trailing after me the short jog home. The cool air breezed over my exposed skin, my heels clutched to my chest.

All I could think of was him. Instead of the cold seeping into me, I felt the warmth of his embrace. Instead of the gravel under my bare feet slapping the pavement, I felt the warm tangle of sheets. Instead of the sharp smell of leaves, I smelt the mixture of mint and sweat that was Maverick.

I laughed, feeling freed. As I reached the house, I didn't even bother going to get the little clothing I had brought, I immediately found the spare key and unlocked the garage. I grappled for keys, any keys I could get my hands on. I pushed into one of my father's prized muscle cars and just drove. My hands didn't shake. I didn't see the flash of broken glass. I saw bright emerald eyes. I heard a shrill ring as I whipped down the side streets of my childhood. My phone. Pete's name flashed across the front. Pete.

"Hello." I said, gripping the phone between my shoulder and ear as I continued driving.

"Grace? What is going on?" Pete's voice sounded only a fraction worried, more curious than anything.

"Pete, I am okay. Pete, its him. I have to see him. I should have known I couldn't come back here. I saw Beck. I went back to the, to the tarmac. I need to see him." The words poured out of me frantic, silently pleading for him to understand.

"I was waiting for you to snap to your senses." I could hear the smile in his voice as I felt my shock. "Gracie, you are never one to give up on something. I know you blame yourself for what happened, and you'll probably never stop, and as much as you think you don't, you deserve to be happy." My eyes blurred with tears at my brother's words. Of course, I would always blame myself. Maybe I didn't deserve to be happy, but I needed to test that for myself. And Maverick was my answer. "Go get him Gracie. I'll cover for you. I love you."

"I love you." I choked out, my voice thick with tears.

I raced down street after street. My mind racing the hour or two it took to get me back to him. I worried over how he would react, worried if he would reject me flat out. I was also determined, telling myself I wouldn't leave till I told him how I felt. I worried about my parents. I vowed to never go back.

Before I knew it, rain began to beat down and pelt the hood of the car I hijacked from my home. The headlights cut through the deep night, the moon barely visible through the down pour. My stomach lurched when I realized where I was. I watched small houses fly by, all blurring together as I searched for the one, I needed to go to.

Chapter Thirty-Two

I lost my breath as I saw it. His jet-black truck parked in the makeshift driveway of dirt. A small porch light left without a porch swathed the spotty front lawn with pale light. All the windows were dark save for the small glow from a lamp in the very top one. I swear I could feel him from where I sat in my car. Feel his hand brush my bare arm. Feel his eyes trained on me. The silence was broken by the steady beat of rain as I tried to steady myself, steel myself for the inevitable rejection I was about to face. When the door opened.

Standing there, squinting out in the darkness was Maverick. His figure was illuminated by the small light, the right half of his body swathed in shadow. I watched as he squinted into the rain, trying to decipher what this car idling in front of his house was. I gulped. Even from far away he was beautiful. His hair was mused as if he had just woken up, his gloriously mixture of tan and inked chest bare. Loose gray sweats hung from his hips, clinging to the hard lines of his muscles. I gulped, pulling the keys out of the engine and stepping out into the rain.

His eyes popped open as he took me in. There I was, clad in my gray dress, already soaked with the rain. My hair held up by an array of pins and curls. My eyes no doubt running with the deep streaks of cosmetics from earlier. I watched as they trailed over me, looking at the pitiful sight in front of him. The dress clung to me more than ever as rain seeped into the satiny fabric.

"Grace?" His voice was like honey, sticky and sweet even though it held a heated question. I stepped forward into the light of the porch light, still far away from him.

"Maverick. It's me." My voice sounded broken and rough compared to the sweet richness of his own. "Look, I know you hate me. I know I messed up. But I can't let you just shut me out. I can't shut you out. I miss you, fuck, I miss you Mav. I went home, I, I ." I gulped as he watched me stumble over the words. "I need you Mav. I need you." I let the broken words hand there in the vast space between us, the rain the only sound for what felt like an eternity. "Mav? Say something."

I stood there feeling naked having just bared my soul to him. He stepped down into the wet grass, his brow furrowed, and his mouth set in a hard line. He surged to me, while I couldn't help but flinch. He just gripped both sides of my face and pulled me into his lips.

All resolve melted away. His hands held me fast, not moving from their place cupping my face. The rain pelted down onto us but neither of us cared. His lips were warm, teasing me in a rush of passion and longing. I melted into the kiss, realizing just how much I missed this boy. My hands grappled to tangle in his hair, pulling the silky strands between my fingers. We were both a tangle of teeth and flesh, gripping each other as if we would be lost without this hold.

The kiss was full of longing, containing what seemed like the hundreds that we had missed when we were apart. Every inch of my being felt ignited, every fiber of my being urging me to get closer to him. I no longer felt numb, I felt like everything was flooding my senses. The smell of mint tangled with the fall rain. My eyes shut against the mist bouncing across our skin. I leaned into his hands urging his lips to come closer. I never wanted to tear my lips from his, never wanted to untangle my fingers from his hair. My mouth opened for him, savoring every sigh huffed into the air we shared.

He finally pulled back, bare chest heaving. I looked up into his eyes a small smile playing at my swollen lips.

"Gray. I am so sorry. I know what you did was to help me. Delilah called a little while ago, she told me everything. I.." But I cut him off, locking my lips back onto his. He let out a deep sigh into my mouth.

"God, I missed you." He murmured against my lips, sweeping me up with no effort. I giggled as he carried me into the house, straight up to his room.

He gingerly set me on the rug, our kiss deepening before he drew back. I watched his eyes flash with hunger as he looked me up and down, the soaking fabric of my dress dripping on the shagged carpet in his room. He reached up his fingertips, tracing the bared skin of my collar bone. My eyes locked onto his gaze as it followed the path of his fingers. Every bit of skin he touched burst out into goosebumps. They found the thin strap of my dress, pulling it down slowly so it slipped off my shoulder. I watched as his tongue peeked out from his lips.

I yearned for his touch. To feel those fingers, trace my bare skin. He moved his touch to the soft fabric of my dress, drawing lines down my side in lazy strokes, his eyes glued to his fingers and their path. His inked chest heaved, panting with the effort of his restraint as he explored my skin. I tingled with his touch, closing my eyes with the sensation of it. I needed more of him.

"You are so beautiful. This dress is just….." Maverick's eyes stayed on me, I couldn't stop the smile that took over my face. "Sorry to have taken you from the ball, princess." He whispered, making my hair stand up. I couldn't wait anymore. I rose up on my toes and brought my mouth within inches of his own.

"Come here." I watched his lips as I said the words, bringing my hand up to trace the small birthmark above his lip. This kiss was softer, sweeter. The rush was gone. We had each other and we weren't letting go. He lowered me to his bed, hovering above me as he brushed his lips across mine. I felt the past month melt away. The threats, the anxieties. All that existed was this little pocket of time. This space that me and Maverick shared together. Our story, together.

***

I woke up snuggled into his chest, the window in front of the small bed telling me it was still night. I let out a deep sigh, burrowing myself deeper into the crook of his chest, scared that I might wake up.

"Are you awake?" He whispered, pressing a feather light kiss to my now free flowing hair.

"Mmmhmmm." My eyes fluttered closed as I relished in the feel of his heartbeat underneath my palm. He let out a soft chuckle into the dark. "Are you?" I asked.

"How could I ever sleep knowing everything I dreamed of these past few weeks is lying, naked might I add, in my bed next to me." His smooth voice drawled, ending in a soft chuckle.

"That was absolutely and utterly cheesy Maverick." I pinched at the swirling ink on his chest. Another chuckle.

"I can't help it. I feel like just being near you makes me want every cheesy moment I can possibly have." My heart swelled with his words. "Gray. We have to talk though. I treated you like shit and I could barely live with myself knowing how I reacted to you helping me, helping my family." He sighed out the words, working to get them out as fast as possible. I just shook my head, trying to find my own words.

"No, I am sorry. I should have told you Mav. I had no right. It was enough for me to even barge in in the first place." He shifted, turning to face me and cup my face.

"Hey, never, ever apologize to me for that okay? I fucked up. You were only trying to help." His eyes were so serious, hard almost, but his tone was soft, pleading. I nodded my head.

"Maverick, I need to tell you something." My stomach clenched with the reality of what I was about to do. I had to tell him, had to let him decide if he could stand to be near me after he knew my truth. He just held my gaze.

"What is it Gray?" His thumb drew a soft stroke down my cheek as a single tear slid down it.

"It's about my," I gulped, "my past."

"If this is about you being the senator's kid, I know. I looked you up after you told me. You had your reasons for hiding it. I am not going to question it." His thumb kept making reassuring strokes while his eyes held me warmly. I shut my eyes as my mouth quivered with the unspoken truth. I shook my head, letting more tears spill. "I meant what I said, none of that matters."

"It's not that Mav."

"Gray, you can tell me anything. It's me."

I let out a shuddering breath. "Maverick, I had to leave. I ran. A few years ago, I was in a pretty dark place. I was in a haze, on pills, high all the time, constantly drunk." I looked into his eyes to find no judgement, only concern swirling in those deep green orbs. As if it pained him to think of me suffering.

"Um, one night, I was with my friends. We were all high out of our minds and there was a lot of alcohol. We were there with a bunch of people. I was reckless. I didn't even think twice." I shut my head shaking my head, but Maverick just leaned his forehead down to rest on my own.

"Gray you don't have to tell me, you don't need to tell me anything." His words were a just a quiet murmur in the night, but they gave me the fraction of confidence I needed. I pulled his face back, looking into his eyes as my tears trailed down my cheeks.

"It was my idea Maverick. I told everyone that we should race our cars, knowing that we all should definitely have not been behind the wheel. Jay was there with me, we got into our friend's car. Him and a girl were in the front seat." I shut my eyes against the image of shards of glass, the scream of crunching metal. "It killed them. I killed them." I choked out the words as they left a bitter taste in my mouth.

"His name was Harvard, remember that friend I was telling you about? I loved him Mav, and I killed him. And a girl named Jill. I killed them."

The room was silent, heavy with the inevitable. I knew he would make me leave. I was a monster. But, I knew it was a possibility, for him to cast me aside like the monster I was, I just had to try. I kept my eyes shut as if not seeing him could delay the inevitable.

His lips softly brushed my own, causing my eyes to fly open in shock. He pulled back, his thumb still making damps circles on my tear-stained cheek.

"Did you hear me? I killed them." My broken whisper hung there as if it were a ripe apple waiting to be picked. But Maverick only shook his head.

"You didn't kill them Gray."

"But, I did. It was all my idea, it would have never happened if I hadn't told them."

"Maybe, but you said it yourself, everyone was out of their mind, Gray. I doubt that you alone took lives that night. It wasn't your fault." His eyes held me in place, coaxing and still brimming with adoration. He wasn't casting me out. He wasn't calling me a monster. "Gray, it wasn't your fault."

The words hit me with the force of a punch. I flung my hands around his neck, hugging him close to my chest. His body pressed into mine as my tears hit the bare skin of his shoulder. If he was uncomfortable, he didn't protest. He just let me hold him to me, wrapping his own arms around me, meanwhile murmuring sweet nothings into my ear.

A strange mixture of confusion, relief, and guilt swashed around in my chest. This boy, he accepted me. I had never realized the fact that I was lacking acceptance, but now that I had it, it seemed so obvious to me. It wrapped around me like a blanket, coating everything wrong with me with a protective layer.

We just held each other, me sobbing softly into the dark air of his room as he pressed me closely to him. He comforted me cooing and murmuring words into my ear, trying to take away my pain. Just a tangle of limbs and flesh, trying to protect each other from the unknown.

***

I woke up to the soft snores coming from Maverick. My eyes felt heavy with the remains of my sobs from the night before. I expected to feel hollow, or even guilty at having not only left my parents but from revealing my past to Maverick. But the constant nagging was absent. I felt content, happy even. I was wrapped in Maverick's embrace listening to his steady heartbeat. He accepted every part of me. I bore everything I was to him, and he didn't shy away. I was still in disbelief. Everything with Maverick just felt right. As if I was meant to be in this small bed, with him.

I looked up into his face. His dark brows were furrowed, his mouth slightly parted as breaths whistled out of him. He looked so young when he slept, all his struggles and pains slipping away with his consciousness. I arched up, strained to lay a light kiss on his cheek. His eyes fluttered with the contact, slowly opening to look my way.

"Good morning, babe." He scrunched up his nose, mocking me. His eyes were still sleepy as he scanned my face, undoubtably making sure that I was okay.

"Good morning, babe." I tried my best impression of his lazy smirk, throwing him a wink. He craned down, planting a kiss on my waiting mouth.

"So what would you like to do today?" He asked me with a sleepy smile.

"Can't we just stay here." I asked him with my own grin, stretching out my feet to feel the rustle of sheets glide across my bare skin.

"Happy to." He rolled onto me, making me squeal with giddiness.

Chapter Thirty-Three

The next few weeks floated by in bliss. We rotated from staying at my dorm to his house, all the while never wanting to spend even a few hours away from each other. Save for class, we were attached to each other at the hip, Maverick even going so far as to hang out at the café and get work down while I worked a shift.

It was perfect.

For the first time in my life, I felt fully accepted, for me. I was able to hold the past at an arm's length rather than carrying the load on my own. I still woke up sweating with the reality that Connor and Beck carried reputable threats, the smell of burnt rubber and sounds of crushed metal choking me, but Maverick was always right there, a warm hand placed on my back and murmuring that everything would be okay. And I believed him.

We saw our friends again, even Jay. Maverick had been icy towards Jay, still recalling that night so long ago, but he eased up for my sake. We all hung out, joking and teasing, forgetting any bumps of the past.

My parents were enraged by my little 'stunt' as they called it. They were appalled at my behavior stating that I had disgraced them even further than I already had. Pete was ecstatic for me, even saying that now I wouldn't even have to worry about being called home. It was a little disconcerting to be practically disowned by my parents, but I couldn't even bring myself to dwell on it. I had Maverick, I had Jay and Mae, I had Pete. That was more than enough.

Enough until it was gone just as fast as it came into my life.

**

On a bitterly cold afternoon, I slung out hot chocolates to the buzzing café, taking special care in drizzling a swish of golden caramel over a deep-set mug. I used my hip to push out from behind the counter, a full tray balanced on my shoulder.

I found Maverick bent over one of his novels, peering over the words while he chewed his full bottom lip. I placed the caramel hot chocolate right in front of him, giving him a quick peck on the head as I went to the rest of my tables.

Before I could get back to my spot behind the counter, I felt a hand on my waist, spinning me till I crashed against Maverick's hard chest. He pressed a deep kiss against my lips, tasting of sweet chocolate and caramel. I smiled at him, watching him as he sauntered back to his small seat, leaving me breathless and wanting more. It was our routine and yet I would never tire of it.

The little bell at the door chimed, revealing Mick Foster. Maverick's cousin scanned the room till he found Maverick, dwarfing the booth he occupied in the far corner. I watched as he strode over to him, his posture ridged. Maverick didn't notice till Mick was leaning over, hissing in his ear. I could only watch as Maverick's gaze become melted steel, his shoulders set in a hard line that matched his mouth. He gave a terse nod before slamming his book shut. I could tell something was wrong, even if the rest of the café was oblivious to the small exchange. I waited by my spot behind the counter for him to come over, waiting to find out what was so urgent.

He faced Mick, talking in harsh whispers with his fists clenched at his sides. He nodded again, gesturing for Mick to stay where he was. Maverick swung his gaze to me, catching me looking at him. I gave him a questioning look and he came over to me.

"What is it? What's wrong?" I asked as my panic started to grow. I could see the rage boiling in his eyes.

"Connor. He is going to take legal action. He thinks," Maverick huffed a sigh, "He thinks that I am purposely keeping Delilah away from him. He thinks that that constitutes as kidnapping." I fisted my hands in my apron at the words.

"Could he do that?" I asked, too much worry leaking into my voice.

He sighed, rubbing a hand down his face. "I don't know Gray." He looked beaten down, tired. "Can you leave, we have to go."

"Of course, let me just let Jenny know." I was already untying my apron, leaving Maverick at the counter to find Jenny.

"Jenny, I got to go. I'll make it up to you, promise!" but I was already walking away before she could respond.

"Alright. Be careful please." She called out from behind me.

I grabbed Maverick's hand and led him towards Mick.

"Hey Grace." Mick's hands were shoved into his pockets. Despite his huge frame and rugged good looks, he looked like a frightened little boy.

"Hey Mick." A feeble hello as my anxiety squeezed at my stomach. "Let's get you two out of here. We have to figure out a way around this. We will figure a way around this alright?" I received silent nods from the both of them and dragged them to the exit of the café, Maverick's hand still grasped in mine and Mick trailing behind us. And I had no idea if the words were to reassure them or me.

I brought them both to Maverick's truck, Maverick still rigid with anger at the prospect of his cousin stripping the safety away from his sister. I could only imagine the rage building in him, I was furious myself. There had to be a way around it. Something, anything that we could do.

I slid into the middle of the bench seat, Mick to my right and Maverick taking up the driver's seat. The muscles in Mick's jaw feathered as we all sat in silence trying to think. Me sandwiched between the two giant men with the heat blasting on my face, making sweat bead at my brow.

"Mick, what exactly did Connor say?" I asked, Maverick keeping his gaze locked on the steering wheel in front of him with his teeth grinding against each other. I reached over to lay a feather light hand on his knee. I wouldn't have even known if he realized until he wrapped his own hand around mine, intertwining our fingers.

"Connor says that as Maverick knew that he was considering taking legal action to get custody, by moving her from an undisclosed location he knew he was going to lose the case. Connor wants to use the whole situation as a case that Maverick is an unfit guardian, going so far as to use the term kidnapping." Mick's face was grim as he spoke the words. I sighed out through my nose while trying to organize the scatter of thoughts clouding my mind.

"But she's emancipated. It's not like Maverick is even considered her guardian anymore. So, he can't do anything right?" I asked, my voice sounding a little too hopeful as I tried to solve our dilemma.

Maverick shook his head, "It's not that simple. Connor doesn't know about the emancipation. He could say that it was faulty because of the upcoming trial or whatever bullshit he comes up with." My eyes widened at the possibility. If they dismiss the emancipation this could have all been for nothing. All the tears, anger, poor Delilah leaving everything she knows.

"But she can fight it right?" I squeaked desperate for a shred of hope.

"Not until she's eighteen." Mick sighed out, looking defeated. "Maverick, you have to start thinking legal options here."

"No shit, Mick. But I can barely afford anything now, how am I supposed to hire a lawyer, never mind a good one." Maverick grumbled, pulling at his hair. Mick snapped his mouth shut knowing better than to push Maverick further.

Maybe he didn't have to hire a lawyer. A curl of dread unfurled in my stomach. I wasn't about to let everything we fought for be rendered useless.

"I have an idea."

***

Maverick pulled out of the lot, his anger blatant with every sharp curve he took. Mick had left, satisfied with my plan and going in to do some research on Connor's legal team for us. Maverick was slightly less enthusiastic about the idea.

"Gray, I can't ask you to do this. I won't ask you to do this." He grit the words out as he pulled into his parking space in front of his house.

"You didn't ask. I offered." I pointed out, hoping my sarcasm would lighten the mood. It didn't.

"Grace." Maverick turned to look at me, his eyes practically brimming with concern and anxiety. I instantly reached out a hand, tracing the ink peeking out from his tight white thermal shirt. He let out a sigh, slumping back into his seat.

"Maverick. I will not let him win. Let me help." My voice was a soft whisper, not so much as a plead but a silent command. He shut his eyes for a brief second as if he wanted to disappear.

"Gray, I know how much you hate it there. And after how it ended last time, how can you be sure they'll help us?" The truth was I wasn't sure that they would. But I had to try. I wasn't going to let Connor strip this family of everything they loved.

"I don't know if they will," my sigh visible in the chilled air of the truck. "But we have to try Mav. We have to." He nodded in response, reaching for the hand not resting on his arm. He intertwined his fingers in mine, pressing our hands to his mouth.

His skin was chilled with the winter air as it delicately brushed across the bare skin of my knuckle. I shivered, not from the cold.

"Ok, we'll try." He looked into my eyes, hand still wrapped in mine before leaning over and planting a deep kiss on my lips. "Now let's get inside because I'm freezing my ass off." He pulled back smirking. I couldn't suppress my chuckle as I swatted at his arm.

Chapter Thirty-Four

We lay tangled in a mess of limbs and blankets, pressed close together to ward off the chill. I snuggled deeper into his chest, listening to the deep breaths that indicated Maverick was on the edge of sleep. I stared off, my eyes tracing the cracked spines of his novels illuminated by the sliver of moonlight peeking through the dark curtains.

Only I couldn't focus enough to read the titles. I had a feeling of dread, as if I were about to lose everything. I thought of Harvard and Jill, how they did lose everything. I was sitting here worrying at the mere prospect. I couldn't lose Maverick. I thought of the accident, as I cradled Harvard's head on my lap, counting his breaths till they stopped. Only it wasn't Harvard in my lap, it was Maverick. I shook my head, trying to get rid of the image, snuggling deeper into Maverick's bare chest. He grumbled at the movement. He was there, with me. He was ok. I rubbed a hand up his muscled side, tracing swirls and patterns of ink.

"Mmmm. What are you up to?" Maverick's sleepy voice startled me out of my trance.

"I'm just thinking."

"About your parents?" just like that he was alert, his arm tightening around me.

"A little. What if they don't help us?" I voiced the fear that I hadn't even realized I had been thinking.

Maverick took a deep breath as if pondering over the question. "Then we find another way." I nodded against him. "Hey Grace. I have been thinking, thinking a lot actually about what you said the first time we really hung out. Remember in the field?" Of course, I remembered. That night was one I would never forget. "You had said that one of your biggest fears was being stuck in the background? That you didn't want to be the background character to anyone else's story." My heart surged a little as he remembered the conversation that had worked to bring me back to him in the first place.

"Yea?"

"Well, I don't think you could ever just be in the background." The word held a sense of shyness as they curled around me. "At least, not to me." I stared down at his chest, watching his quick breaths. I could tell he was staring up at the ceiling, worrying his lower lip as he pondered.

"You forced me into the foreground." I whispered against his skin.

He let out a sheepish chuckle. "I'm not too sure about that. If anything, you just rewrote the story." The words settled into the night air, as if they were suspended in a glimmering curtain around us. I lifted my head, wrapping my hand around his chin and forcing his head to look at me.

"I love you Maverick." The words slipped out. I watched as a shock of surprise flitted across his eyes. Watched as it was quickly replaced with a look of pure bliss and a smile stretching.

"I love you Grace." Something shot through me with the words, making every cell of my being explode and bubble as if it were a glittering glass of champagne or if I was struck by lightning. I genuinely couldn't describe the feeling as anything else.

I pressed my lips against his, as if I could taste the words he had just spoken. His tongue brushed across my bottom lip, eliciting a deep moan from me. My fingers found his hair, tugging at the locks as if I could pull him closer. He moved his mouth to my jaw, peppering it with kisses before moving to my neck.

"I love you Gray." He mumbled the words across the flesh of my neck. I didn't think I could ever grow tired of hearing the words.

"I love you Mav." I smiled as he brought his face back up, hovering just above mine. His eyes were as light as I have ever seen them, any trace of pain just gone. He rested his forehead against mine, his breaths raspy and smelling of mint and the smell that can only be described as Maverick. I could never get over the feeing I got when I was wrapped in his arms. Or just being near him. I was tied to him by some invisible strand. It seemed as if an electric current passed between us, connecting us. And I couldn't get enough.

My past vices had stripped me of my sense of life. I had driven myself mad on pills, alcohol. And now, my new addiction was hovering just above my lips, murmuring words like the sticky sweet of honey. Only it heightened every fiber of my being. I wasn't suppressed, rather I was exaggerated. Maverick made me a better person. And he was mine. I was his. I couldn't wait any longer and pulled his mouth to mine.

***

The next morning, we loaded up our stuff into Maverick's truck and embarked on the drive back to my home. After the revelations of last night, we both seemed lighter, relieved in a way. We were in this together and nothing could change that. I was still slightly racked with nerves at the prospect of revealing the entirety of my past to Maverick. I couldn't help it, I was anxious despite everything we had been through that he would come to his senses and realize who I really was. The idea of watching him walk through my parents' home, vulnerable to their judgement made me shudder.

I hadn't told them we were coming. I only sent a quick message to Pete, telling him to get Delilah and bring her to the house. She needed to hear what was going on. He just agreed, no questions asked. The drive seemed quick, Maverick taking the turn onto my road made my stomach clench and my heart pound. I clenched my fits in my lap.

Maverick let out a low whistle, "I know you told me you were rich, but… wow." He let out a chuckle as he eyes stared in awe at the large houses lining both sides of the street. He shot me a quick glance, doing a quick double take as he took in my nervous appearance.

"Hey, you okay?" one of his hands lifted from the steering wheel, wrapping around my own. I gave him a tight-lipped smile in return.

"Yea. Yea. I'm okay just worried." I whispered, returning my gaze to the towering houses on perfectly manicured lawns.

"It'll be okay Gray." His voice held a note of uncertainty, but I chose to ignore it and try to believe his words. I watched as the truck began to slow, Maverick scanning both sides of the street for my house, I almost didn't want to tell him.

"That one on the left." I pointed to the massive house; Pete's car parked on the curb in front. The cold air stung my eyes as I uneasily jumped down onto the gravel. I met Maverick at the front of his truck, graciously accepting his outstretched hand. I pulled my hoodie tighter around me, clutching it closer to me with my free hand. I watched as my exhalations curled in the air in front of me, choosing not to focus on the fact that each step brought me closer to showing Maverick my past. Maverick gave my hand a reassuring squeeze, to which I only could manage a slight nod. Was I supposed to knock? I didn't really know the protocol for when parents practically disown their children. Maverick kept his eyes on me, waiting to see what I would do. He didn't urge me to knock, or to waltz right in. If I wanted to leave right then, I had known that Maverick would leave with me.

I raised my fist, tapping the elegantly carved door. Maverick moved closer and slipped an arm around me, an unspoken promise that he would protect me from whatever we would face behind that door. I heard the click of heels across the tile in front of the door, each one making my anxiety grow.

The door snapped open. "Hello…." My mother stopped as her eyes doubled in size. Her mouth literally dropped open. "Grace? What are you doing here?" The words weren't as hostile as I thought, most likely caused from her shock.

"Mom? We need to talk to Dad." I leaned into Maverick for extra courage as I tried to find the words.

"We?" she hadn't seen Maverick before, which I am not really sure how she missed his towering frame leaning into me, but when she did, she scanned him up and down, her eyes growing even larger if possible. I watched as her pale throat bobbed with her deep gulp of air.

"Hello Mrs. Edison." Maverick extended the hand that wasn't wrapped around me to my mother. She looked at it for a second before delicately putting her hand in his large one. "I am Maverick, very nice to meet you." He shook her hand before she quickly withdrew from his grasp.

She looked horrified at the tall mass of muscle in front of her but Maverick only grinned. The silence was palpable as we stood there, waiting for her to move aside and let us in. Or to kick us out. I imagined how my mother must be looking at us. Maverick all muscles and bits of ink curling out from under his winter coat. A beanie was pulled snug over his head but not large enough to conceal the large mess of dark hair. He was all steel and hard lines, and likely terrified my mother. Then there was me, engulfed in one of his hoodies and a pair of my signature shredded jeans. I could practically hear her disgust with each breath she gasped through her nose.

"Uh, Mrs. Edison? I am not trying to be rude or anything but if you are going to ask us to leave please hurry. It's freezing out here." Maverick bounced on his toes with his words, that grin still plastered on his face. My mother scrunched her nose in disgust before stepping aside, gesturing for us to come in. She took in the wet state of his boots.

"Shoes off please, you can wait in the living room for your father." My mother barely gave us a second glance as her heels clapped against the tiled floor in quick strides as if she couldn't get away from us fast enough. I watched as Maverick struggled with his boots while his eyes took in the house. The giant house felt too large, too haunting especially as Maverick took in every detail around us.

"She seems like a lovely woman." He snorted into the too empty space. The sound bouncing around the walls around us. I chuckled at his sarcasm. It helped to know he would be here with me to face my family. Even though I felt vulnerable and scared over what he would think when he found out the reality of my upbringing.

"Come on." I grabbed his hand and pulled him to the large stiff couch that took up the formal living room. Dark wood accents shone with fresh polish. The large bookcases in the corner sported hundreds of books and an array of antiques that my mother had collected over the years. Not even a speck of dust occupied the shelves.

"Grace?" I heard Pete's voice before I saw him, ducking into the room. His eyes snapped to mine, and his face immediately brightened with a smile. "Grace!" He surged me, picking me up in his strong grip and twirling me around.

"Hey Pete!" I laughed. I patted his broad shoulders, aware that a suddenly sheepish Maverick sat on the couch behind me. "Pete, you remember Maverick."

"How could I forget. My jaw hurt for a week. Hey man." Pete was joking but I couldn't help but wince at the memory of their fight. He extended his hand out to Maverick.

"Yea, I'm really sorry about that." Maverick stood up, matching Pete in height. It was weird seeing him standing up and talking to my little brother. Especially now that violence wasn't part of the equation.

"Hey no worries. To be fair I came after you first. And I also got a few good hits in." Pete winked and the two shared a laugh.

"You sure did." Maverick rubbed at his own jaw as if her remembered a ghost of the pain from that night with a grin. I rolled my eyes at the two comparing blows.

"I hate to break up this little reunion." Maverick instantly whipped his head to the doorway, going rigid. "Hey Mav." Delilah held her clasped hands in front of her, looking shy.

Before she could get out another word, she was wrapped in Maverick's arms. He buried his head into her shoulder just holding her. Pete moved to stand next to me bumping me with a shoulder and a smile. Delilah let out a little sob as she wrapped her frail arms around her brother.

"Oh my God. Delilah. I missed you so much. It's too quiet without you bitching at me." Even though the words were light, I couldn't overlook the fact that his voice was thick with tears.

"My bitching? Yea ok." Delilah pulled back and rolled her tear drenched eyes at her brother.

"Hey don't swear." He reached out and ruffled her hair, earning him another eyeroll.

"Hey Grace!" she broke off from her brother and tackled me, nearly knocking the breath from me with the impact.

"Hey kid." I hugged her back, looking over her shoulder to see Maverick watching me, a soft smile on his face as he watched us.

"Alright can we find out the reason you guys are here now? Or should we wait in eager anticipation some more?" Pete chuckled, flopping down on the couch. His arm rested on the back, no doubt waiting for Delilah to fit into the spot next to him. And she did exactly that.

Maverick watched in shock as Delilah settled next to my brother, grabbing his arm and placing it on her shoulders. She pecked his cheek. Maverick's mouth dropped. He looked like a fish as he moved his mouth up and down looking for words. I walked over to him grabbing his hand.

"Bigger issues at hand here overprotective brother." I whispered into his ear before brushing my lips on his stubbled cheek. Pete and Delilah seemed oblivious, whispering and giggling on the couch. "She's not a kid anymore." I poked him in the ribs.

"Who said she could date some random…" I swatted at his arm before he could finish, reminding him that that was my little brother he was referring to. "… uh, fine young man." He stammered.

I chuckled, pulling him toward the opposite end of the couch. He kept his eyes on the two. All sense of amusement died though when I looked up and saw the harsh features of my father's face, his grey eyes like ice. I stilled. Maverick sensed my shift in mood, snapping his gaze to me before stilling as he followed my gaze.

My father cleared his throat, causing everyone in the room to sit up straight and alert, all sense of relaxation or joking vanished.

"Explain to me right now why you are here with this," my father gestured to Maverick making sure to glare at the hand I was resting on his arm, "this boy. Why you are here at all. After what you pulled the last time." His voice came out low and intimidating. I could sense Maverick's rising temper. My mouth felt dry, my tongue turned into sandpaper.

"I.. um…" I stumbled over my words as my father just continued to glare at me. Maverick reached behind me, setting his hand on my lower back.

"Well? I am waiting." He snapped.

"Dad." Pete warned, moving to sit up, with Delilah still at his side, holding his arm.

"Peter, stay out of this. It does not concern you." My dad snapped, never taking his eyes off me. I looked to Pete, shaking my head to tell him to stop. Maverick's hand pressed harder in my back as I watched the muscles of his jaw feather.

"I came to ask for help."

My dad huffed, rolling his eyes. I knew that was probably it for Maverick.

"Mr. Edison, or Senator Edison. I get that I am in your house, looking to you for help. But so help me God, if you ever, and I mean ever, speak to Grace that way again…" Maverick growled out from next to me, getting ready to stand up.

"You'll what? Hit me? You'd be arrested before you could even land a punch son. And you will not tell me how to speak to my daughter." My father pushed as much disdain as he could behind the words. Maverick began to open his mouth with a retort, but I gave his arm a squeeze. He looked to me before relaxing a fraction, still tense enough though that he could be at my father's throat in an instant.

"Dad. This is important. Please." I begged, the words tasting like ash on my tongue. I hated to sound so weak.

"So was the Gala. The event that you ran out of and made a big scene. The night you stole my car. The night you left me, and your mother heartbroken over the fact that their first born had such utter disrespect." The words were too calm, not revealing any of the anger he felt. But his eyes said it all. They simmered with silent rage. Like molten steel swirling in blazing heat. "And now you are back, with this boy, to ask for my help?" I gulped at the words.

"Dad, that's enough." Pete barked the words, startling even me. My father looked to him with a mixture of shock and anger.

"Excuse me? Peter, did you just tell me enough?" But Pete didn't shrink from under our dad's gaze.

"You heard me." Pete was practically bristling. Delilah sat next to him, her eyes the size of saucers as she wrapped her small porcelain like hands around his large arm.

"You will not speak to me like that in my house." His voice held a new edge as his anger shifted from me to my brother.

"And you will not speak to my sister like that. She only left in the first place because you made her. She has been trying so hard to fit into your perfect world, and you don't even care that it is killing her." Pete's voice was loud as the words rang through the room.

My dad sucked in a breath, taking the words like a blow. I heard my mother start to speak. I hadn't even realized her small frame standing behind my father in the doorway. He held out a hand behind him to tell her to be quiet. "I never forced her to leave. She did that when she got involved with those kids' deaths." I winced at the words, seeing Harvard's and Jill's faces flash before my eyes.

"Have you even questioned why she was there to begin with?" Pete fisted his hands, the veins in his neck prominent with rage as he gritted out the words. "The only reason she was there that night was because you were too busy with whatever it is that you thought took precedent over your kids." The words hit my father like a blow, my mother's face streaked with tears.

"Peter.." My mother sobbed before clutching a fist in front of her mouth.

"No Mom. It's time you both realize what you are doing here. You are trying to cast out Grace for just trying to find a place in this world that doesn't fit your ideals. Are you really going to kick her out of our family for trying to escape from your suffocating image?" The words came out sharper than I thought possible from Pete.

My father stood in silence for a few seconds as if pondering what to say next. His eyes slid to mine, and I was surprised to find them glassy. Was he, was he actually crying? "Everything I have ever done for this family was to give you all the best opportunities possible." The whole room felt charged with expectation. I held my breath for the final blow. He was going to kick me out. Or scream. Or.. something. But instead, he just looked at me, suddenly looking tired.

"Grace, do you actually feel that way? Like I failed you?" My father sounded utterly broken, making my heart pang with sympathy I didn't realize I had.

"You didn't fail me Dad. You never failed me." My own vision was starting to blur with tears. "But, it wasn't easy trying to grow into the role you wanted me to. I blame myself every day for those kids that died. I get that I am the ultimate screw up, ok? I know I am a total disgrace. But it still hurts that you throw it in my face every two seconds. No, you didn't fail me, but you make me feel like I failed you." My voice cracked over the last words, making Maverick pull me closer to him. He used the pad of his thumb to wipe away a tear that escaped.

"It's ok Grace. I am here. Hey, I am right here." Maverick whispered against my ear, stroking my hair back from my face. "Mr. Edison. We came here for your help. Please, can you just. Can you just hear us out?" he sounded bitter as he clutched me to his chest. My father just nodded for us to continue, still looking shocked from Pete's proclamation.

I looked over at Delilah, grasping my brother's hand and watching us. I let a deep breath out of my nose. "Delilah, Connor is trying to say that Maverick kidnapped you. He doesn't know about the emancipation. He is going to take legal action."

Delilah looked as if the wind had been knocked out of her. Pete pulled her stunned frame into him, locking his arms around her as if he would fight anyone who tried to get near her.

"But he can't. I mean she's emancipated whether he knows it or not." As Pete spit of the words, his grip on her tightened. I watched as tears slid down her face.

"He is trying to say that the emancipation is faulty because it was done with knowledge of a legal battle over guardianship." Maverick said the words lightly, hugging me to his side while he watched his sister's face carefully. She looked pale, like she did the night I had first met her. Before I even knew what I was doing, I walked over to her, grasping her hands and kneeling in front of her.

"I won't let anything happen to you Delilah." I turned to see my Dad, still standing in place with his shoulders slightly slumped. "That's why we're here. To see if you can help. See if there was anything that you could do to help her."

His brow furrowed over his deep gray eyes, suddenly looking old and crumpled. He fidgeted with the end of his tie as if considering possible solutions. He finally drew out a sigh, shutting his eyes for a second.

"I can try." His deep voice still held a sound of defeat, but my heart swelled at his acceptance. I pulled myself up to a standing position, dropping Delilah's hands and walking towards my father. He seemed taken off guard at my sudden approach, still raw from Pete's words. I stood in front of him unsure what to do.

"Thank you." I whispered. He gave me a grim nod, before dropping his gaze to the floor and walking out of the room. My mother's once perfect makeup was streaked down her face with her previous onslaught of tears. With trembling lips, she nodded to me before following my father out of the room.

Chapter Thirty-Five

After trying to calm Delilah down and assuring Maverick I was ok, I found myself padding in sock clad feet to my father's study. I found him at his desk, head buried in his hands while gray strands of hair peeked through his fingers. His glasses were haphazardly thrown over a large stack of books and scatters of papers. The dim room smelt of cherrywood and tobacco. I walked toward the desk, causing him to lift his head as I sunk into a deep backed chair directly in front of him while he watched me with wary and tired eyes.

"I just wanted to thank you again. And see if there was anything I could help with." I tried to give him a smile, but I was sure it was unconvincing. He just nodded, trying to give me his own grim smile.

"Well, I looked over some documents. Legally speaking, Connor himself holds no hold over whether or not Delilah stays as her own legal guardian. His parents hold real no case. If anything, a judge would look down

on them for abandoning these kids to their own vices."
My father ran a hand through his hair, eyes scanning
over his papers. To say I was relieved was an
understatement. With this news came the reality that
Delilah could stay here and be safe.

"She can stay in the Maine house for as long as
she needs. She really is a bright girl you know." My dad
smiled a little as if he were reminiscing over a distant
memory. "She reminds me of you when you were a little
younger." He huffed a sheepish laugh. I reached out
toward his hand, grasping it in my own. He looked up,
his eyes meeting mine with question in them.

"Thank you. You don't know what this means to
me." I felt the tears start to well up in my eyes.

"I have to ask you something though. I am not
trying to force my opinion on you or anything, I just
want what's best for you. I am sorry if it didn't always
seem that way. But that boy you brought? Why him?"
for once his tone was totally nonjudgmental just curious.
I couldn't help but smile. The change from his attitude
earlier was drastic, but it didn't leave me unsettled, it left
me hoping.

"Um, I'm not sure exactly. You know in the
beginning he was obnoxious." I zoned out, smiling as I
remembered my first encounter in the kitchen of a frat
house with Maverick. "But he reminded me of me, I
guess. We started to talk, and he was able to handle my
attitude which is more than I can say for most." That
elicited a laugh from my father. "And I, I love him." My
mouth widened as I thought of the night before. The way
his eyes lit up with the words. How the words tasted
when they fell of his lips. I picked at the frayed edges of

my jeans, tucking my bottom lip between my teeth. I peeked up at my father to see his own closed lip smile. And for once it reached his eyes. It brought me back to my childhood. Flashes of running through waves with him trailing behind him. When he tried to braid my hair after and ultimately failing.

"Grace. He sounds perfect. And, you sound, um, happy." His eyes clouded slightly with the words, making his smile fall. "I am just so sorry I never realized. That night when I saw you covered in blood and dirt, you reeked of alcohol. I just felt so ashamed. Like I should have been there. But instead of blaming myself, I blamed you. I never meant to make you feel like you were unloved or unaccepted." His eyes were downcast. I gave his hand a light squeeze, trying to bring his eyes back up to mine.

I decided that there was nothing left to say, just looking at the man who raised me, hand in hand. I felt the tears start to choke me as I nodded. He patted my hand with his own surprisingly warm one.

"Alright, go get some sleep. I assume that you will stay the night?"

"Of course." I stood to leave turning around at the doorway.

"I love you Dad." He looked up in a haze, tears brimming his eyes with light.

"I love you too." And I left feeling light with acceptance for once in my life. I was accepted by my father.

***

I shut the door to my room, savoring the cool feeling of the wooden door pressed against my back. I let out a sigh as I recalled every word that I had just shared with my dad.

"How'd it go?" Maverick was suddenly in front of me, planting a kiss at the base of my throat. I sighed with the feeling.

"Actually, really well." I brought my hands up to rest on his back. His lips explored the skin against my neck, mumbling words I couldn't process over the feeling of his lips on my flesh. My eyes fluttered closed as I savored the sensation. "He told me about what he could do for Delilah." With that he snapped his gaze up to me. He cocked his eyebrows, tensing with anticipation. "He can help her." He huffed out a deep breath he had been holding. He crushed me against him in a hug.

"Thank you Gray. Thank you so much. God, I just. I love you so much." He murmured against my hair making my heart flutter. His heart pounding against my skin as I held him close to me. His own minty scent mixed with the smell of crisp apples and cherry wood that filtered through the room, filling my heart with a sense of nostalgia.

"I love you." I whispered into his shoulder. He pulled back, his eyes looking soft and dreamy. His lips hovered inches from my own, his broad hands cupping my chin.

"Hearing you say those words does something to me Gray. It's like I won't ever get tired of you saying it."

I smiled lazily at the words because I knew exactly what he meant. I slowly closed the distance between our lips. The kiss was slow, no rush pushing us forward, as if we had all the time in the world. He tasted like the cold winter air as my lips molded with his own. His thumbs brushed my cheeks, causing me to sigh with each brush of the pad of his thumb. Every inch of me screamed that I loved him. Maverick. Maverick was like the missing piece of me. I needed him. More than I needed anything. I brought my hands up, wrapping them around to rest at the base of his neck. Maverick pressed harder, deepening the kiss with a soft sigh into my mouth. I knew he felt the same.

He understood every part of me, more than anyone would ever would. He accepted me wholly and I couldn't ask for more. He pulled back suddenly, making me immediately miss him.

"This feels risky kissing you in your parent's house." He waggled his eyebrows with a childlike grin. I laughed, pushing him down onto my bed.

He gazed down at me as I hovered just above him, eyes trailing all along my body. His hands slipped under the fabric of my shirt, fingers grazing my bare skin. I hissed a breath, savoring the feeling of him touching me, the warm strokes left on the soft skin of my stomach.

"Remember that night in your dorm, when you were showcasing these tattoos of yours," his voice was husky as his finger grazed the inked skin of my ribs. I could only nod in response as my eyes fluttered closed with the feeling. "All I could think about was touching them," another stroke of his finger as he dipped his head planting a kiss on the thin fabric separating his lips from the ink. "And kissing them." He rolled up the fabric, gently sliding it off over my head. Heat flared instantly in my stomach as his lips brushed the sensitive spot on my ribs. "Especially those secret ones of yours."

I could only moan with the contact before crashing my lips back onto his.

***

The next morning, we struggled with the idea of having to say goodbye to our families once again, showering and snagging a quick cup of coffee in an attempt to avoid the inevitable. I hugged my mother, tears still streaming down her face in her usual dramatic fashion. My dad looked at me with a new sense of understanding, reaching out and giving me a quick squeeze on my shoulder.

"Thanks again, Dad. I'll try to get home again soon." I gave him a sheepish smile.

"Please do Grace." Maverick came up next to me, placing a hand on my back. My father shocked me by extending a hand out to him. "Maverick. Take care of her."

Maverick's eyes filled with an undistinguishable emotion, grabbing the extended hand with a quick shake. "I will. Thank you for helping my family." Both men gave nods. I watched as my mother pulled Maverick into a forceful hug, knocking some of the breath from his chest with the impact. I couldn't stop my smile as he tried to pat her back and pry away from her grasp.

Pete and Delilah stood by the door, hand in hand.

I pulled Pete into me, "Thank you for yesterday. Seriously. I don't know what I ever did to deserve a little brother like you." I squeezed my eyes shut to try to stop the tears from flowing.

"Take care. And next time warn me that you are going to start the next World War." Pete gave me a squeeze with his usual goofy grin. I let go, reaching for Delilah.

"I'll see you later kid. In the meantime, don't take any of his shit." I punched Pete's arm.

"Thank you again Grace, for everything. Watch out for my brother?" She asked in her clear innocent voice that worked to mask her true sassy-self. I crushed her to my chest again.

"As long as you take care of mine."

Maverick walked up to Pete, extending his hand out to him. "I'll see you. And watch out for my sister, seems like you have been doing a good job so far."

"Of course, man. Hey, don't put up with too much of my sister's bullshit. She's all talk." Pete winked and both boys shared a laugh. Maverick walked over next to where I stood with his sister. Her full bottom lip trembled as she looked at her older brother.

"Don't cry. Shhh. Come here." Maverick wrapped her small shaking form in his wide arms, her broken sobs muffled by his hoodie. "You keep up the good work ok? I'll come see you soon. I promise." Her platinum head made a nodding motion as she continued to sniffle.

She pulled back, whipping at her eyes. "You hold on to her Mav. She's perfect for you." She talked to him as if she were a mother scolding her son. I watched as he looked to me over her shoulder, his eyes filling with love.

"Trust me, I will."

The ride back home was bittersweet as we realized we didn't know when we would see our family again but knowing that we had not only helped Delilah but helped my family in the process. I felt happy, light. Sitting there with Maverick's hand resting on my thigh as we drove home, I felt at peace for the first time in a while.

As we drove on, I found myself nodding off, lulled to sleep by the steady motion of the car and the reassurance that Maverick was next to me. I snuggled up pressing my head lightly to his shoulder as he drove us back home.

Chapter Thirty-Six

"Shit."

I didn't know how long I had been asleep, but Maverick's sudden anger made me instantly alert. A starless night settled around us, the only light coming from the same porch light that showed me Maverick those weeks ago, only this time it illuminated a different figure.

I squinted through the dark, trying to decipher the details of the face in front of me. Blonde hair was slicked back, catching the faint glow from the light. It gave him an eerily ghostly look. His complexion pale while his blue eyes looked wild and sunk in. His head snapped in our direction, rage over boiling at the sight of Maverick's truck.

Connor.

Maverick threw the truck in park, hopping down with ease. His posture was rigid with rage.

"Grace, stay in the car." He didn't even look at me as he spit out the order. My chest tightened with anxiety.

"But Mav…"

"Stay in the car!" He yelled before he slammed the truck door. I shrunk back in my seat, startled at the tone that Maverick had used. He had never spoken to me like that before. I watched as Connor staked toward Maverick, his finger jabbing in his direction. I heard the muffled sounds of their yells. Both men stared each other down, breath clouding in front of them with the cold air.

I itched to get out of the truck, to go to him. I felt the need to be there, to protect him somehow. He couldn't fight him. Not now. He shouldn't even give him the satisfaction. We won. We won. He doesn't need to fight his cousin anymore. But Maverick wasn't the type to forget past wrongdoings. He wasn't usually forgiving.

The altercation continued, my mind springing to its conclusion as I saw Connor shove Maverick, barely making him take a step back. I swung open the door, running for the two.

"Enough!" I squeezed into the space between Maverick and his cousin, my hands braced on his chest. Only he wouldn't look at me. His eyes were fixed on Connor, his hands thrown to his sides in fists. He grinded his teeth, eager to get to Connor.

"And here she is, the slut to save the day. My dear cousin gets in your pants and you suddenly become his permanent plaything?" Connor sneered behind me. I remembered how his words split me in two at the prospect of him revealing who I am and what I did to the man in front of me. Maverick's heart pounded, his breaths coming out in deep rasps.

"Shut the fuck up. Right now." Maverick growled, but I refused to loosen my hold on his chest.

"Maverick calm down. He can't do anything." I tried to keep my tone even despite my own anger bubbling into my chest. This pompous ass was trying to get Maverick to snap, he wanted him to attack him.

"You sure know how to pick them cousin. Now tell me, is it because she is a good lay or the prospect of money that gets you. Because it's certainly not for her kindness, she did murder two kids in cold blood." Something in my chest broke at the words. Harvard. Jill. My hands slipped a fraction, losing their hold for only a split second. But it was enough.

Maverick surged forward, moving around me and tackling Connor to the ground with a horrendous smack. He pinned his cousin to the ground, Connor giving a sinister grin while blood poured from his nose and onto his sky-blue sweater. He just kept his hands braced on Maverick's shoulders, not even trying to dodge the onslaught of punches being thrown at him.

Maverick's bloody fist repeatedly connected to Connor's face as a thin laugh fell from Connor with each blow. It only worked to further enrage Maverick. I surged forward, not sure what I planned on doing, only knowing that I had to do something. Maverick looked up for a brief second, seeing me come closer to the fight. Connor took that as is opportunity. He wriggled himself free before standing to his feet, swaying slightly. Maverick was up in a second, already approaching his cousin. I yelled to him but to no avail. Connor shoved at him, swinging his fist and landing one single punch on Maverick's jaw. His head snapped to the side, blood spraying from his mouth.

"No! Get away from him!" I urged my feet forward, grabbing fistfuls of the thick cashmere of Connor's sweater. But he turned, his hand connecting with my cheek with an ear deafening slap. The force of the blow pushed me to the cold earth, my fingers stinging as shards of gravel cut into the skin of my bare hands. My cheek burned with the sting of Connor's hand. I gingerly touched it, looking up to find his smug smile above me.

"Grace!" Maverick scrabbled to get a hold on Connor, throwing him back onto the ground. I sat, numb with shock as Maverick landed punch after punch, Connor's gasps and flesh hitting flesh the only sounds in the empty night air. I pulled my legs closer, still cupping my cheek with wide eyes.

"Get the fuck out of here and don't come back!" Maverick's grip was wrapped around the shredded blue sweater, pulling Connor's near limp body toward him. His head lolled to the side, but he blinked slowly looking to the side to spit out a glob of blood and spit. "Do you hear me! Never. Come. Back." Maverick screamed in his face, veins bulging. Connor just nodded; his hazy eyes filled with hate. Maverick threw him back to the ground, stepping up and over him.

I watched as Connor crawled to his unstable feet, swaying as he stumbled to his car parked on the street. I barely even noticed Maverick at my side. I startled as he took my hands in his, examining the shredded skin. I winced as he gently prodded the tears adorning my skin. I felt the tears flow, my cheek and skin burning.

"Grace. I am so sorry. I... Are you okay? Tell me you are okay." His voice was full of panic as he scanned me from head to toe, his eyes hardened as they landed on my cheek, no doubt sporting a deep red mark. I couldn't think. I couldn't move. I collapsed my head against his chest, crying softly into the torn fabric of his dirt crusted hoodie.

He didn't even hesitate to wrap his arms around my shivering body. He lifted me up, effortlessly cradling me in his arms and bringing me into the house. He carried me to his bed, laying me down against the soft comforter, wordlessly leaving me to fetch a wet cloth and a bottle of cleaning solution.

"Gray, give me your hands okay? This is going to sting a little bit, but we have to clean out these cuts." His words were soft, coaxing me to listen. I held out my trembling hands. He grasped them, steadying them in his own graspm cradled them, his eyes darkening as he looked over my blood-stained palms.

He gingerly dabbed at the skin, making me wince in pain. Every stroke burned but I knew he was working as gently as he could, prying the stray pieces of gravel out with as much care as he could. When he finished, he lay my hands down on the bed, turning to find himself new clothes then the blood and dirt-stained ones he wore. I watched him with heavy eye lids as he worked to put a fresh shirt on, wincing slightly as he lowered it. He had a deep cut above one eye, the blood already wiped clean.

My cheek still burned with the ghost of the blow. I let out a soft whimper and he was there, right at my side. He brushed the pad of his thumb over the sore spot on my cheek as he looked into my eyes. All that was there was pain and anger, and concern. I just wanted him closer. I reached up, interlocking my fingers with the ones gliding over my blotchy red skin.

I scooted over in the small bed, gesturing with a small movement of my head for him to lay with me. He wordlessly shifted, the only noise the shrill groan of the springs as he settled down, his eyes never leaving mine. We lay there in the dark, staring into each other's eyes, scared to look away. I felt the tears drip down my face, soaking into the comforter under me. He caught each one, wiping them away from my burning cheek. We lay there in silence, letting the weight of what happened settle over us. We fell asleep that night facing each other, our hands intertwined.

***

My head throbbed with a dull ache that came with crying and the memory of the blow from the previous day. The sunlight filtering through the window only made it worse. I reached out next to me, needing to feel Maverick. His presence alone could make me feel instantly better. But my hand found nothing but empty air and the crumpled mattress, cold with having been left alone for a while.

I shot up, immediately wincing as the healing skin of my hands stretched and my head throbbed. I felt my cheek, finding the skin to be searing with heat, slightly swollen. I rubbed at my eyes with the back of my hands. I looked around the room, to find no traces of Maverick.

"Maverick?" I started to feel the gnaw of anxiety claw at my stomach, making the ache in my head intensify. The door opened, Maverick walking in rubbing a towel over damp hair. He wore jeans, no shirt and bare feet. Along his jaw lay deep bruises, the small cut above his eyebrow an angry red.

"Are you okay?" He clutched the towel in front of him, his hair hanging limp across his forehead. I gingerly put my fingers to my temples.

"I have a killer headache." He reached behind him, scanning his small bureau for a bottle of Tylenol and a water bottle. He found both and forced them into my hands.

"Let's get out of here. I think you would be comfier in your own room. And not to mention Mae is going to kill me, anyway, let's not make her more mad by keeping you away from her." He tried at humor, but it didn't reach his eyes. It made me instantly uneasy.

"Um, ok. That's fine." I shut my eyes as I nodded, happy to feel the ache already subsiding. He rested his big hand on my knee, bringing his lips to brush across my forehead. The usually normal gesture felt different this time, as if it were laced with regret, weighed down by sadness. He cupped my uninjured cheek before returning to his bureau to find clothes. I couldn't stop the nagging feeling in my stomach.

The whole ride back to the dorm, Maverick stayed quiet, glancing at me every few seconds as if he was checking to make sure I was still there. Everything around us felt tense, too wound up as if the slightest movement could make us snap.

"Mav, I don't blame you for what happened, it wasn't your fault you know that right?" I knew that that was what he was thinking. He thought that he had dragged me into this, that it was his fault Connor hit me.

He let out a deep sigh. "If it weren't for me, Connor wouldn't even know about you. You wouldn't have gotten hit; you never would have been threatened. I almost feel like you would have been better off if you never met me." His mouth was set in a hard line, eyes glued to the dingy windshield in front of him.

My head snapped to him at the words. "Never say that. Never say that to me again, do you understand? I wouldn't take back a second I have had with you for anything. I will always choose you Maverick. Always." He closed his eyes for a second before returning them to the road with a sigh.

He didn't look at me as he whispered, "I love you Grace."

Something about the declaration felt off, as if he was guilty as he said the words, but I swallowed down my fear. "I love you Maverick."

We sat in tense silence for the rest of the drive, Maverick pulling into his spot in front of my building. I looked to him expectantly, peeking to make sure he was okay.

"I just have to grab something out of the back, meet me in the front?" Maverick fidgeted with the keys as he spoke the words, avoiding my eyes.

"Um, okay. Yea. I'll meet you in the front. Don't be long okay? It's cold." I jumped out of the cab, not able to ignore the dread building in my chest.

As soon as I shut the door behind me, I heard the locks click down.

I whirled for the door, looking at Maverick and his pained expression.

No.

No.

"Maverick?" I pulled at the door, knocking on the glass. "Maverick?" My voice came out as a desperate squeak. He couldn't be doing this. He thought this was some self-righteous sacrifice. His mouth was set in a grim line as tears slipped out of his eyes. He just shook his head at me. My mind buzzed with panic. He couldn't be doing this. He thought he was protecting me, protecting me from himself. But who was supposed to protect me from myself?

"Maverick! Please." The words poured out of my trembling lips. "Don't do this."

He shut his eyes, turning the key in the ignition, and making the truck hum back to life. He stared straight ahead, pretending not to hear my desperate pleas. I watched the tears stain the front of his jacket.

I was losing him.

I ignored the pounding of my head and burn in my hand as I banged on the window, my cuts opening back up. "Don't do this to me Maverick. I can't." I was sobbing now. I was numb, I couldn't even feel the deep chill wafting into my hoodie. I only wanted to feel him.

Taking in a deep shuddering breath, he threw the truck into reverse. I hung on, my hands flat against the door, refusing to let him do this to us. He had a pained expression on his face, but he refused to look to me, His shoulders slumped, his head dropping as he put the car in drive. The tires rolled picking up speed, but I was right there with it, jogging to keep up. My hands fumbled, sliding off the ice-cold exterior. "Maverick!" I yelled, breaking out into a full run to keep up with the truck. But he didn't slow down. He didn't stop.

I was sprinting now, urging my own legs to keep going. But I was losing him. I couldn't keep up. He was too far ahead from me now. My legs burnt as I tried to keep pushing. It was useless. He was gone. I slumped down, right there in the parking lot. The cold tar bit at me through my leggings as I curled my arms around my knees. I was alone. I had nothing, no one. He was gone. I felt nothing, was nothing, without him.

***

I sat in that parking lot till my body spasmed with shivers. I dragged myself up, not caring about the blood running down my hands, or my tear-stained face. It didn't matter, not when he was gone. I hoped he was feeling as miserable as I was. I knew why he did it, I knew he thought he was saving me from himself, but he had no right to make that decision for me. I couldn't help but feel enraged at him, bitter over the fact that he just left me, after he promised me he wouldn't.

I don't remember walking up to my room or turning my key in the lock, but there I was looking at Mae and feeling like I was spiraling out of control.

"Grace? Oh my God. Grace what happened to you?" Mae rushed toward me abandoning the laundry she was folding. Her eyes flew to my cheek. "Did he do this to you? Did Maverick hit you?" Her voice was full of rage and dripping with accusation. I shook my head; I must have been out of tears by now, yet they still slowed freely. "Oh Doll." I clung to her as she wrapped me in her arms, the scent of vanilla encircling me doing little to calm me down.

She guided me to my bed, slipping under the sheets as she cradled me. All I could do was imagine it was Maverick holding me, murmuring to me that it would be okay, that he loved me.

I love you Grace.

That wasn't made up, it was real, but if it was, he wouldn't have abandoned me. If I was so easy to toss aside why was I sitting there feeling destroyed?

My thoughts were interrupted by the shrill ring of Mae's phone, she shifted, reaching for it where it rested on my desk.

"It's Bo. I'll call him later." Mae looked at me, swiping my tear-soaked hair out of my face.

I shook my head, "No answer it. It's okay." My voice croaked out of me, sounding just as miserable as I felt.

"Are you sure?" She asked, her phone still ringing in her hand. I nodded, sinking my head back down into her lap.

"Hello? ..... Yea she's here," She sucked in a breath, "Shit. Ok. Why would he do that? Okay. I'll see you soon. I love you...." She hit the end button, pushing my hair back and smoothing the messy tangles as best she could. Bo had obviously told her what happened. And he obviously heard from.... I gulped down another sob.

"Grace, it'll be okay. I know it doesn't feel like it. It will get better though." I just clung tighter to her, willing my sobs to stop. I felt as if my chest were caving in, like everything was crashing down around me.

I stayed there for a long time, listening to Mae's attempts at console me. Even though I still felt nothing, numb to everything. Bo came around at some point with Finn, trying to overlook my haggard appearance and get me to choke down some food. I wasn't hungry though. Even the thought of eating food made me queasy. Just to satisfy them though, I nibbled at a burger, fake smiling a tight-lipped smile when I could. They didn't believe it for a second, yet they refused to comment which made me grateful for their company after all.

I was exhausted, trying to battle my thoughts of Maverick. His face as he left. *I love you Grace.* I couldn't pretend to be fine, I couldn't act as if nothing was wrong. I fell into my bed after nibbling on my burger just enough for my friends to be somewhat satisfied.

Finn shifted from his place on the floor, striding over to give my shoulder a squeeze where I was slumped over in my bed. "Feel better bud, alright. Maybe tomorrow I'll stop by with something a little stronger than a milkshake." He gave me a sad smile I couldn't even try to reciprocate. I just nodded my head as he walked towards the door. Bo decided to stay the night, offering to help keep me distracted with a "shitty movie marathon".

Mae and Bo cuddled up on her bed, while I curled in a ball on my own, feeling utterly miserable with the absence of Maverick. I craved his touch. I would do anything to hear his soft snoring whistling next to my ear, or the cackling laugh he let out when I snorted. My chest felt hollow with the memories. How could I have felt so full, so loved just the other day? I felt complete, whole. And now I was back to being a disaster. I cranked up the volume, silently crying until I drifted off into a restless sleep.

Chapter Thirty-Seven

Two weeks dragged by, and no word from Maverick. Mae was insistent that I would feel better, with each day I would get a little better. Only with each day I felt less and less like myself. Time just dragged on leaving me feeling more and more alone. I called him twice, finding myself at a loss for words each time the dial tone told me to leave a message. I didn't want to cry anymore; I was sick of feeling weak and sitting back while others made decisions for me. Instead of focusing on how lost I felt, I homed in on my anger.

Each moment was filled with a burning desire to find Maverick. I didn't know what I would do when I found him, but I knew that I wanted him to feel like I was. Even thinking of him made my blood boil and my vision fill with red. He forced me out of his life to protect me. Yet in the process, he was killing me.

After those bitter two weeks, I vowed to find Maverick. I was going to explain to him that he had no right to make that decision for me. I wanted him and I knew he wanted me. He would have to accept the fact that we couldn't control everything, but we could control what we did.

I sat on my bed, picking at my comforter as Mae droned on about some girl in her math class. Jay sat perched on the other end of my bed, mindlessly flipping through some magazine of Mae's offering nods here and there. But as per usual, I didn't hear a word. I knew she was telling me the story to distract me, but it wasn't working. All I could think about was him.

"Mae." I looked up as she immediately stopped talking, not even caring that I had interrupted her. "I need to find him." Jay's instantly left the magazine, eyes landing on me.

Mae's eyes went a little wide before she furrowed her brows with a pout. "Doll, is that a good idea? It sounds like it's over." She tried to put the words as delicately as she could, but they still stung.

"Grace, Mae is right." Jay slid to sit up, scooting closer to where I sat. "He left Grace. It's not your fault, it's his, but he left." Jay lifted a hand to my shoulder as he said the words. I pushed it off, suddenly resenting their sympathy. It was suffocating. They didn't understand why Maverick had done it. He didn't just stop loving me, he thought he was doing it for me. "Grace, I'm sorry...."

"Just stop." I snapped at him, startling him and Mae. I had seemed a husk of myself and even if I was showing utter rage at least it was something. "I just need to see him. Look, I'm not some pathetic girl pining over someone who doesn't want me. I just need to talk to him."

Jay looked away, suddenly finding the stained carpet interesting. Mae just gave a silent nod, a sense of understanding filling her eyes. I knew she didn't get it, she thought I needed closure. Maybe I did. More importantly though, I needed to tell Maverick how much of a dumbass he was being.

"Do you think that you could ask Bo where he is going to be?" My tone was even, calculating. It came out with a slight edge as if I were commanding rather than saying.

"I'll try. Hold on." Mae picked up her phone, punching in a few keys before mumbling into the receiver. I flopped back down next to Jay with a huff. Jay still just stared at the floor. A little wave of guilt washed over me. I reached out, punching his arm.

"Hey, I'm sorry okay? Jay look at me please?" When he turned to me, the pain mingled with sadness brought me back to that night, him holding Jill's body. I blinked away the memory.

"I am just so sick of seeing you getting hurt, Gracie. Between what happened with Harvard and Jill," he winced as he recalled that night, "to me hurting you. Your parents. Now this? I'm worried you can't take much more Grace. You try so hard to act like you just don't care, like things don't affect you. But, you aren't invincible." He turned to face me trying to convey the weight of what he was saying.

I was not invincible. I knew I wasn't. Didn't I?

"You hate being weak Gracie. I know you. Having feelings isn't weak though. As cliché as it sounds, it's okay to let it out, healthy even. It doesn't make you weak." I held his unwavering stare, not really sure what I could even say. My throat constricted with the oncoming tears. I just nodded, accepting his hug as he wrapped me into his arms. Mae still murmured on the phone behind us.

"Ok, Ok. I will. I love you too. I'll see you soon." Mae sighed the words, her stress evident. I swiped at my cheeks retracting myself from Jay's arms. "Looks like we are going to a party." Mae smiled, only it didn't reach her eyes.

***

We piled into Jay's car, sealing ourselves in against the bitter cold night air. Maverick was going to be at the frat party tonight. My heart fluttered at the idea of seeing him while my stomach lurched with nerves. I felt Jay's hand wrap around mine, giving it a quick squeeze before returning to the wheel.

"Are you ready for this?" He asked as he pulled the car into park in the long line already cluttering the street.

"As ready as I'll ever be, I suppose." I glanced over at the house, its usual buzz of drunk college students doing nothing to excite me. My palms were slick with sweat despite the chill in the air. Mae leaned up from the back seat, placing both of her hands on my shoulders and giving me a squeeze.

"We'll be right there with you." She whispered before planting a kiss on the top of my head. I sucked in a deep breath, before opening my door and stepping out to the street. I was instantly hit with the smell of artificial smokes and stale beer. I scrunched my nose, suddenly feeling more nervous than I had been.

Flanked by Jay and Mae, I made my way towards the house. The cold did nothing to ward off the swarms of people studding the front lawn. Smoke billowed from their lips as they cackled over plastic cups brimming with alcohol. I stared at the open door, the vibrant lights neon against the otherwise lightless house. Maverick was here. I stepped into the house, not sure what to expect despite the fact that I needed to find him.

The house was bustling with sloppy girls, swigging out of cups as if their lives depended on it, batting their eyelashes at anything with a pulse. I scanned the room, searching for those deep emerald eyes. I saw Finn and Bo, leaning against a door jam, talking in low tones to each other. Just as I saw them, they saw me. Bo tensed, walking towards me with Finn on his heels.

"Hey Grace." Finn said sheepishly as if scared if he looked at me the wrong way I might shatter.

"Grace, I don't think this is a good idea, especially tonight…" Bo started, his arms crossed over his chest. As much as Bo was my friend, his loyalties lied with Maverick. He might have been dating one of my best friends, but that did not mean he had any debts to me. The realization stung a little bit.

"Where is he?" I asked, mocking his posture to show I wasn't going anywhere.

"Grace, it's not a good idea. You know why he did it." Bo lowered his voice after glancing at Mae and Jay behind me. His eyes instantly softened as he looked at his girl, but it wasn't enough to change his mind.

"Bo, you know what he did was stupid. I am fine. I can handle myself and make my own decisions." I gritted out as my temper started to rise. "So, I'll ask you again, where is he?" Before he could answer, my attention snapped to the doorway of the small kitchen.

Bo noticing the shift in my attention, followed my gaze, heaving a breath at what he saw. There leaning against the chipped wood of the frame, staring into a cup stood Maverick. He wore a tight black tee despite the cold, the ends of his tattoos tickling the edges of the sleeves. His hair was messy, dark smudges cradling his eyes. He looked awful. My mouth dropped, my mind racing with thoughts as my heart pounded against my chest.

"Grace.." Mae started to warn me, but I was already pushing past Bo, rushing to where he stood. I stopped a few feet away, my breaths coming out in heaves. Bodies pushed around us, trying to absorb me in the sea that crowded the makeshift dance floor. I stood my ground. I watched as Maverick brought the cup to his lips, a few drops getting stuck on his full lower lip.

"Maverick." I had sworn that I had whispered the words, the crowd instantly absorbing the sound. Maverick froze. He lowered the cup, dangling it by his hip as his arm went slack. His shoulders slumped as he turned on his heel slinking back into the kitchen. I was already following.

"Maverick." I said it louder knowing that he could hear me now as his shoulders stiffened. He just kept walking forward. "Maverick!" I grabbed the fabric of his shirt, spinning him so he could face me. Only, he didn't meet my eyes. He looked anywhere but. I stood there, desperately gripping the thin fabric, silently begging him to look at me.

"Maverick. What are you doing? Why would you leave me? Huh? You told me you never would, didn't you? But the second something happens; you turn back on your word." The words tumbled out of my mouth, my tone a mixture of anger and desperation. He met my words with silence, the only indication that he heard me was his grip tightening on his cup. I didn't mean it. I didn't feel the venom that laced my words. I just wanted him to feel how I did.

"So that's it huh? Its over then? You can't even bring yourself to look at me?" I shoved at his chest, causing him to take a step back, his teeth grinding. His eyes were pained, blood shot with lack of sleep. "You son of a bitch! I told you everything! I showed you who I was! I even told you I loved you." I kept pushing at the solid muscles of his chest, tears burning my eyes. He stayed still, not even acknowledging that I was speaking to him.

I shook my head, vision blurred, "I was so stupid, so stupid for thinking you were any different." I shuffled back, watching the defeated look take over his features. I got nothing. Maybe he didn't love me. Maybe it was all just a lie. My fingernails dug into my palms, breaking the skin. A bitter taste rose in my mouth, my stomach burning with rage and devastation. I pushed my way through the writing bodies, not even sure what I was looking for or what I was going to do.

He didn't even look at me. I chuckled a bitter laugh. He never loved me. I felt so stupid.

"Grace!" Mae stumbled, grappling to get a hold of my arm. "Grace what happened?" She took in my disheveled state.

Another dark chuckle escaped my lips. "You were right, he never cared about me after all." My voice was blurred by tears.

"What do you mean, Grace? What happened?" She grasped my shoulders, to root me in place.

"Nothing, just, forget about it. Let's get out of here." I could tell she didn't want to drop the conversation, but she didn't want to push me either.

"Ok, let's get Jay." She looked around, spotting him and tugging me by my hand to get him. He stood by the open door, just staring out into space.

"Jay, we got to go." Mae's voice startled him from his own thoughts causing him to turn.

His expression instantly darkened as he saw me. "Grace? What happened? What did he do?" I just shook my head, too choked up to speak.

"Look Jay we just have to get out of here, just give me the keys, you stay with her in the back seat, try to calm her down."

I would have been upset over being coddled, but I was too devastated to care. Jay gave a grim nod before wrapping an arm around me. I looked back into the throng of people once more, my eyes settling on deep green ones before turning back around and followed Mae and Jay to the car.

I felt nothing, not the cold sting of the air, or the continuous glances from my friends. I just didn't care enough. I wordlessly slid into the seat in the back, barely even noticing as Jay wrapped my hand around a water bottle and Mae pulled out of the space.

I felt the tears streaming down my face but didn't even bother to wipe them away. Mae continuously glanced at me in the rearview mirror, her dark eyes heavy with worry. I didn't move, I wasn't even sure I was breathing.

"Shit, Grace. You are scaring me. Shit." Before I even would have been able to respond, her phone started to ring.

He didn't love me. He never did.

"Hello? Bo? Yea I have her. It's not good Bo, she isn't even talking she's....."

And then everything came screeching to a halt. The force of the impact whipped my body to the side, striking against Jay's. Shattered glass glittered through the air, framing Mae's phone as it flew by my face. Everything was warped metal, shattered glass. Time stopped. Mae's eyes scrunched against the onslaught of debris. Jay's horror-stricken face as he reached toward me. The squeal of tires as we whirled, skidding to slam into something solid. Then black.

***

The wail of sirens was ear shattering. Everything moved as if it were suspended in honey, warm and fluid. The cold concrete at my back seeped into my skin, and yet I couldn't even shiver. My head was pulsing, my eyes weaving in and out of focus. I used every ounce of effort I had to look to my right, seeing Mae sitting up, clutching her mouth. Tears stagnant in her eyes as Bo wrapped her in a hug. A single stream of dried amber streaked on her forehead. Her hair sprinkled with glittering glass, shrouding her, making her look almost holy. Bo smoothed back her hair as they both looked out. Were they looking at me?

My thoughts were sluggish, disheveled. Jay lay a few feet away, face illuminated by flashing lights. He blinked slowly, sucking in deep breaths, surrounded by swarms of men in black, all prodding at him. I wanted to call to him, but I could get my tongue to move. It felt like concrete, my throat sandpaper. My limbs tingled with exhaustion, begging me to close my eyes, as if I were to be lulled to sleep.

Hey Birdie. I smiled at the sound of his husky voice, draped in cigarette smoke and lust. I missed him.

"Harvard?" I wasn't even sure if I spoke the words.

"Grace? Grace?" His broad hands cupped my broken body, as if they alone could stitch it back together. I smiled at the thought. "Gray please." Something wet splattered on my cheek, disappearing into a pool of crimson next to me. Eyes like emeralds, warming me to my core. My eyes fluttered closed at the thought.

"Maverick." I whispered into the cold night air.

"I'm right here baby. Please stay with me." I offered a closed lip smile, my eyes quivering to stay perched open as I took in his handsome face, the way the flashes of blue and red shadowed his features perfectly. I focused on how badly I wanted to run a finger down that nose, over those full lips.

"Sir you need to step back." I didn't recognize the voice and was lost as to who its owner was. All I could think about was the big hand gripping mine. Why was I so heavy?

"Just. Please take care of her."

"We will sir you just need to step back." And just like that his hand was gone, leaving me to spiral into the darkness.

Chapter Thirty- Eight

My eyes rolled, feeling the soft sheets wrapped around my legs. Fluorescent lights flashed across my vision as my head pounded in my skull. I flinched as I reached my hand up, gingerly grazing over a large bandage at my temple. *Harvard. Jill. Jay. Mae.* I shot up, too fast apparently, as black dots swirled across my vision. The sharp scent of disinfectant and stale blood teased at my nose, knocking the air from my lungs.

"Hey, hey. Grace. Take it easy." Finn sat at the chair by my bed, but instantly moving to my side as my world careened out from under me. I looked down to find my clothes ripped, stained with blood. My breath caught in my throat. I was okay. I tried to force myself to take deep breaths. The tar mac stained with blood. Harvard on the ground. Gasoline.

"Grace. It's ok. You were out for a bit." Finn held onto my shoulders guiding me back to rest on the propped-up backing of a medical bed. I was still in my

clothes, no hospital gowns, no wires. I sighed slightly
with the small relief. I tried to speak but my throat felt
like it was burning. I clutched at it, wincing at the
sudden pain.

"Here, here. It's water." Finn put a cool glass in
my hand, keeping his grip on my shoulder. I greedily
gulped down the cool liquid, willing it to calm my
haggard throat. I pushed the glass back into his hand,
noticing the sting burning my head. I reached up to the
bandage again.

"There was an accident Grace. You guys were
lucky. None of you were badly hurt. You got a pretty
nasty gash on your head," he gestured to my head,
saving me from having to ask my questions myself. "Jay
and Mae are banged up, nothing serious though. You can
all go home by the afternoon."

"Afternoon?" My voice came out as a raspy
croak. My eyes snapped to the window suddenly
noticing the soft sunlight of mid-morning. I spent the
night here?

"Yea. They wanted to keep an eye on you guys
over night. You were kind of out of it. A drunk driver t-
boned you guys." Finn rubbed the back of his neck. How
long had he been here?

"Where's Bo? Does he know?" my chest
tightened with the memory of Mae on the phone.

"He was on the phone with Mae when it
happened. We bolted from the party. He was there
before even the cops got there." Finn chuckled, trying to
lighten the mood. But I couldn't focus.

"Where are Mae and Jay?"

"They are in recovery. Nothing too bad. Jay has a broken arm, few cuts. Mae got off with a few scrapes and bruises. Bo is with her and Jay is just down the hall."

"Can I see them?" I was desperate to see them, alive. All I could see was Harvard and Jill's crumpled bodies replaced by my friends. The thought sent shocks through me. I needed to see them.

"Of course you can, but first let's get you checked out." Finn offered a tight-lipped smile.

"Grace, there is something else that you should know. Maverick is the one that drove us."

With that I stayed completely still, the breath knocked out of me. Maverick?

"He was the only one sober." Finn started to explain. How could he have been when I saw him nursing that cup? Seeming to see the question forming on my lips Finn started back up, "he hasn't had a sip to drink since..... you know." His gaze hit the floor.

"Where is he now?" The words came out a whisper.

"He is in the waiting room. He slept out there. We tried to get him to leave, said you wouldn't want to see him, but he didn't quit. He wanted to make sure that you were safe first." The thought of him waiting for me after blatantly ignoring me and casting me to the side shattered what little heart I had left.

My mind warred with confusion as I tried to decipher my emotions. I was thrilled at the thought of his presence but still filled with rage over his abandonment. I gripped the thin blankets under my aching form, battling a wave of nausea as it washed over me. I couldn't worry about him right now. My friends. I needed to be there for them.

"I have to go. I have to go see them." I mumbled as I swung my legs over the bed. I staggered, swaying as my head spun.

"Grace, maybe you should sit back down." Finn was at my side, gripping my elbow to ensure I didn't fall flat on my face.

"No, Finn. I have to go. I have to go see them…" I mumbled. I couldn't think straight. I couldn't focus. Maverick was here. Harvard's cold eyes. Jay reaching toward me.

"Grace." The stern voice echoed from the doorway, not from Finn by my side. My eyes snapped to him. There he stood, clad in a jean jacket over his stained black tee shirt from last night. He looked more out of place than he did last night, the deep red of his eyes practically glowing with exhaustion.

His mouth was set in a hardline, his face all hard edges, but his eyes looked wary, tired and heavy. Something burned deep in my gut, only I couldn't decipher the mysterious emotion as rage, relief, or just nausea. "Sit down. Before you hurt yourself." He sighed the command as if it pained him. And in that moment, I knew, it was rage. I strode across the room, injuries and dizziness forgotten for the favor of going after Maverick.

He didn't move, didn't even flinch as I came at him hands clenched by my sides.

"You don't get to tell me what to do. Ever. You left me remember. Now I am going to go and see my friends, you can sit here and brood over the fact that I am no longer yours to order around as you please." I spit the words in his face. Yet I got no reaction. He took it all without blinking. I huffed in frustration, the soles of my filthy shoes smacking against the spotless tiles.

"Grace!" I heard Finn yell, but I wouldn't stop. I was bristling with my encounter with Maverick, adrenaline pumping through my veins and making me forget about the pounding in my head. I needed to find my friends.

"Grace?" Bo popped out of a room on the corner, Mae tucked under his arm. Finn caught up to me as I froze. Mae looked to me, a deep scrape chiseled into her high cheek bone. Her hair was wild, stray strands standing up on end.

I felt my face crumple as I looked over Mae's stained jeans, seeing the bloodied band aids dotting all of her olive skin. Neither of us spoke as I surged forward and threw my arms around her. Bo stepped back, allowing me full access to her. We sobbed into each other's shoulders. Both of our bodies racked with sobs as we embraced in the middle of the hospital's hallway.

I pulled back, scanning over her damaged face while she did the same assessment on me. "Are you okay?" My voice came out shaky, thick with tears. Her own face crumpled as she nodded.

"Are you okay?" She sniffled.

"Yea. Yea. I'm okay." I pulled her back into my chest. I didn't care who saw us, all I could think of was Jill, her face replaced with Mae's.

"Ahem." We both looked up to see Jay, sporting a fresh black eye and a black cast to match. Relief flooded me as I saw him. I knew he was replaying Harvard and Jill's death just as I was. He gave us a crooked grin, trying to mask his pain. "Am I interrupting?" We both chuckled through our tears, hobbling over with stiff muscles. We all embraced, Finn and Bo watching with wary smiles. Maverick lurking by the doorway to the room I had just occupied. Relief flooded me. They were okay. They were okay.

"We should probably get you guys back home. Come on, I had one of the guys drop off my car." Bo moved behind Mae, tucking her back under his arm.

"Looks like I am going to be relying on you for some rides for a while now." Jay rolled his eyes as he followed the two of them to the counter to check out.

"Wait. Grace, let me drive you home." Everyone visibly cringed at Maverick's words. I turned to him, ready to spit venom.

"Maverick, come on she literally just got discharged from the hospital." Mae said from Bo's side, his grip tightening on her. But his eyes stayed glued to me. I glanced at Mae, hoping to find disgust or anger or something I could use to throw at Maverick, but she was just as empty as I was.

"Please Gray." His voice cracked over my nickname. I shut my eyes against the sight, knowing that all my resolve would disappear with one look at those eyes heavy with grief.

"Why should I? You abandoned me remember?" My voice came out harsh, yet again he didn't flinch.

"I know I messed up Grace, just, please. Let me drive you home. I need to make sure you get home safe." His words crushed me, every word coated in pleas.

"Bo can get me home just fine." I started to turn away, but he was right there, wrapping a soft yet firm hold around my wrist. "Please. Grace. Let me explain." I looked to Mae and Jay, standing in front of me. Both battered. Mae looked at me knowingly, just giving me a nod of her head. Confirming what I already knew.

I huffed out a sigh, turning back to Maverick. "Fine. Fine. I'll drive with you." Relief overtook his features as he slowly released his grip on my wrist. With once more glance at Mae, I followed Maverick out to his truck.

***

I felt uneasy, not sure what I should do, what I should think. We walked in silence. When we got to the car Maverick wordlessly wrapped his strong hands around my waist and set me in the passenger seat. My skin burned with the memory of his touch. *He left me.*

After shutting the door, he climbed into the driver's seat glancing at me as he turned the engine. He watched as I winced with the purr of the machine coming to life.

His hand reached out as if he were about to hold my own before he quickly retracted it, laying it back on the wheel. The air was full of charged silence, neither of us knowing how to start. What to say. I stared out the window, watching the blur of slush covered woods and bare trees swaying with the winter breeze. Soft gray clouds loomed over head, threatening snow. I fidgeted with my hands, my head throbbing and my chest tight with the dam of words I was holding back.

I didn't know if I should scream at him, if I should slap him, or tell him how much I missed him. I could have easily died last night. I could have suffered the same fate as Harvard and Jill, and yet here I was sitting and grappling with my emotions as the boy I loved drove me home in silence.

"Gray. I… I don't even know what to say." His voice came out gruff as he rubbed at his forehead. "I fucked up. I know that. I should have, I shouldn't have…." He stumbled over his words looking utterly defeated. I had known why he left me. He wanted to save me from himself, but it didn't mean I forgave him. He treated me like I meant nothing to him when I saw him. "Please say something." He pleaded with me.

I kept my stare on the dingy windshield, trying to decipher my own thoughts. Did I know what to say?

"I know why you did it."

He huffed out a sigh of relief, I couldn't tell whether it was the statement in itself or the fact that I had actually spoken to him. "I know why you did it, but you had no right to." I could feel the tears start to edge my eye. God, I was so sick of crying.

"I know Grace, I thought I was doing what was best. When I saw you after he hit you I…" his grip on the wheel tightened, turning is knuckles white. "I wanted to kill him. I saw that bruise and your hands. And I never wanted to see anything like that again."

"So, what you decide to leave me?" the words came out harsher than I meant them to, causing him to flinch.

"I know. It was messed up. But I know you deserve better than what I can give you. I couldn't even protect my own sister! I didn't want to drag you down too." The words hit something deep within me. "Then when I heard about the accident, Grace I was so scared. I was so scared I lost you."

I remembered pushing at his chest, shoving him before leaving him alone. Just like he had done to me. My cheeks suddenly burned with shame. I was a hypocrite.

I hadn't even noticed as we pulled into the lot in front of my dorm, the weight of our words palpable in the cool air of the truck. He still stared out the front window, hands gripping the wheel. Everything that I had faced, Maverick was the hardest thing I had ever had to undergo. I fought to keep him, fought for our families. He knew everything about me, and he stayed. He had thought I was too good for him.

Ironic.

I glanced at him, worrying his lip between his teeth. *I love you Grace.* In his eyes I saw sunsets and giggles. Words from his worn-down paper backs. I saw pain, brokenness. I saw myself.

I tentatively reached out my hand, laying it on his arm lightly. His head whipped around, his eyes searching my face with a mingled sense of hope. With him, I felt whole, I felt right. I wasn't one for clichés, for that story book ending. And yet, maybe Maverick was mine. Maybe I was his.

I reached my hand up, rubbing the pad of my thumb over his cheek. His eyes fluttered closed with the touch. The warmth from his cheek spread into my hand, my arm like pins and needles. My palm itched with the light scruff dotting his chin.

"Open your eyes." The soft command slipped out, and immediately followed with his eyes finding mine. Like a summer field, all sunshine, like soft pale grasses blowing with the summer breeze. I brought my lips to his, just barely grazing the soft skin. I instantly lit up with a new fire.

His hands moved, cupping my own face. We moved our lips together, everything fluid and easy, like we were meant for each other. I loved him. And I don't think I could ever stop. Our touches were soft, no rush following. Just content with being there together.

This was it.

This was how my story was meant to end, wrapped in Maverick Foster's arms.

I pulled back, watching the flick of love glisten in his eyes. I caught an escaped tear with my thumb.

"I love you Mav." I whispered.

"I love you Gray." That birth mark quirked to the side as he gave me his signature grin, bringing our lips back together.

"But if you ever leave me again like you did, I will end you Maverick Foster." I said against his lips.

"I don't doubt it for a second." he chuckled.

Acknowledgements

Wow. I can't believe the fact that this is it. It's done. This book took... a lot. Lots of tears and rewrites and even more encouragement.

Thank you to my parents for pushing me and supporting me to keep on keeping on.

Thank you to my annoying brothers, I knew you supported me throughout the whole process even if you don't want to admit it.

Thank you to the only person I let read this book (you know who you are) and driving me to be a better writer.

Thank you to all my friends listening to my constant book ranting.

Thank you to God for giving me this passion and ideas to create this book.

And thank you, for picking up this book and supporting me.

You will never understand how much you all mean to me.

It's not over yet.....

The story will continue.

CPSIA information can be obtained
at www.ICGtesting.com
Printed in the USA
BVHW081637050521
606419BV00004B/724